ARCHIVIST
WASP

Best of the Year:
YALSA Best Fiction for Young Adults,
Kirkus Reviews Best Teen Books, *Book Riot*,
Buzzfeed Best Fantasy Novels, ABC Best Books
for Young Readers

Los Angeles Times Summer Reading
Locus Recommended Reading
Norton Award Nominee

Praise for *Archivist Wasp*

★ "A ravishing, profane, and bittersweet post-apocalyptic bildungsroman transcends genre into myth. In a desolate future, young girls marked by the goddess Catchkeep fight to the death to become Archivist, needed but feared and shunned for her sacred duty to trap, interrogate, and dispatch ghosts. After three years as Archivist, Wasp is weary of killing, of loneliness, of hunger, of cruelty, of despair, so she barters with a supersoldier's ghost to find his long-dead partner in exchange for a chance at escape. But looking for answers in the land of the dead only reveals that everything Wasp knew was a lie. Equal parts dark fantasy, science fiction, and fable, Wasp's story is structured as a classic hero's journey. Her bleak and brutal world, limned with the sparest of detail, forges her character: stoic, cynical, with burning compassion at the core; in contrast, the rich and mosaic (if capricious and violent) underworld overflows with symbol and metaphor that tease at deeper meanings never made fully explicit. Meanwhile, the nameless ghost's history, told through disconnected snatches of memory, encompasses heroism, abuse, friendship, and betrayal in a tragedy only redeemed by the heart-rending convergence of their separate narratives. Names (and their absence) form a constant leitmotif, as identity is transformed by the act of claiming it.Difficult, provocative, and unforgettable—the most dangerous kind of fiction."
Kirkus Reviews

"Now the story becomes clear for what it is: a story about agency, freedom and revolution. All of sudden, this book Mad-Max-Fury-Roaded me, like a boss. SO! Incredible characters – fleshed-out, human, complicated: check. Beautiful writing: check. Plot that develops like it was written for me: check. A cool mixture of Fantasy and Science Fiction, because ghosts but also super-soldiers: check and check. Reminiscent of everything I love but completely its own thing, a SF YA like I haven't read in a while, *Archivist Wasp* is a book I will treasure."
Ana Grilo, *The Book Smugglers*

(*continues overleaf*)

"With understated skill, *Archivist Wasp* twists myth, fantasy and science fiction into a resonant tale of erasure and absence — and an aching reminder that regaining what has been lost isn't always the answer."
> Jason Heller, NPR

"Goes off like a firecracker in the brain: the haunted landscape, the sure-footed, blistering prose — and, of course, the heroine herself, the most excellent Archivist Wasp."
> Kelly Link, author of *Get in Trouble*

"Call this novel YA, call it science fiction or science fantasy, call it a new mythology. But by all means, call it compelling."
> Tobias Carroll, *Vol. 1 Brooklyn*

"This isn't your typical YA novel. With myth, mystery, and heart, it is a post-apocalyptic world unlike anything you've ever read. Perfect for fans of Anna Dressed in Blood and science Fiction."
> *YA Books Central*

"This is a lean, mean book with a lean, mean main character, and among all the post-apocalyptic dross, it's pure gold."
> *Geekly, Inc.*

"GLORIOUSLY appealing and what I most like: Nicole Kornher-Stace's *Archivist Wasp*. Throw this book in the face of anyone who suggests that the dystopian YA genre is all tapped out!"
> Jenny Davidson, *The Explosionist*

"Young adults will be able to relate to Wasp's inner turmoil and her battle to understand a world full of inexplicable hatred and violence. The fast pace and graphic action will draw in reluctant readers. VERDICT A must-have for dystopian fans who prefer to avoid love stories and pat endings."
> *School Library Journal*

"A gorgeous, disturbing, compelling book with a smart, complicated heroine who bestrides her post-apocalyptic world like a bewildered force of nature. Reading it was a wild ride and a thoroughly satisfying one."
> Delia Sherman, author of *The Freedom Maze*

ARCHIVIST
WASP

a novel

✝

NICOLE
KORNHER-STACE

Big Mouth House
Easthampton, Mass.

Big Mouth House
150 Pleasant Street #306
Easthampton, MA 01027
info@smallbeerpress.com
weightlessbooks.com
smallbeerpress.com

Distributed to the trade by Consortium.

Third Big Mouth House Printing
May 2016

Library of Congress Cataloging-in-Publication Data

Kornher-Stace, Nicole.
Archivist wasp : a novel / Nicole Kornher-Stace. -- First Big Mouth House
edition.
pages cm
Summary: "A postapocalyptic ghosthunter escapes her dire fate by joining the
ghost of a supersoldier on his quest to the underworld"-- Provided by publisher.
ISBN 978-1-61873-097-8 (paperback) -- ISBN 978-1-61873-098-5 (ebook)
[1. Fantasy. 2. Ghosts--Fiction.] I. Title.
PZ7.1.K68Ar 2015
[Fic]--dc23
2014046381

Text set in Georgia.

Printed on 50# 30% PCR recycled Natures Natural paper
by the Maple Press in the USA.

Prologue

T he knife. She'd lost the knife. Now she was as good as
  dead.
     Frantically she scanned the sand around her. No knife.
How far off could it have landed? She squinted to see farther
out, but the crowd's torches were too far back for the blade
to catch their light. She swore under her breath. Fractions of
a second passed while she, Wasp, three years Archivist and
terror of the upstarts, actually froze. They were probably the
last fractions of a second she had left.

There was a pause as the other girl, this year's third and
final upstart, realized what had happened. As the crowd
began to shout. An Archivist disarmed! The Catchkeep-priest
in his high chair raked his gaze across them and their shouts
hushed to murmuring, showing the Archivist-choosing day
its due respect.

Still, out of the corner of her eye Wasp could see spectators
jostling to the front of the ring, parents lifting children on
their shoulders for a better view. She knew there'd be a few
in the crowd secretly betting now: would she try to fight
unarmed? Would she run? Would she stand unmoving in her
pride and let the upstart cut her throat?

The upstart staggered to her feet, bleeding freely from
half a dozen wounds, and bobbed behind her own knife,
watching Wasp cagily.

Still Wasp stood there, her pulse banging at her wounds, sweat cooling on her skin. Somehow, it was almost a relief. It wasn't like she'd ever thought she'd die easy. That was a luxury Archivists weren't really allowed. Getting it out of the way now might not be so bad. She thought on what she'd miss in those last moments, bleeding out into the sand. It wasn't a long list.

Not a split second too soon, reflex grabbed her, dragged her back. The upstart's blade slashed the air a thumb's width from her jaw. The slick hiss of its passage sounded daunted. It'd meant to empty out her throat.

Dumb luck. It couldn't last. The upstart was getting cocky now, slashing wide and wild, riding high on the vision of Wasp's death and her own ascension to Archivist in Wasp's place—and Wasp had to fling herself back hard from the next swing.

Not hard enough. The knifepoint caught her lip. She tasted blood. Momentum and lightheadedness caught her feet in the sand and she faltered a few steps and went down.

The crowd's sudden silence beat at her like wings. Respect for the goddess Catchkeep whose ritual this was, but respect too for Catchkeep's Archivist, soon to die. Soon enough they'd be dragging her from the sand, reading the holy words over her as her corpse was sectioned out like an orange. Meat for Catchkeep's shrine-dogs, powdered bones for the planted fields, a skull on the shrine-wall with a green stone in its mouth. The bloodied sand of her drag-trail scraped up and kept, for luck.

And Wasp would dwindle in their sight until she was no monster any longer, not marked from birth as Catchkeep's own and holy. Just a girl with a knife, infinitely breakable, and for days they'd amuse each other with the story of that breaking.

But she knew all this already. It was a decision she'd been making over and over for three years now, and she always reached the same conclusion. She hated being Archivist. Hated being forced to choose between killing upstarts to keep the sacred role she'd grown so tired of and letting herself be killed so that the upstart who killed her could take up that role when she was dead.

But if there was one thing she was terrible at doing, it was giving up.

Use your head, you carrion, she commanded herself. *You relic. Think.*

She'd lashed out. Her blade had bitten deep, then skittered against ribs, caught and twisted. Flung. She had not heard it land. If she went looking for it now she'd just get tripped and gutted like a deer. She'd have to improvise.

The upstart hung back, unsure. It wasn't for nothing that Wasp had been Archivist for so long. Even with Wasp disarmed, blood-drenched, and downed, the upstart was still one wrong move from having the hair cut off her corpse's head and interwoven into Wasp's many-colored braids, a trophy among trophies.

Far above, the sixteen stars of Catchkeep's constellation twinkled down on Wasp, all innocence. She ignored them. So Catchkeep's ritual trapped her here, staring down her death as sure as if she had her eye pressed to the barrel of a gun. She didn't have to *like* it.

Meantime, the upstart seemed to have reached her decision. She began half-stumbling half-charging at Wasp, moving like she had shackles on her ankles and a mad dog at her heels. She had the knife gripped out at arm's-length, elbows locked. No art in it. No grace.

She needed none. She only had to fall.

Like a ghost to a saltlick, Wasp thought. *Stupid as snot.*

Wasp waited for her moment, then kicked out hard, heard something in the upstart's leg give way. The upstart cried out and plunged down, knife first, her aim knocked perilously out of true.

Wasp caught her mid-fall, one knee in her ribs, one fist in her hair, and eased the upstart down to kneeling. One leg splayed out at an ugly angle, but the upstart made no sound. The upstart's knife-hand snapped up, too quick to draw a gasp from the crowd, and Wasp snatched her wrist and broke it. She caught the knife as it fell free.

She seized a handful of the upstart's hair and the upstart flinched away, expecting her own knife in the throat—but Wasp only wiped the blade clean on the upstart's ponytail, then palmed the hilt, still slick with fear-sweat, and watched the girl thoughtfully.

What she was supposed to do at this point was cut the upstart down, preserving her role as Archivist unchallenged for another year. For three years she had done precisely that. She could still see the face of every upstart she'd killed. Still woke from dreams in which they died all over again, woke nauseous and sweaty and scrubbing invisible blood from her hands.

She was sick of it. She was beyond sick of it. There had to be another way.

So many eyes on her. The crowd's. The Catchkeep-priest's. The upstart's. Catchkeep's Herself. Wasp kept hers straight ahead. She turned and walked to the edge of the sand and threw the upstart's knife as far as she could into the lake. It flew out into the dark and splashed.

Voices behind her, outraged now. Calling for a bloodletting, as was Catchkeep's necessity and the people's right. If the ritual had ever ended before with two girls alive, Wasp didn't know when, and it seemed the crowd didn't either. Well, let them squawk. She was done listening.

The upstart had stayed where she had fallen, hugging her wrist and screaming through her teeth. She gathered like a cornered hare as Wasp approached, but did not try to run. *Some pride in that*, thought Wasp, used to chasing upstarts across the sand as they fled her knife.

Wasp stood looking down at the upstart. She wondered if the upstart had gone into this fight gladly, her eye on becoming Archivist, or whether she, like Wasp, was only fighting to survive, because the least of evils couldn't possibly be death. She wondered what the upstart thought she'd miss when she was killed. Whether her list was longer than Wasp's. Wasp wasn't sure whether or not she hoped it was.

The upstart's wounds weren't immediately life-threatening. If she got to the midwife's for stitching, fast, and had the leg and wrist set, and nothing became too badly infected, she'd get out of this alive. Certainly Wasp would be punished for her disobedience, but she was long since used to that.

She collared the upstart and hauled her to her feet.

"Come after me," she whispered, "and I will see to your ghost personally."

She let go, and the upstart dropped deadweight to the sand. *Stay down,* Wasp thought at her. *Please stay down.*

The upstart stayed down.

When the crowd tried to block Wasp's path, she shouldered through. One of the gamblers grabbed her arm but let go fast when he saw her eyes.

"Kill her yourself, then," she spat at them, knowing as well as they did that interference in the fights was forbidden, even by the Catchkeep-priest himself, and they wouldn't harm an upstart any sooner than they'd heap filth on Catchkeep's shrine.

Then she walked away across the lakeshore, not looking back along the beach toward where her people watched her, not looking up into the stars toward where Catchkeep did, and kept on walking, leaving a red trail, until the world around her darkened and she went down face-first in the sand.

Chapter One

A s it did every year in the days that followed the Archivist-choosing day, Wasp's recovery routine kicked in each morning even before she'd come completely awake. It was her third year as Archivist, after all, the third year she'd stayed at least a week in bed so the wounds could knit themselves to scabs, then scars. By now, the steps came to her easy as breathing.

One. Check the bandages.

The smallish ones on her neck, legs, and shoulders, then the wide one at her side where the third upstart's second knife had gone in and stayed—until Wasp had pulled it out and flung it at her head, ruining an ear. Also the set of neat stitches tracking down her lower lip to her chin, and the other one cutting across the old scars on her cheekbone and up into her temple.

For the first few days, this was as far as she had gotten before pain and exhaustion had overcome her, and she'd spent those days drifting in and out of healing sleep, in and out of less productive nightmares.

Today, all seemed sound.

Two. Sit up.

This took longer than she would like, and she expected any moment to feel the pull and gush down her hip where the deep wound had reopened. She dreaded this, of course, but more than that she dreaded another round of festering and a fever high enough she could practically boil water on her forehead when she tried to treat the newly opened wound herself. Exactly a year ago she'd nearly killed herself doing exactly that, but she was fairly sure she'd do it again. A choice between a moment with a heated knife and a bottle of spirits and a rag to scream into, or letting the midwife back at her, didn't seem to her like much of a choice at all.

There was a pull, but no gush came.

Three. Stand.

The fracture in her ankle screamed but held, and a glance at her bandaged side in the light discovered no bloodstains, no greenish watermarks of pus. She took a deep breath, gritted her teeth against what was coming, and bounced a little on her toes to see if they'd take her weight.

If she ground down hard on whatever desperate messages her ankle was firing at her brain, she could push through or outstubborn the rest.

"Finally," she whispered.

Four. Get back to work.

Her injuries were different (and, alarmingly, more plentiful) than last year's, so, as she did every year, Wasp improvised, inching her way back out into the world.

Two weeks in bed had taken their toll. Her arms felt weaker, somehow stiff and rubbery at once, as did her legs. When she bent down to touch her toes, the muscles in the backs of her thighs began complaining even before the wound at her side got its say. Squatting over her pissing-pot was agony. So she tried to stretch her back and instantly her side felt like someone had stuck a pick in it and twisted.

She paced a bit, feeling like a caged cat, trying to outwalk the pain. She wished she could limp back into bed. Sleep, dream, let the Catchkeep-priest set the upstarts at each others' throats until whoever was left standing became Archivist in her place. There would be another soon enough at this rate anyway.

But there was the backpack in a corner, and *there* were the jars and knife and saltlick, and she never would have gotten away with it. Wasp knew quite well that two weeks abed was already enough of a display of weakness, without adding any more wasted days on top of it. She knew what the dozen surviving upstarts must be saying about how long it'd taken her to beat the three who'd drawn this year's short straws, and how many wounds they'd given her. How Wasp just wasn't what she used to be. How next year it'd be her on the wrong end of the knife. It had to be eventually. It always was.

She couldn't keep that day from coming. But she could push it out of reach a little longer.

So she limped her way over to the far wall, where the painting was.

The bones of the painting were nails, hammered straight into the wall to pick out the stars of Catchkeep's constellation. And around them She had been outlined in thick black paint, all teeth and legs, Her back curved like a rainbow, caught in mid-leap over a shadowy abyss. On one rocky shore of it a woman stood, tiny in comparison with Catchkeep, Who spanned the wall. She held an open jar out in front of her with both hands. Gray fog drifted from the jar, up toward Catchkeep, forming into figures that clung to Her back as She carried them to the far shore. That shore itself was misty, hard to make out—but green, greener than anything Wasp knew. She wasn't even sure what had been used to paint it.

In little drips of color that same green was radiating off of the gray figures, drifting back toward the woman. There was a book by her feet, and the greenness went there and infused it with a glow. From there it floated off behind her in threads to tint the shadows at her back. On her side of the abyss, it was the only color whatsoever.

Catchkeep Herself was black and red. Stepping close to Her you could make out the outlines of handprints, darker where they overlapped. Wasp's first day as Archivist, they'd rushed her here before the blood of the fallen Archivist could dry on her palms, and to the painting she had added the shape of her hand, which was the shape of her predecessor's death. Sometimes she wondered where that Archivist's handprint was in the painting, whose blood had made that mark. Sometimes she wondered which part of Catchkeep her own blood would redden, whose hand it would be in the shape of.

Wasp didn't need to come close enough to read the words painted in above Catchkeep's beartrap of a head. She'd known them by heart for years. Every day she went out to do the work, she stopped here and said the words first, like every Archivist before her. Now more than ever, she needed them to keep her safe.

She bowed her head before all that long-dried blood.

"I am the Archivist. Catchkeep's emissary, ambassador, and avatar on earth. Her bones and stars my flesh; my flesh and bones Her stars. Mine is the mouth through which the dead world speaks. Mine are the hands that record what the dead world left behind. Mine are the eyes that hold vigil, so that the old world's death does not return to kill the world anew. Protect me, Catchkeep, until another stands before You here, as I stand where another stood. Protect me so that I can do Your work, until my flesh fails, until my bones fail, leaving only Your stars, which light the earth forever."

She felt like a fraud even saying the words. In freeing the last upstart she was supposed to kill, she had spit on the very rituals she was calling upon now to keep her alive.

But she could still do the work, and she'd keep on doing it until she found a way to break free. It seemed to be enough for Catchkeep. After all, Wasp had lost count of her attempts to rebel against the Catchkeep-priest and escape, and Catchkeep hadn't yet come down out of the sky to murder her.

Besides, it wasn't the work she minded. It was everything else. Next to that, the work was downright soothing. What could the dead do to her that the living did not do already?

She shouldered the backpack and stuck the harvesting-knife in her belt. Pulled on her shoes. Gulped down half the stale contents of her water-jug and poured a cupped handful to splash her face. Eased off the bandages, all but the big one at her side, which her shirt would cover. Stuffed some flatbread and raisins in a pocket to eat while she walked. Stopped, one hand on the door, to glare over her shoulder at the room: cot, shelves, braided rag-rug, not much else. A few hanging strings of wild garlic, peppers, apples, drying or dried. A few changes of homespun clothing. The box that held her field notes. Everything but the food had been handed down from dead Archivists, inherited with the little house itself. No knowing how many Archivists had patched and mended those clothes before her. From the look of them, plenty. But Archivists had been adding field notes to that box for four centuries. In them was all the knowledge they had ever gained from their studies, going back and back to when the first Archivist was given the harvesting-knife and learned what it was for.

The upstarts never touched the field notes. Nor did the Catchkeep-priest. They were the only line of communication between that long line of Archivists, and the only way each one learned how to do Catchkeep's work was by reading them. It wasn't like any old Archivists were left alive to teach the new ones.

And then there were the jars. There had to be at least a hundred, crammed on the shelves that lined three walls of four. Clay pots and wooden boxes, made by town crafters or traded for, made up the majority. Much rarer were the glass jars, found out in the Waste. Some with only hairline cracks or chipped rims, some still with the matching screw-top lids that were so precious that scavenger kids would fight over who brought them to the Catchkeep-priest, for they were usually worth a decent meal in trade. Never mind that the Catchkeep-priest only ever took that meal out of the upstarts' share, never skimming from his own.

As though aware of her eyes on it, from somewhere among the jars there came a rattling. As she watched, a row of empty glass ones began to clink against each other, pushed gently, rhythmically, by something from behind. Well, if they fell and shattered, the Catchkeep-priest would have her hide for a coat, bones for buttons, and she knew it. Quickly she scooped those off the shelf, then located the rattling jar behind them and stretched, hissing through her teeth as she went up on tiptoe to bring it down. It was a reddish clay one, the size of her two fists pressed together, with a tooth-shaped chip near the base. With a sinking feeling, she remembered it. The patience of the thing inside it astounded her.

"Morning, troublemaker," she told it, and set out, cradling that jar as carefully as she would old ordnance or a pail of rain, for Execution Hill.

She threw open the door on the autumn and the woodsmoke from the warn-fires and the half-frozen mud and the rotten-sweet windfall smell from the valley—and the first thing she saw was not the warn-fires or the orchard or the valley for that matter, or even the mud, but the Catchkeep-priest, rummaging among the cairns of offerings the people had left by her door as she'd slept.

Apart from what she managed to forage herself, those offerings were all that would see her through the winter, for there was not a shopkeeper who would trade with an Archivist, not a townsperson's roof under which an Archivist was welcome. That was *her* bunch of wild onions. *Her* horseleather gloves. *Her* nettle-yarn scarf. *Her* sharpening-stone. And there *he* was, picking through her things with those soft long daintyfingered hands that had never seen a callus or probably so much as a blister in all their days on earth.

He had two shrine-dogs with him, hulking and silent. For once, they did not snarl at her. They were much too occupied with eating a loaf of bread the Catchkeep-priest had picked out of her things for them. One, finished, raised its head, and the Catchkeep-priest cooed at it and flung some eggs and jerky he'd unearthed. The shrine-dog set to, slobbering, and the Catchkeep-priest turned to regard Wasp, who forced her face to show only apathy.

He was nibbling at something else he'd found. A pear, and a ripe one, from the smell of the juice Wasp could see running down his wrist. Her mouth watered. She spat.

She would not let him rile her. It was only food. She could find more somewhere, if she looked hard enough. Another cart of offerings would come eventually. She would not show weakness. She would walk on by.

She'd never gotten what was coming to her for disobeying him, disobeying Catchkeep Herself, letting that last upstart live. He was forbidden to kill her himself, but Wasp was sure he'd thought of some way to try to stomp her back down into her place. He always did. She could think of no other reason why he should be here.

Even nearing him, her palms went clammy and she had a sensation like someone had dumped a bucketful of worms down the back of her shirt. He smiled and the sensation intensified.

"A fine morning to you, lazybones," he said, bending to her height. "To think I was beginning to forget that pretty face."

He'd found a kind of necklace in the heap: bits of old glass, remnants of shotgun shells, tarnished rings and yellowed fingerbones, all strung on somebody's lost cat's sun-dried sinews. It looked like the contents of any out-turned pocket of any scavenger kid in the Waste. There was a tiny locket on it with a blue-and-white enamel windmill on the front. He popped it open with a sticky thumbnail to hold it glinting before her.

A shard of mirror trapped a fraction of her face and proffered it. Part of a dark eye. Part of a dark eyebrow. Part of a snarl of five-colored hair, not hers, darkened with two weeks of grease, falling not quite over the eye, not quite over the four long scars, paler and pinker than her skin, that ran the full length of the right cheek, temple to jaw, with which Catchkeep marked each upstart in the womb to do Her holy work—

She grimaced at her grimace. "Pretty face yourself," she mumbled, and began to walk past him. He set a hand to her arm and despite herself she stopped. It was a gentling hand, such as she'd seen him use on the shrine-dogs when they'd gone wrong with too much Waste or too much holiness, a gentling hand to the top of the head while the hidden knife slid in under the jaw and—

"That's better. Now let me look at you. Catchkeep's champion. Wrecker of upstarts. Glorious horror." His tone changed, honey to oil. "Long fight this year. Long heal. What must they be saying."

"Nothing I can't answer," said Wasp, staring straight ahead as the dogs began to growl. They didn't seem to like her tone.

"Today, maybe. Today you have a fresh fierce face to show them. No blood. No bandages. No footholds by which to climb you. No handholds by which to tear you down. But in a year?"

His inspection of her paused. His hand was very near the deep wound in her side. Did he remember it? Her pulse ticked in her neck. Of course he did.

"But in a *week*, when this has festered and you are babbling on the midwife's cot?"

His fingers dug in, very slightly, and the air went out of her. She could have sworn the dogs were grinning.

"Or in a *day*, when this ankle, which you are too proud to have set, finally gives out on you, and the whole market watches you hobble up your hill like somebody's toothless granny?"

He drew his foot back, gave that ankle the tenderest of kicks, and Wasp saw stars. She bit down on the cry.

He laughed. Gave her head a little pat, like hunters pat a bear-torn dog's that did its best. Began to walk away. "Won't that be a pity."

"Too bad you're not allowed to fight me yourself then," Wasp snapped, and when he stopped walking she instantly regretted it. She'd let him rile her. She really was losing her edge.

"No point in dirtying my hands on you," he said. "All I have to do is wait. And I am very good at waiting." Half display of wastefulness, half contempt, he turned and lobbed the pear-core at her.

She was meant to stand and let it strike her. She swatted it from the air.

The Catchkeep-priest watched her for a moment, smiling like a shark, licking juice from his fingers thoughtfully as he took those few slow steps back to face her. She expected him any moment to kick her ankle for real, breaking it along the fracture, or tear that ominous wound at her side back open. Or black her eye for her, or split her lip along its stitching. Give the upstarts some fresh blood to mutter over.

Could she take him in a fair fight? She wasn't sure. He wouldn't fight fair, though. Then again, neither would she. She tensed, gauging. If she was fast, she could maybe blind him. Not outrun him, not like this. Not that she *would* run. She'd never taken a wound to the back in her life and she wasn't starting now.

The window was a few seconds wide at most, and narrowing, before he got the upper hand.

She touched the harvesting-knife at her belt and, just like that, the point of his blade was at her throat. He peered down his nose at her with scholarly interest.

"Well, look at you, with your fire up. Such terrifying confidence for someone who couldn't even finish her last fight."

That last upstart, the third this year. Who Wasp had disarmed. Whose knife Wasp had thrown in the lake. Who Wasp had let live.

For an upstart, or an Archivist, to be killed was to be erased. Swallowed into history. Turned ghost. Already the other upstarts would be forgetting the ones who had died. Their names would be the first thing to rot from their bones.

Aneko, Wasp thought. *Her name is Aneko.*

"That fight was finished," Wasp said, her voice thickening so that she had to wring it out of her throat. "You want them cut up like chickens, take them to the butcher."

Heal clean, Wasp wished at her, wherever she was convalescing. *Then run.* Let the Catchkeep-priest say what he would to her. This time, she had won.

"Well, that's the thing of it, Wasp. You see, I *took* them to the butcher. And the butcher lost her nerve." He shook his head sadly. "Do you know it took that poor girl four days to die of her wounds, raving of fever and thirst in the street?"

It struck her like a punch to the stomach. She hadn't known. She hadn't known at all.

"How is that charitable?" the Catchkeep-priest continued, but Wasp could barely hear him over the rush of blood in her ears. It was all she could do not to leap at him with the harvesting-knife. "What are you proving? She's still dead, and people are saying her ghost will walk for all time because it's caught in-between and Catchkeep can't take it across. Nobody's happy about this, Wasp." He chuckled. "Well. Nobody but the upstarts. Next year they'll be fighting over those short straws. What a gift you're giving them. Making things so *easy*."

His knifepoint went in, just enough to draw blood, and he gave it a delicate quarter-turn, bringing Wasp up slightly on her toes. He smiled.

"Hate them, if it helps. Hate me. Hate every person in this town and every ghost outside of it. But you were entrusted with the tools to do the work, and you will do the work. It's not like much is asked of you. Catch ghosts. Take notes on them. Send them on to Catchkeep. In exchange, your roof is sound. You don't break your back taking rotations boiling water or working the gardens. You're untouchable to every person in this town who'd rather just stick a knife in you and leave you for the bears. Is it really so terrible?"

They only want to do that because they're scared of what I am, Wasp thought. *Because of what you've made me. Because they can't deal with the ghosts themselves. Because they have to give me offerings, when they have nothing to spare. They hate themselves for needing me.*

But she'd said all this before. It had made no difference then, would make no difference now. Same for everything else she wanted to tell him. *I never asked for this. I never wanted this. Well, maybe I did once, but that was a long time ago. All I remember wanting is out.*

The Catchkeep-priest saw in her face all the things she was not saying. "If you don't like it," he said, "then next year's fight, don't fight *back*. Until then, you belong to Catchkeep, which means you belong to me, and you will jump when I say."

The jar in her hand started shifting in her grasp. His gaze went from her face to it and back. She almost managed not to flinch. "The fact that you have not yet sent that one on to Her is an embarrassment to Her and to us all," he said. "Ghosts don't like to be kept waiting, my girl, and neither does She." His smile was kindly, forgiving. She didn't trust it for a second. "When you are finished, do us the kindness of coming down from your hill to break bread with us. Your sisters are all so *anxious* to see the results of your convalescence."

Slowly, deliberately, he lowered the knife into Wasp's field of vision. It was not his knife.

There was blood dried onto it. Sand dried onto that.

Somebody'd found it after all.

"Take it," he said, holding the knife out toward her.

She swallowed hard. "I don't want it."

In answer, he set the flat of the blade to her cheek, drawing it softly down along the scar to where it ended at her throat. Flaking dried blood against her skin. "I didn't ask."

Wasp grabbed at it, too fast. Anything to get it off her face. Sliced a finger. Didn't care.

"Really you should have just cut her throat," the Catchkeep-priest mused. "This much blood, you'd think it would have been quicker. Half a *week* you left her wandering, yowling like a cat in heat. Children following her with pockets full of stones I could not let them throw. However long their mothers begged." He shook his head at her, all sorrow. "All you had to do was walk up to her and finish what you started. But no. I hope your little nap was restful, Wasp. I do. I hope your dreams were sweet."

He patted her cheek and walked away, dogs at his heels. As soon as he was out of sight around the rocks, Wasp dropped the knife, then stuck two fingers down her throat and retched. Nothing but bile to bring up. She brought it up all the same and spat on the tamped dirt path where he had stood. No use. Everything still smelled like that pear.

Wasp's tiny house sat on a high hill, perched on a heap of boulders like a nesting hen. From there, the path switchbacked down and down, bottoming out in the valley where an ancient orchard had long since gone to seed and metastasized into a stunted woodland, its maggoty apples a lifeline some years, a staple every year, to the pieced-together little salvage-town of Sweetwater that clung to its westerly edge. All the trees leaned hard one way, toward a lightning-blasted spit of rock.

It was jagged and black and its peak was twice as high as Wasp's house on the other side.

It was the one ridge in the whole valley where the people raised no warn-fires. The one whose rock was never used for building, though it was dense and tended to break in clean lines and chunks of it littered the Hill's foot where they had tumbled or been blasted out for that purpose by those long vanished. Now nobody dared touch it, for it was sacred to Catchkeep, so it was the Archivist's property.

Her first year, Wasp had come upon a young couple living with a week-old baby in a sort of lean-to by the market. The baby was a grayish, squalling, starveling thing with more skull than face, and the mother's milk had run dry. There was no food but what they stole, no fire whatsoever. Wasp had brought them the best of her latest batch of offerings, a pot of honey and some bread and cheese, and gave them her permission to use that dense black rock to build themselves some shelter.

When he found out, the Catchkeep-priest had whipped her to within an inch of her life, and it was a long time before she tried again to help anyone but the dead. She never saw that couple and their staring skull-baby again, except in dreams. She had not come upon their ghosts yet, either, but she figured it was only a matter of time. She wondered whether they would come to her starved or stabbed.

The black peak's name—Execution Hill—was an old one. The name was in the field notes, and the field notes did not lie.

On a good day, it was two hours' walk down from her house and across the orchard to the foot of the Hill. This was not a good day. She picked her way down the path, her legs slogging, her feet slipping on the scree. She wasn't letting herself think about her ankle.

Still, the day was clear, and she'd missed the sharp sweet smell of the warn-fires. It was getting cold. Soon she'd be cracking cat-ice on the puddles when the catchment bins went dry. And soon a brush fire in a smoky hearth and the terrified charity of the people would be all that stood between her and the winter. She could starve to rattling bones and the people still wouldn't take her in any sooner than they would a rabid dog.

With the hills now behind her, and the Catchkeep-priest somewhere among them, presumably wending his way back to town, she allowed herself to slow. Still keeping her breath measured. Still not letting herself limp. Still not betraying that the muscles of her calves were already quivering with the effort. That she'd eaten the flatbread and raisins and her head still swam with hunger. That she'd like to sit and breathe that clear cold air awhile and hoard it in her until it began, from inside out, to scrub her clean.

The orchard opened out before her and she headed in. At the first row of trees she stopped to fill what space was left in the backpack with apples. She kept one back to eat, spitting maggots as she walked.

She would have liked to sit beneath the trees a while instead. It might have been her last chance to do so before the snows came. But she knew the Catchkeep-priest was right. No ghost liked to be kept waiting.

Chapter Two

W asp was never sure whether it was because the Archivists' presence drew them, or because their presence drew the Archivists, but the ghosts always came up thick as suns-and-moons on Execution Hill. The field notes theorized that since deaths had happened there, there ghosts remained, each pacing out its circuit like a dog on a chain too short for comfort. Each with its dream (some previous Archivist had written) of a long drop on a short rope, or an axe to the neck, or a half-dozen bullets sinking themselves, warm as kisses, in its flesh. However it was they'd killed people here, back in the world Before.

But then there were the ghosts that didn't fit in to that theory. Infant ghosts, blue-faced with crib-death. Ghosts that had visibly died from illness or old age. Ghosts traveling with the company they'd died in: singly, or in pairs, or whole bouquets. Gangs of starving children. Families. Traveling like any wanderers on any road, linking hands and lighting fires against the eyes out in the dark. And nobody knew why.

Various Archivists had added their guesses to the field notes, but until somebody captured a ghost that could *talk*, guesses were what they'd remain. There was even a list, worn and soiled from the hands of countless Archivists, of questions one was supposed to ask a ghost, if a ghost was ever found who could reply. Name of specimen. Age of specimen. Description of surrounding environment during specimen's lifetime. Description of specimen's life, work, family, friends, enemies. Does the specimen recognize other ghosts? How does the specimen decide where to appear in the living world? Where does it come from when it appears? Where does it go? How many found objects in the Waste can the specimen identify? Did the world die during the specimen's lifetime? Place and manner of specimen's death. Manner of the world's death, if known, in as much detail as possible.

Wasp was no nearer than her predecessors to filling any of those answers in. As far as she could tell, the dead conversing with the living was a thing that happened in stories. Carrion Boy slinking down out of the stars to scare dreamers into a year of wakefulness, or the Chooser giving people advice that was like as not to get them killed.

But she was the Archivist, and it was her job to get those answers or die trying.

You uselessness, the Catchkeep-priest would say. *You misery. Why do we keep you? You're no solace to anyone. You couldn't unpuzzle a snarl in your hair.*

"You keep me," Wasp muttered to herself, kicking windfalls, "because none of you can kill me."

Long years had passed since Execution Hill had frightened her, though today, the prospect of the climb was almost enough to turn her on her heel and send her home. She could still see the remains of the narrow old road that spiraled up, or did once, to a high broad stage-like ledge seventy-or eighty-odd yards from the ground where she stood. The road was mostly crumbled now, a path at best, punched into powder by some storm, or the weight of years, or maybe the same blast of lightning that had clawed the scar into the face of the Hill.

She was not frightened anymore. Now she only felt affinity. "That's right, you bitch," she told it, unconsciously setting one hand to her own matching scar, Catchkeep's mark. "I'm still here."

Wasp tore a strip from her sleeve and bound the lid to the jar, then the jar to the pack, and climbed.

She did not come here often. At first the Catchkeep-priest didn't even know she could climb to the ledge, thought she'd be daunted by the crumbled path like so many other Archivists before her and choose to catch her ghosts elsewhere. That information had proven useful to her, her first year: this was where she'd hidden from Catchkeep's shrine-dogs, the first time she'd attempted escape—it was here or else the lake, rocks in her pockets, and the lake had almost won.

And then the dogs had treed her on the ledge, hunger had forced her down eventually, and all she had to show for it anymore was a pain in her heels when it rained, from when the Catchkeep-priest had dragged her back in triumph through the town, spitting, slashing, half-starved, and smashed her feet between two stones.

Sheer dumb luck, or stubbornness, she'd healed. But the place tended to leave a bad taste in her mouth after that. Still, she was the only one she knew of who could climb the thing, and so it remained her location of choice for disobeying direct orders.

Today, though, as much as she'd like to, she wasn't planning on disobeying anything. After what she'd done on the Archivist-choosing day, Wasp's educated guess was that pushing the Catchkeep-priest any further right now wasn't exactly going to end in her favor. But she'd already had enough of people today, and the ledge was still one place where she could go where she was guaranteed to be left alone.

In the end, she made it up there gracelessly. She almost broke the jar several times and almost fell to her probable death at least twice. But it was worth it when she hauled her screaming muscles up onto that high black ledge, her hands leaving sweaty palmprints on the rock, and she looked down knowing that the Catchkeep-priest, if he were standing at the foot of the Hill, would be the size of a beetle to her eyes, and that a lucky dropped rock would end him.

She set the backpack down. Against it, the jar tried to wiggle from its bonds. The lid heaved and clacked a little but stayed shut.

"Easy, easy," she told it. "Not much longer now."

As she spoke, she was untying the knots holding the jar against the pack. Out of the corner of her eye, she could see a low pale huddle, keeping as far away from her as the ledge allowed. She would not look at it. She did not look at it. Not yet.

Instead she kept talking, low and sweet as she was able, knowing that the ghost in the jar couldn't understand her words, unsure whether the soft steady noise of them might calm it anyway. Working the rust of two weeks' disuse from her voice. "Sorry about the wait. Locked in there for so long, nothing to look forward to except me destroying you when I finally let you out." The knot came loose and she sat on her heels a minute, imagining those smooth clay walls all around her, too narrow to stretch her arms or comfortably sit. "Well, if it helps, we're not so different, you know. I just live in a bigger jar, and they give me a fighting chance when they let me out of it. But if I win, I go back in. You're better off. You get cut loose. One way or another." She lifted the lid off the jar. "Anyway, come on out. I promise I'll make it quick."

She gave it a moment. Nothing happened. She peered into the jar. Just a silvery blur, sunk to the bottom like fog.

She'd never seen a ghost so weakened. For all she knew she wasn't going to be able to get it out of the jar. Could she still send it on to Catchkeep if it was stuck in there? It had never been covered in her predecessors' field notes, and today was not the day to be screwing things up. She took the notebook from the backpack and settled in to wait, thumbing back through the few field notes she'd taken on this ghost the day she'd caught it.

found at the baker's house.

There'd been salt at the baker's house, she remembered. Salt despite the ban. Idiot. She was tired of cleaning up after stupid people.

throwing-things-ghost. nasty. annoying. looked like it died violently. attacked the baker's wife. howling so loud the baker's ears bled.

It had been dripping silver, slinging gouts of silver as it smashed facefirst into walls. The baker's sleeping-room would never be the same.

tried to attack me, got put down.

Her eyes strayed from the page to the jar, her brain unwilling to match the ghost that had crushed the baker's wife's face like an eggshell with the washed-out used-up squashed bug of a ghost she had here.

useless for study. going to give it a day to calm down, then see if i can get anything out of it.

It'd had no discernible gender. No clothing. It had barely been person-shaped. Many decent specimens tended to mime the moment of their deaths, over and over, allowing Archivists to guess at least at what had killed them. Not this one. Beyond a mouth, it hadn't even had features to its face. Just a blur of light and rage.

Wasp had found it tearing up the baker's house two days before the Archivist-choosing fight. Being forgotten in its jar on her shelf for two weeks while she'd healed had calmed it down, all right, but it looked much the same. Only smaller. Less angry. Like a fire that had nearly gone out.

She stuck a finger in the jar. Poked the ghost, and her finger sank in to the first knuckle. No response.

There was still a little space left on the page. She wiped her finger off on her leg and took out a charcoal.

too weak now to even take shape. left in the jar too long? no fight left in it. almost dead. if that even happens.

conclusion: ghosts wither in captivity.

She read it over. It wasn't anything groundbreaking, but it was an observation she'd never seen written up before, and that had to count for something. At least it might save her a beating when she reported her day's work to the Catchkeep-priest. Maybe.

Weak and insubstantial as the ghost had become, being here, in a ghost-place, seemed to be lending it a bit of strength. As it stirred and stretched at the bottom of the jar, sending out stubby appendages from its mass, Wasp put the notebook down and began readying the items for the ritual that would destroy a ghost that had given its Archivist as much information as she was likely to get out of it. In this case, almost none. Waste of time, really.

She was moving quicker now. No point in being cruel, letting the ghost come into its strength only to annihilate it. Not when all it had to do was get out of the jar.

She took the firestarter out of the backpack, and a handful of dried leaves. A tiny plastic vial of water and another of milk followed those. The milk was long since soured, but that didn't matter. She set these down on the ledge in a rough circle in front of her, then put the jar, ghost and all, in the center.

All she needed now was blood.

She eased into a crouch as smoothly as her shaky muscles allowed. Something hissed a white streak up her leg, ankle to thigh, but she set her face and waited it out. The harvesting-knife was at her belt, and an eroded crater of black rock was by her feet, stained with rusty brown.

A flick of the blade against her thumbtip and the blood ran down. She held it out over the crater and waited as it dripped a tiny pool, hardly big enough to drown a bug.

The line she'd cut into her thumb had crosscut old scars from days and months and years of bloodlettings. She'd long since run out of empty spaces to slice into. *A map,* thought Wasp, who had seen one once. *A map to nowhere.*

The ghost in the jar roused a little, scenting. Farther back, other ghosts rose and settled in a mass. Out of the corner of her eye she watched them watch the blood run, watched them watch her raise her bloodied hand and lick it clean.

The silence curdled now. Clung to her crawling skin like the tarry rains of spring and did not lift. She didn't need to look to know the ghosts were straining toward the pool and toward her backpack as far as their roots allowed, as if she were Execution Hill itself and they the orchard curled around its heels.

She looked away from the jar for a second, just long enough to replace the notebook and charcoal in her backpack—and when she looked back at it the ghost was, impossibly, climbing out.

It was the size of Wasp's hand, and glowed dully silver. It was shaped like a person, or like a person as drawn by a small child. A cutout-shape person reduced to vague particulars—body, arms, legs, head. It was faceless, hairless, genderless. It gained its stubby feet and stood tilting its oversized skull at her. Wasp knew that stance. When it strengthened enough to bring its eyes in clear, they would be looking at her with the bland inquiry of an infant. If they could even see her at all.

What baffled her was that it was out of the jar in the first place. The saltlick was still in its box in her backpack, and the blood was two feet away. Where was it getting that much strength from?

She had two options. Hurry up and destroy the ghost before things got complicated. Or wait to see what it would do.

Her job was to destroy it. Send it on to Catchkeep, Who would carry it to that far green shore. She'd seen enough of this ghost to know she wasn't going to learn anything from it. She was just drawing out the inevitable, not to mention putting herself at risk. She'd had to fight this specimen once before, and she wasn't up for a second round today.

There had been Archivists before her who enjoyed destroying ghosts. There might well be another when she was dead. Wasp wasn't one of them. Something about how most ghosts never seemed to want to stay still for the ritual, kept trying to drag themselves out of the circle and back toward where they'd popped out of nothing into the living world, flopping against their salt tethers like fish out of water. In the stories they all went on to Catchkeep joyfully, but whatever Wasp saw in them, she didn't reckon it was joy.

Not that it mattered. That was the work, and she had to do it. The least she could do, here, now, with this ghost at her mercy, was to show it some and get this over with fast.

She drew the harvesting-knife.

Oblivious to Wasp's approach, the ghost took a step back, staggered a little, windmilling the paddles of its arms, then proceeded to toddle in a slow circle and fall over.

As it lay there, its mouth came in.

It was saying something.

Wasp sheathed the knife so fast she almost took off a finger.

She dropped to her knees and snatched up the little ghost. It weighed literally nothing. She'd long since gotten used to the instantaneous visceral shock of touching one, halfway between frostbite and vertigo. The ghost smushed its face against the clotting at her thumb, then took a tentative little lick. Then another. And another. At first the ghost's tongue felt like nothing, absolutely nothing, but as the ghost battened on her, strengthening, she became aware of a scraping sensation, as though she were a hide the ghost was tanning. Tomorrow it would be a nasty bruise, her thumb would be green-purple to the webbing, and she'd have to think fast to keep it hidden from the Catchkeep-priest.

She didn't mind the pain. Whatever ghosts might do to her, she at least knew where they stood. They didn't hurt her to benefit themselves, like the upstarts, or because they wanted her to suffer, like the Catchkeep-priest, whose hate she never fully understood. Ghosts were just hungry, lonely, lost. Desperate and confused. These were all things she could relate to. And out here, among them, was the only place she felt safe—not because none of them ever harmed her, but because they never wished her harm. They barely even knew she was there.

As it drank, the ghost began to grow. By the time she set it down and it inched on its belly to the pool and started lapping, it was the size of a weanling pup. It drank and drank, pausing only to . . . glance? . . . over its shoulder at her with a blank silver face in which the only feature was a wide red mouth. When the pool was emptied the ghost stood the size of a two-year-old child, and its eyes had come in.

It blinked at her, not inquisitively, not anything. She had no idea what it was seeing, but whatever it was, it wasn't her. It stood there, its mouth releasing unformed mewing sounds in no language Wasp knew.

Wasp held her breath, listening.

And the hazy outline of the ghost sharpened off a little, and the sounds clarified with it. The same few syllables, looping over and over. It sounded like a name. It could have been anyone's. A lover's, a child's, a friend's. Wasp's mouth twisted, scorn or envy.

Then she realized what she was witnessing, and scrambled for her notebook.

two-weeks-caught ghost
weakest Ive ever seen
no salt no blood but walking talking
She underlined *talking* three times, then circled it twice.

talking louder now with the blood in it but this thing went from silver smoke-blob to climbing out of the jar in a three-count on its own and that was before any blood any salt any reason
Underlined *on its own*. Underlined *reason*.

shouldnt be happening
stupid to destroy without further study.

Like it mattered, sparing something already dead. Stupid that she should feel relieved, but she always did. She'd just have to destroy it later, once she was done with—

She glanced up, frantic for a second because the ghost was not where she had left it. Then she caught sight of it, meandering back along the ledge, its hand twisting at the air as if turning invisible doorknobs. Wasp watched as it reached the others and began to play with its shape, stretching and shrinking, stopping when it was roughly the height of most of the ghosts in the group. It stood among them as they patted its arms and face, which had grown fingers and a nose, respectively. It was looking into the face of each ghost in turn, still repeating those syllables that might have been a name. The last syllable had a little upward tilt to it now. As if it were asking a question.

Wasp stared, charcoal forgotten in her hand. A ghost was *communicating with other ghosts?* This was big. This was very, very big.

"Hey," she whispered at it, feeling stupid.

Of course, the ghost didn't respond. She'd mostly known it wouldn't. Ghosts couldn't talk to people, not even Archivists. She had a whole box of field notes to prove it. It was only a very, very strong ghost that could do something like attack a person, but even then it did so mindlessly, like a tantruming child kicking at the floor.

She tried again. "Hey there. I'm not going to hurt you."

Nothing. No surprise there. But she could still recapture the ghost for study. See what she could get from it. Give its death a purpose. It would be the same purpose that a struck spark gives firewood, but it was better than none.

She was just reaching for the jar when the ghost found a crack in the wall and shrank down some more to disappear inside. She leapt after it, too late.

Wasp dropped her head into her hands, swearing as colorfully as she knew how. It was a good few minutes before she calmed down, but she had to. When a tiny spark of hope shone out from the shitheap of her life, she had to focus on it. It was the only way she was going to get through another year of this without losing her mind.

The ghost was gone, but it could have been worse. She would have loved to study it further, try to figure out what it wanted, and, more importantly, what had given it the *strength* to want it in the first place. No point in worrying about that, though. She was losing the light. She'd tell the Catchkeep-priest she'd destroyed the ghost like she was supposed to, and catch another one to study. It'd have to be a good one, to make her less pissed at herself than she was right now. But she also had the notes.

It was rare that she was *supposed* to release a ghost, but what she was meant to say when she did so was this:

I am the Archivist. Catchkeep's emissary, ambassador, and avatar on earth. Her bones and stars my flesh; my flesh and bones Her stars. I am She who bears you, She who sustains you, She to whom your dust returns. You have lived well. You have died well. I release you. Do not ghost my way.

What she did say was:

"Back into the soup with you, troublemaker. Next time, pick someplace smarter to haunt."

Destroying the captive ghost had been only one of her appointed tasks today. She was also supposed to catch another. The midwife's niece wanted a baby, but was suffering from an uncooperative womb. An egg would catch, and clot, and grow, then lose its grip and trickle out, and the midwife's arsenal of tricks was to no avail. The midwife had prayed to the Chooser and come away with the notion that an *animated* clot might have the will to hang on as a new body pieced itself around it. She'd gone to the Catchkeep-priest with her petition and her offerings to Catchkeep, and the Catchkeep-priest had given Wasp the job of finding her a ghost.

In Wasp's experience, the townspeople were terrified of ghosts, and with good reason. Unlike Archivists, they weren't under Catchkeep's protection, and Catchkeep's dominion was ghosts. It was very, very rare for someone to come *asking* for a specimen for personal use, but it did happen. There was trade in ghosts to neighboring towns, for instance—once or twice a year, maybe, the Catchkeep-priest would barter a bottled ghost for Chooser knew what, and one time Wasp had seen her predecessor catch a particularly nasty specimen and tether it in the town gardens to keep the scav kids off the perimeter fence. The harvest that autumn had doubled.

But Wasp was not her predecessor. She didn't have a fraction of that kind of love for the work. As an upstart, Wasp had been sent up to the Archivist-house on an errand for the Catchkeep-priest. All she remembered about the Archivist she'd go on to replace was that she'd left salt-trails running *to* her house, at least half the jars on her shelves were not only full but also blood-streaked on their inside walls, and she'd been in the process of squeezing a cut finger for a hungry ghost when Wasp had knocked. When the Archivist had grinned at her, Wasp had shuddered at the sharpness of her teeth.

Wasp wasn't in the habit of keeping ghosts around for long, and she wasn't looking to start a collection. She might have three full jars, at most, on any given day. Her method was as pared-back as possible. Cut, capture, carry home in jar, take notes, bring back in jar, destroy. No reason to prolong suffering, even of the dead. When they'd come to her asking to tether a scarecrow-ghost as her predecessor had done, she'd done it—but after a few nights of its howling drifting up her hill, she'd snuck into the gardens and cut it free. When they asked her to catch another, she'd obeyed. When that one and the next two also disappeared, they stopped asking.

So Wasp would catch a child-ghost for the midwife's niece. She had no idea how the midwife was planning to put this ghost in a living woman's womb, or whether a ghost would even want such a thing, and what a ghost might do in that case to show its displeasure if the idea was not to its liking. She wasn't sure she wanted to know. Still, before and after her doubts she was the Archivist. She had a duty to her people. The fallout from their decisions wasn't her business. Not unless the ghost got loose.

The other ghosts were still milling around the crack in the rock, oblivious to her inspection. Most were ankle-height or less; a few topped out around her knees or thighs. The tallest one she'd ever seen stood half as high as the ledge, but she'd only seen it once. Where it'd gotten the strength for that trick from, she had no idea. She'd been an upstart then, and had kept well away.

Thankfully, her thumb had stopped bleeding. Not that any of this batch of ghosts looked particularly threatening, but the blood had been known to bring it out in them, and things were weird enough today already without adding a brawl on top. She'd bandage it. Meantime, she'd better get moving and distract them, just in case.

Wasp rummaged in the backpack and came out with the little plastic box containing the saltlick. She set it down near the nearest of the ghosts, putting herself between it and the bloodstained pit of rock. The ghosts nosed forward, browsing at the air—one or two taking a step, then others following, and a scuffle erupted at her feet as the ghosts descended upon the dish.

It still startled her, how violently the salt drew them. The field notes said it was because it put the ghosts in mind of their former flesh. That to them, it was the salt of sweat, of tears, of blood. It drew them because it made them remember being alive, made them hunger for everything they'd lost.

She sketched the feeding ghosts in her notebook, her mind on the one she'd let slip through her fingers. It fascinated and depressed her, the way the ghosts moved, pacing their confines. Sounding their boundaries, back and forth. She saw much of herself in them, so she never watched for long.

Today there were eight lone ones and what looked to be a rare set of three. What with their ability to change size at will, it was always hard for her to tell the ages they'd been when they'd died, but by the way two of them were nudging the third one on before them toward the saltlick, shielding it against the others' jostling with what they most likely still thought of as their *bodies*, Wasp's best guess was that this used to be a family.

As the salt took hold of them, their faces began to resolve: first the features grew, claylike, then refining—their hair grew out, straight or curly, then darkened or lightened from that dullish silver—their eyes grew pupils, irises, and color slowly began to bleed in. Their heights and sizes began to stabilize, to calibrate against each other. It *was* a family, she could see now. Or used to be. Two females and a tiny male, maybe three or four years old at time of death.

It might be weeks before she found another child-ghost so young. And she hated unfinished business.

Keeping her eyes on the lapping ghosts, one hand reached behind her blind and felt around on the rock for the jar, while the other hand drew the harvesting-knife free of its dogleather sheath at her belt. The knife was as long as her forearm, forged from some bright metal, with a guard like a sword and a grip wrapped with the same dogleather as the sheath, and worth more than everything else in her little house combined. The shape of the blade was irregular, the hilt longer than the handle of a knife of similar size would be, and the point was unevenly tapered, as though the true point had broken off and this was what was left. But it was a ritual blade, not a weapon, and it served.

When she readied it in position, the low autumn sun caught on the sixteen dots of darker metal inset along the blade: the six larger ones, the size of a wild blueberry; the ten smaller ones, the size of a clover-seed. Vaguely they described a wedge-shaped head, a jaw like a beartrap, a barrel chest, long legs, a lashing back-curved tail.

Years ago, when she stood bloodied on the lakeshore above the previous Archivist's cooling corpse, and was presented with this blade, it was held out to her in such a way that the constellation on the blade caught and returned the light of the matching constellation in the sky. Catchkeep.

The harvesting-knife felt strange in her hand now after two weeks without it. Strange and yet as familiar as any other part of her. She took a step toward the child-ghost, and it turned.

This part used to frighten her a little. The sea-change in the ghosts' eyes as the salt waylaid them. The look on their faces, like they woke from a nightmare to find that the monsters had followed them back out into their cozy beds. It had not taken her long to realize that the only monster they were seeing was her.

The child-ghost turned back to the saltlick. Its parent-ghosts didn't seem to have noticed her at all. For the thousandth time she reminded herself of what the field notes had taught her: that when she harvested a ghost, the ones it had traveled with wouldn't even know it was gone, no longer had the minds with which to understand the loss or the hearts with which to feel it, any more than a hand feels the loss of a pared fingernail. That ghosts, essentially, were recorded information rewinding, playing, rewinding. Skipping and resuming. A resource to be tapped and nothing more.

She wished she knew whether that were true.

Knife in one hand, jar in the other, she was kneeling behind the child-ghost ready to slice it free and lid it up when she realized: there was only the one jar. Only the one jar, which she was about to fill with a ghost that had died too young to be of any use to the field notes.

It wouldn't be the first time she harvested a ghost she didn't have much hope of learning anything from—but usually it was not her first day on the job after half a month in recovery, she hadn't just lost the ghost she *should* have been bringing back to study, and she hadn't forgotten to bring enough damn jars with her on a hunt. And she didn't much relish the idea of coming back up here to try again tomorrow.

If she took the child-ghost for the midwife's niece, she would have made good on that particular duty, but otherwise she'd be returning to the Catchkeep-priest emptyhanded. And that was not a place she wanted to be.

But then she thought of the child-ghost, and wondered whether the midwife was right and it was possible for it to be reborn. She thought of the children she had seen chasing each other around town and concluded that, as far as she could tell, children liked to be alive. It was her best guess that this one might have liked it, too. She only hoped it wouldn't come back as a baby girl with Catchkeep's mark on her cheek.

She glanced at the child-ghost, the parent-ghosts. "Paring a fingernail," she said, either to them or to herself, and decided.

A quick swipe in a ring around the child-ghost with the harvesting-knife and it shrank back to ankle-height, weakened. Free for the picking. She set down the knife, closed her hand around the ghost's waist, and pulled. It came free of the rock with a sound like uprooting weeds from mud and she dropped it into the jar, looking anywhere but at its face.

Where she found herself looking instead was into the eyes of the two parent-ghosts. They had turned from the saltlick and were staring at her with a look that she had seen rather often on the living but very, very seldom on any ghost. Complete awareness. Utter hate.

It froze her. These ghosts, these nothing little ghosts she'd disregarded, actually had the strength to turn their backs on the salt without her say-so. It flew in the face of everything she knew.

"No," she whispered, as her palms went clammy and her heart began to race.

First she'd released a ghost from two weeks' confinement, which was apparently beyond long enough to wither it like a leaf, but somehow the ghost had found the strength to remember. To search. To attempt to speak. To communicate with other ghosts, if Wasp's observation was correct. And then there was the look in the parent-ghosts' eyes. Which was now in the others' eyes, too, as all the ghosts abandoned the salt to turn their faces upon her in unison, as though alerted by the sudden racket of her breath, the sudden stink of her fear.

She'd read warnings in the field notes about clusters of strong ghosts. One on its own meant a difficult catch, but a first-class specimen. More than one meant trouble. No catch at all, and maybe a dead Archivist. It had happened before. She had a pretty good idea where this was going.

It wasn't these ghosts that were the problem. Not any of the ones on the ledge, not the one she'd lost.

It was worse.

Chapter Three

Slowly she set the jar down and gripped the harvesting-knife, wondering if it would defend her. Eyes scanning the ledge for the ghost that she knew had to be there, somewhere: the one that brimmed with so much careless, reckless strength that it was running over with power, it was *shedding* power—and the others were drinking it up by the roots like rain.

Stupid. She'd been stupid. So focused on some little ghosts' weird behavior that she didn't notice the bigger picture. Didn't even *look* for a bigger picture. Stupid and careless and too hung up on hope, which had gotten her precisely nowhere thus far. And now she was going to have to think fast if she didn't want to get herself pasted on the rock with all those notes she'd been so pleased with up until about fifteen seconds ago.

She could have kicked herself in the ass. Saved this mystery ghost the trouble.

She couldn't see it. This thing was strong enough to slap her dead like a fly where she stood, and she couldn't see it. How could she not see it? It had to be there. Maybe she was rusty from being so long out of the field, but that didn't explain it. Without the salt to bring them into focus between worlds, the blood to give them strength enough to put their faces on and speak, most ghosts were too weak to do much of anything aboveground, but *this* one—wherever it was—with this kind of strength radiating off of it, it should be huge, it should be, she didn't know, glowing or something, it should be *obvious*—

Her hand was too sweaty now to have any kind of sure grip on the knife. Quickly she passed it to her off hand, wiped her damp palm on her leg. For a fleeting second a childish urge welled up in her and she nearly shouted for help. But who could hear her? And, hearing her, who would come? The matter of her death was between her and Catchkeep. To the townspeople she was the Archivist, faceless, nameless, a goddess's eyes and ears and hands. They honored her as they had honored those who'd come before her, and they would bury her likewise. And pull another Archivist up after her, climbing on her corpse.

On the ledge by her foot, the child-ghost's jar was beginning to tip back and forth, teetering and righting. A thin wail, high and pure and so tiny, reached Wasp's ears.

She should not have been able to hear it. It should not have been there to hear.

"Shit," she whispered, backing a step.

At the cry, the staring parent-ghosts now broke from the saltlick entirely and bolted for the jar, swiping at the lid. There were sigils on that jar and their hands should pass through. They did not pass through. There was a melodious clinking as the lid rolled away off the ledge and was lost, and from the jar the child-ghost emerged into its parents' arms. They bore it away between them, and for the first time in three years of hunting and harvesting Wasp could actually *see* the oozing silver trail, half snailslime half brine, that a ghost left behind from where it had been cut free.

Wasp had seen strong ghosts before. She had seen a ghost as tall as a tree, a ghost bigger than her house, a ghost that had emerged from the rock still wreathed in the live fire that had killed it, which ignited where it touched, and singed her backpack as she'd leapt away. She'd read the stories in the field notes, the cautionary tales of Archivists who got too cocky and were found in unrecognizable piles, bones cracked to get at the salt in their marrow, silvery footprints leading away.

She had been punched in the face by a ghost, nearly trampled by another, had a few try to drink her dry of blood like something out of a story from the Before.

But she had never seen anything like this.

There was something behind her. She whirled and there was nothing there.

Invisible? she thought wildly. *Can they even—*

She stood a moment, scanning the ledge, her heart banging at her ribs like it wanted out. "Nothing," she whispered. The sound of her voice comforted her. She said it louder. "It was nothing."

She turned back and was lifted bodily from the ledge and slammed up against the wall.

The air flew out of her with an ugly sound. For a second she hung there, too stunned both in her muscles and her mind to fight.

This ghost was stronger than her. Stronger than the Catchkeep-priest. Stronger than the shrine-dogs, who were bred to reach two hundred pounds of solid muscle, their heads as high as her shoulder.

She could not get it in focus. Had she hit her head that hard? It was still holding her pinned against the rock face of Execution Hill. It would have made much more sense if it wasn't a ghost at all, if someone had followed her up here, someone from town who had finally decided to try their luck at doing her in, maybe a friend of that last poor dead upstart, wanting revenge, or a friend of one of next year's, looking to better someone's chances. It wasn't like she lacked for enemies. But there were the other ghosts, all turning toward it, half-yearning half-terror, and there was a sort of dark light rising off of it like steam, feeding back and back along the rock where the other ghosts drew it up shuddering, and anyway since when had anyone in town been an upstart's *friend*—

"Start talking," said the ghost, its voice perilously calm.

Wasp's mouth fell open. If this wasn't already wholly beyond the realm of her experience, it certainly was now. "I— what—"

The ghost stared at her. She stared back.

Chooser help her, she was about to die and some part of her mind had detached itself to take field notes.

male specimen. died young. not all that much older than me really.

weird voice, gone rusty, like it doesnt get used much.

some kind of uniform. dark. boots. havent seen it before.

gray eyes. angrylooking. mostly. something else in there. hurt? shocked? down deep. cant really make it out.

dont look like ghost eyes.

The ghost narrowed them at her. "Clarify."

It sounded like the Catchkeep-priest when Wasp was halfway between a failed escape attempt and a whipping. Only much, much worse.

It was now or never. She slashed up hard with the harvesting-knife and the ghost let go. She tucked her legs to hit the ledge rolling and came up blade-first, strangely disoriented and shaking her head to clear it.

To her satisfaction, there was a long tear in the ghost's coat-sleeve, issuing a steady runnel of silver. The ghost either didn't notice or didn't care.

Off behind it, one or two of the other ghosts, full to bursting with that strange dark light, exploded into silver sparks like a dry scorchweed blossom stomped. The others scattered back into the rock.

"Back off," she shouted at it. Her voice shook, but her knife-hand did not. "That's not a warning I give twice."

The ghost advanced a step and froze there. Its image seemed to stutter somehow in mid-stride, flickering. When it spoke again, its tone of voice had changed.

"We're leaving. Right now."

Wasp was reaching her limit. She burst out laughing. "The hell we are."

The ghost just gave her that wordless stare. She'd thought she'd seen hauteur on the Catchkeep-priest before. That was nothing, nothing at all, to this.

She calculated. Her chances didn't look good. There was the saltlick, and there was the jar. The jar whose lid had gone over the edge and was now two hundred feet below, clay shards among scree. The saltlick which she'd have to get through the ghost to reach. Even with all her tools at her disposal, and uninjured, could she bind this thing? She was beginning to sorely doubt it.

"The plan changed," said the ghost. "Get up."

Get up?

"Look, I don't know where you think you are," she said carefully, "or who you think I am, but—"

The ghost took another step. Wasp knew the look in its eyes. It was the look she gave upstarts on that final approach before they came under her blade. She threw her body aside as the ghost strode toward her, nearly tipping herself over the ledge. The harvesting-knife came up bloodied, and so did her forearm. She hissed annoyance between her teeth and began sidling around, trying to interpose her body and blade between the saltlick and the ghost. It wasn't much of a chance, but it was what she had. They circled like brawlers. She couldn't see this ending well.

She was two steps and a blind grab from the saltlick when the ghost drew a blade of its own.

Wasp flung herself back out of immediate range, her mind racing. This ghost could bring things *through with it*? Apparently so, for it was now coming at her with a sword, and it had a gun on its belt as well.

It was too much. It was beyond too much. And she wouldn't make it to the saltlick at this rate, not without losing limbs on the way. If, that is, the sword could cut her. She wasn't sure. But she knew where her guess was going.

She backed another step, which took her up against the wall. Her eyes fell on the blood welling up out of the gash on her arm, then to the blood still on the harvesting-knife.

It wasn't a weapon. She'd never used it as a weapon before. She'd never had to really *fight* a ghost before, sure as hell not like this, anyway. And to stab this ghost, now, with her blood on the blade, was a Ragpicker's gambit if ever she'd seen one.

Wasp went to wipe the blade on her sleeve—and stopped. She was thinking of those lesser ghosts, all exploded, and how they'd drunk up this ghost's shed power until it had overloaded them. Thinking this ghost had to have a limit, too. Wondering where it was. Whether she could reach it.

It would have looked like a worse idea if she had anything else to choose from short of jumping off the ledge with a prayer.

However, the ghost's reach with the sword was easily twice what hers was with the harvesting-knife, and Wasp had serious doubts about getting inside it now, let alone getting the ghost inside *her* reach. Still, she had to try. Without warning she dropped to the ground, under the swing of the ghost's blade, and stabbed her own bloodied knife down through the top of the ghost's boot until the point hit the porous rock of the shelf and wedged there.

She must have hit her head harder than she'd thought, because as the knife came down she thought she saw something, for a split second, there and gone before it could be identified, darting from her mind like a fish the net had missed—

A shudder went through the ghost as the holy metal and the blood took hold, and she pulled the knife free, blinking in awe. She hadn't thought it would *work*.

It couldn't last long—a few seconds at most—and Wasp didn't want to stick around to wait for it to wear off, the ghost's awful strength to come raging back, her choice either fighting a losing battle or fleeing down the mountainside like a whipped dog. Which wasn't any choice at all.

In one motion she swiped the saltlick, dropped her hip to sweep the ghost's legs out from under, planted a knee on its chest, and pressed the salt to its mouth, grinding it in with the heel of her hand. She scattered more around it where it lay. Jar or not, blood was blood, salt was salt, the knife was the knife, and she'd hung her hopes on worse before and lived.

"By blood and salt I bind you," she gasped. "You will follow."

The effect was instantaneous. The ghost lunged at her and came up short, collared by the empty air. Wasp crouched a few paces back, knife at the ready, for all the good it would do if the last trick up her sleeve had failed.

Slowly, slowly, something changed in the ghost's face and it began to see her clearly. It was drawing itself up now to its full height, looking at her the way she would look at a snake in her path, if she couldn't identify it as one that might bite her or one she could eat. Wasp was amazed to realize that, just as she had suddenly been able to see the goo the child-ghost had bled from its cut roots, she could now also see the way the salt and blood eddied around this ghost's feet, carried on the current it exuded. It didn't thrash at the shackles, didn't draw on her again. It stood like a stone, and Wasp hated herself for being humbled by some dead thing's dignity.

It was powerful, so powerful. But she had caught it. It was hers. Until she said otherwise, it would stay.

When she thought of all those unanswered questions in the field notes, what answers she might glean from this specimen, she felt a little dizzy. So what if she'd lost the other ghost? She could toss her notebook off the ledge right now and it wouldn't matter. Archivists had gone up against powerful ghosts like this one and been broken against them, or fled. If any had captured one successfully, there was no record of it in the field notes.

After three years of observation and study and guesswork, *here* was a ghost she could *learn* from. It was like nothing she'd experienced. Nothing she'd even known was possible. It had been a long time since she'd seen anything that looked so much like a way out.

She may have had a long fight and a longer heal, as the Catchkeep-priest had so helpfully pointed out, and maybe she was starting to lose her touch, as she'd suspected from the number of wounds the last batch of upstarts had given her. But after this, she wouldn't be showing them weakness. She wouldn't be showing them a has-been Archivist, rusting to garbage in her little house on the hill. She would be showing them one of the most potentially useful discoveries that any Archivist had likely ever made in four hundred years and counting. She would be showing them something so huge, so important, that she might be able to trade it for her freedom. She would—

"So I take it you are in the business of hunting ghosts," the ghost was saying. It watched her levelly, its eyes unfathomable. The pain and shock was gone from them, Wasp saw, gone or quashed. "Excellent. Then I could use your help in finding one."

If the rock of the Hill itself had spoken to her directly, it might have caught her less off guard. This ghost could see her. It could speak to her. It had . . . come *looking for her*?

It wasn't possible. It couldn't be possible. But there the ghost was, staring at her. Not through her. *At* her. Waiting for a reply.

"I think," she said slowly, "we might be able to come to an agreement."

Chapter Four

It was getting on for sundown when Wasp had picked her way back down the Hill, hoping against hope she wasn't so late for her meeting with the Catchkeep-priest that he'd go looking for her at her house and find her coming across the orchard, stumbling with exhaustion and accompanied by a ghost, salt-snared but jarless, walking on its own two feet.

They crossed the orchard in a silence that was not quite hostile but nothing like companionable, and Wasp would have felt more like she was escorting a prisoner, as was the case, if anything in the ghost's demeanor had suggested it. Beside it, she felt diminished and vaguely ridiculous, like a lapdog it had let off-leash to growl at rabbit holes. The ghost didn't seem to be much for small talk, which suited Wasp fine. Her mind was racing. The ghost wanted her to . . . *find* another ghost? She didn't even begin to know what to make of it. An hour ago she was nearly beside herself because she'd witnessed a ghost dumbly mouthing repeating syllables in the general direction of another. Here, now, half delirious with questions, it was a long walk back to that simpler place and its simpler confusions, and the door to it was shut.

The Archivist part of her brain, meantime, would probably only stop cycling through its function when the part that controlled her breathing went, or her blinking, or her heart, or her stupid improbable plans that never held water and would probably one day get her killed.

This part carried on muttering field notes to itself, oblivious.

of course I cant do what it wants. but that isnt the point. the point is that ghosts dont ask people to do things. ghosts cant talk to people. ghosts sure as shit dont go looking for other ghosts, sure as shit dont go asking living people to run their errands. Ive never seen two ghosts so much as nod at each other before today, let alone—

conclusion: I am dreaming.

Wasp tripped over a rock, stumbling hard on the bad ankle. Amended it.

hurts way too bad to be dreaming.

How Wasp was going to explain to this ghost what she wanted in return for helping it, and how it would react to that news, and what she would do when it did . . . she hadn't figured that part out yet. She was working on it. Her best guess, though, was that it wasn't going to respond well when she asked it to go willingly into study and interrogation. And smooth talking was never her strong point. For now, all she knew was that she wasn't letting this preposterous thing out of her sight. She'd already lost one ghost, one plan, one hope today. Over her dead body she'd lose another.

Luckily, when she reached her little house on the hill there was no sign of anybody. Something about the ghost made her want to keep it secret. It almost would have been easier to return from the Hill emptyhanded, because now when the Catchkeep-priest asked her what she'd caught today, she was certain she'd lie. She thought of the Catchkeep-priest circling this ghost like a vulture, questioning it, dissecting it with his eyes, and the idea made her want to punch a hole in a wall and she wasn't sure quite why.

By the time she reached the door her whole leg from the bad ankle up was one throbbing ache, and to put weight on it was a coin-toss: would it give out, would it hold. She had resolved not to limp and failed miserably. She faltered up the last of the long path and listed between the toppled heaps of offerings by the door. There she stopped.

It came to her that she was standing in a choosing moment. Ghosts didn't get into her house unless she let them. She didn't have to let this one. She stood there, in that choosing moment, weighing *dangerous* in one hand over *useful* in the other.

Well, everything was dangerous. She couldn't say the same for useful.

"Stay back a second," she said, and reached high with the knife to cut down the bundle of ghostgrass that hung above the door. A few steps behind her there was a dark, scorched-looking ring drawn on the rock the whole way around the house's footprint. Wasp went to that next, and squatted down awkwardly on one ankle to draw the knife over the line in a slicing motion, twice, as though she were cutting a gap in the circle three feet wide. "Walk where I walk," she said, and stepped over the ring, through the gap, not touching the marks.

The ghost watched her. The look on its face, on a living person, might have been quizzical. "Keeps ghosts away," said Wasp. "I'm the only one in town allowed to have salt. It's too rare and too dangerous. For ghosts, this place must light up like a warn-fire. When they find it . . ." She shook her head. "It's not pretty." A pause. "No offense."

She went inside and began to light the lamps, whatever use a ghost would have for them. She dropped the backpack, washed her face, rubbed some soap through her hair, bound her arm, found a clean shirt with sleeves long enough to hide the bandage and the gash.

If she didn't know it was beyond the Catchkeep-priest's ability to capture ghosts, she would have sworn he'd put this one in her way to test her. She imagined him poking it into her path with a stick, gingerly, as if it'd bite. The townsfolk gambling: could she bite back harder?

"Don't break anything," she told it, and left.

†

A mile later, she reached the shrine. She stood a moment, gasping up the blood-and-ash-and-flowers smell of the place, so that by the time she circled around to the living-quarters she was only a little out of breath. The Catchkeep-priest opened the door before she knocked, one finger keeping his place in some old book, and looked sidewise down at her, taking her in at a glance: favored leg to salt-caked nails to lacerated cheek to baleful stare. The shrine-dogs padded to the door to bristle at her and the Catchkeep-priest kicked at their legs until they backed down.

"Busy day," he said. She guessed it was a question. She didn't answer it. He didn't mention that she was late. She hadn't expected him to. It wasn't his way. His way was to keep her waiting until the hammer fell. She'd walked the last quarter-mile with her hands shoved in her pockets to hide the trembling.

From inside the house she could smell fresh bread and some kind of garlicky stew, and she became suddenly, acutely aware that she hadn't eaten since that morning.

The Catchkeep-priest opened the door wider and stepped back. From deep in the room she could hear the upstarts laughing, she assumed at her. "Come in, come in."

His voice was mild enough, but then she saw his eyes. She went inside.

She hated everything about this room: its long table, the shallow curtained sleeping-alcoves along the walls, the great room of the Catchkeep-priest's quarters between the upstarts' and the shrine. If a ghost was a recording of a memory, as some believed, and Wasp pulled back the curtain from the third alcove on the right, she might find the wide-eyed bloody-handed ghost of herself, hugging her knees and shivering, trying to unremember the sound of her little dagger sinking hilt-deep into girlflesh, the day she earned her name. And in the alcove two up the line from it might be the ghost of the upstart Naomi, who'd snuck into Wasp's alcove after that fight, though she was risking a beating to do so, and sat in silence holding her hand, never complaining, though Wasp's nails dug in until they drew blood and were stained with it for days. And in the alcove almost directly across the room from hers, the ghost of the upstart Becca, who'd taken her own handmade shiv to the big veins in her thighs that same night, because Wasp had drawn the short straw first and cut the Archivist down before the other upstarts got their fighting chance to do the same.

Not to mention the ghosts of four hundred years' worth of dead upstarts before them, and of those who had lived, for a time, but in whom something somewhat less essential than a beating heart had died.

Wasp wasn't sure where the three latest dead upstarts had slept: Mariska, Suzie, Aneko. She might have stopped before those curtains, laid down some roadside flowers in her mind. They hadn't died well.

Puzzling at ghosts only brought to mind the one she was hiding among the empty jars in her no-longer-empty house, and she schooled her face fast before the Catchkeep-priest could read it.

Upstarts scooted down the benches from her, muttering amongst themselves at her approach. Either it was her imagination or there was something new in their voices since the Archivist-choosing day had passed—disdain for the relic who'd kept her title but ended her fight by fainting in the sand, too thrashed or too soft to finish what she'd started. She was becoming mortal in their eyes. Replaceable. Killable. And there was no coming back from that.

Her hair, weighted with the inbraided hair of one dead Archivist and eight dead upstarts, swung loose from its pinnings as she took a seat at the long table. It fell around her, heavy as a pelt, its smell of death outlasting all her soap. The upstarts stared at it, particularly at the multicolored ends they all must recognize, and thought of the three short straws they hadn't drawn.

The Catchkeep-priest set a bowl before her, served her with his own hands from the breadboard and the stewpot. Under the weight of the upstarts' eyes, she ate. The Catchkeep-priest waited on her, served her seconds, and settled in across the table, steepling his fingers.

"It's so *good* to have you back with us," he said. "It's been, oh, much too long."

The upstarts leaned in, hanging on her words less than on her fear.

"Yes," she said.

"We were beginning to dread you weren't coming back out of that hovel of yours this time."

She could feel the upstarts breathing down her neck.

"Well, I did," she said.

"And it looks as though you fell foul of some mishap. Your first day back to work." He *tsk*ed, and Wasp braced for what never came. "A pity."

Wasp, unable to think of anything witty to rejoin with, said nothing.

"You have always been blessed with a spectacular talent, our Wasp. It is our honor and our pleasure to hope it does not forsake you."

Around her, a dozen upstarts were all wearing the same smile. It stretched their Catchkeep-given scars, made the smiles look even wider than they were. Wasp's flight instinct stirred and started kicking. She fought it down.

"Yes," she said.

"You and I, Wasp, we're so *much* the same," he said, eating bread-bits with little birdlike pecks. "We have burned our pasts, our futures, our very names away in the service of something greater than ourselves. Can these green girls be faulted for desiring to serve as we serve?"

Unless Wasp missed her guess, what the upstarts desired even more than that was to cut out her liver and wring it out into the sand and read their fortunes from the patterns of gore it left there.

"No," she said.

The Catchkeep-priest nodded sagely, sipping stew-broth from a real spoon.

Wasp wished he'd choke on it. She had plans for his ghost.

"But the work won't wait, will it?"

"No," she said.

"Not like that poor ghost," he said, and Wasp's heart started beating at its bars so fast and hard it left her short of breath, but: "Left to suffer in that jar for so long," he continued, and she calmed. So he didn't know. Not yet. "No light, no air, no salt," he said, and the upstarts shook their heads as one. "It's a good thing you put it out of its misery."

"Yes," she said.

"Why not show a little grace to your inferiors," he said, his voice light and warm and utterly menacing. "Tell them how you did it."

He was baiting her. Maybe he knew she hadn't destroyed the ghost after all. Maybe he didn't. Either way, she could take it or push back. And her tendency favored pushing.

"They can figure out how to do it themselves," she said. "When it's their business to do."

A hiss went round the table. Wasp set her jaw. Let them come at her. But it was not the time and place for bloodshed, and they all knew what happened to upstarts who picked fights on the side, on the three hundred sixty-four wrong days of the year, so they stayed.

In a year, though, when the time came, they would still remember. And the ones who could, the ones who drew the short straws, would try their very best to make her pay.

"If," said the Catchkeep-priest, beaming now. "*If* they become Archivist. *If* they can defeat you first to do so. I suspect that what you mean is *if*."

She had challenged them, and he was challenging her back. To tell the truth now was to court a whipping. All she had to do to get back out of it was open her stupid stubborn mouth and say *no*.

She met his eyes.

"Yes," she said.

There was a pause as the Catchkeep-priest dabbed at his mouth and put his napkin down with a sound like a withered flower dropping from its stalk. "Ah, Wasp. It is *so good* to have you back."

"So I've heard," she said

"You are, after all, the most gifted Archivist I've ever seen. Truly we'd be lost without you."

"Thank you," she said. She was getting wary now. Talking to him reminded her of walking on a frozen pond. The ice would hold until it didn't. It was anybody's guess when that would be.

"To say nothing of those poor ghosts. Why, that one you destroyed today, for instance. Where did you catch that one again?"

"The baker's house," she said.

The upstart sitting beside the Catchkeep-priest muttered something under her breath, and, without taking his eyes from Wasp, the Catchkeep-priest grabbed the girl behind the head and smashed her face into the table. While the upstart sleeved at her split eyebrow in silence, he kept on talking as if nothing had occurred.

"The baker's *kitchen*, as I recall," he said. "And what was it doing there?"

"It was after the salt," she said.

"You *think* it was after the salt. No, no, don't give me that vicious look, everyone at this table respects your expertise. But I think the baker's wife, with the broken jaw from when your gentle ghost flung a chair at her head—across the *house* from where the salt was kept, I could add—might think differently."

"And this is why people don't *keep* salt in their *houses*," Wasp gritted, her temper coming out in a slow leak. "This is *why* there's a *ban*. I don't have time to clean up after every slag-for-brains who thinks it's safe to disobey it."

There. It was out. She'd backtalked the Catchkeep-priest in front of all the upstarts. Their gazes were darting between Wasp and the Catchkeep-priest, expecting calamity.

The Catchkeep-priest only laughed, apparently delighted. But Wasp could see something very different in his eyes. It was only a matter of time before he found out about the ghost in Wasp's house. She'd have to decide what to do with it soon. Tonight. Right now would be good. There was no guidance in the field notes for this kind of situation.

She couldn't get it out of her head. The damned thing had almost sent a ledgeful of ghosts into full-on riot. It had *spoken to her.* How long had it been waiting there? What did it *want?* She thought of it sitting there on the ledge in the rain, suns and moons rising and setting above its head. Waiting for her to drag her ass up the hill so she could find it. So it could find her. It was all terribly strange.

"—are expecting great things from you this year," the Catchkeep-priest was saying. "Don't disappoint us. There's a long winter coming. We would so hate to see you starve."

And he touched his cheek at the place where the four long slashes of Catchkeep's holy mark would have been if he were Wasp, and kissed those fingers to her. If she were standing over a warm corpse, in the sand, blood dripping from her knife in the starlight, and the Catchkeep-priest were someone else, it would have been a salute. From him, here, now, it was a promise she would fall, and soon, and another upstart would spring up where she had fallen, as corpseroot was engendered of the dead.

It was also a dismissal, so she tossed down her crusts and left the hall, the gazes of the upstarts drilling through the back of her head. It took all her willpower not to slam the door behind.

Safe in the cold again, she assessed her damages. This meeting could have gone way, way worse, as she was well aware. The fact she'd gotten out of there in one piece was pretty much exhilarating. Not a word out of him about the ghost she should have caught for the midwife. Not a word asking about what she'd been doing up the Hill instead. By now she recognized what he was doing, but it didn't make it any easier to bear. Not when she was sitting across a table from him, his gaze going right through her, like he was seeing past her to the Archivist he could torment when she was killed, and the Archivist past that one. Until then, he'd keep her guessing, on her toes, not knowing which disobediences he'd let slide and which would bring the fallout crashing down. At least it worked beautifully on the upstarts. She despised that it probably worked just as well on her.

She wound back around the front of the shrine toward the road, and an upstart was there waiting. Pure reflex, Wasp's hand went to her harvesting-knife. It wouldn't be the first time an upstart broke ritual and tried to better her lot against Catchkeep's law. As far as Wasp knew, it would only be the third. Still, she couldn't be too careful.

This upstart was a young one, unblooded, fresh from whatever house had adopted her until she'd come of age to join the training at the shrine. Wasp didn't even really know her name. Sarah? Sairy? Something like that. Her Catchkeep-mark wasn't as neatly drawn as Wasp's, its four lines running in an unclean parallel, as though Catchkeep had trembled in raking the unborn upstart's tiny face with Her claws.

The upstart was holding a blanket, threadbare and soft, more patches than weave. "Cold night," she said, and tossed the blanket to Wasp, not meeting her eyes. "Aneko was my friend," the upstart went on, softer, staring at the brown grass between her cloth-shoed feet. "Every night since she drew that stupid straw, she had nightmares about fighting you. After you got her knife away, you could have—could have cut her down. You didn't. Maybe some of us look at that and see weakness. Maybe some of us see something else. She's gone now, but I'm—you know, I'm sure she—" A noise came from inside, and the upstart stiffened like a spooked deer. "You didn't see me."

Wasp was holding the blanket practically thumb-and-forefinger, practically at arm's length, unsettled at this unexpected kindness. "Thanks," she managed, but the upstart was already gone.

She thought to leave the blanket there, at the shrine. She'd rather be cold than beholden. But the upstart was right. The night was bitter. And leaving the blanket there to be found would probably only earn the upstart a beating. Wasp slung it over her shoulders and went.

Chapter Five

S omewhere on that long dark lonely walk through town and then from it, away from all the lit-windowed houses where people ate warm food around cozy fires, and the blind-windowed houses where they were snug asleep, toward the single point of light among the rocks that was the one light she'd left burning, a wind came up and picked the clouds from the sky like scabs.

Suddenly the night loomed very close. Despite herself, it gave her pause.

There was Catchkeep, of course, lolling in Her sixteen stars; and there was Ember Girl, Whose heart was the blue star called the Beartrap, Whose head was the nebula called the Spool. Near Her, Carrion Boy bent His head in deference or treachery to the crows, and lower down, half-concealed behind the hills as though She waded through them to the thigh, stalked the Chooser in Her clacking cape of bones, with the Ragpicker following bent-backed behind. And beyond the horizon entirely, hidden by the turning of the year, the One Who Got Away stood with His/Her chin held high, perpetually triumphant.

By the position of the stars, she'd been gone longer than she'd planned. The walk out of the hills and down to town had taken the better part of two hours, on top of however long she'd wasted there—to no point and purpose she could discern, apart from the Catchkeep-priest never missing an opportunity to try and take her down a notch in whatever way he could. She wondered, if she'd let the midwife set her busted ankle in the first place, whether the Catchkeep-priest would have bothered fabricating a reason to make her walk those uphill-downhill miles on it.

What *was* strange was that the light in her house hadn't gone out. Or else it had and the ghost had lit it anew, though it had no need of light itself and it didn't seem too inclined to do her any favors. More likely, it had upset the lamp and the distant point of light she saw was actually her house going up in flames.

Wasp started walking faster, inasmuch as she was able. She kept her mind off the pain by breathing deeply with each step on the bad ankle, sniffing for a fire. Beyond the woodsmoke drifting back uphill from town, there was nothing. By the time she made it to the crossroads—one path stretching back through town behind her and dead-ending somewhere far ahead among the rocks, the other wending away to left and right, skirting the hills on its way to towns she'd never seen—the bright point that was her house had resolved to windows, lit from within.

It looked warm and welcoming. It looked like any other house. Not the cold stone hut of a goddess's puppet, respected, shunned, and feared—but a normal house, where normal people lived their normal lives. The surreality of it stunned her in her tracks.

After a moment she began picking her way toward those yellow windows, wary, as if stalking unpredictable prey. Up into the hills she went, along the footpath that was barely wide enough to admit the cart that trundled up from town twice a month, laden with the people's offerings. Past corridors of blackberry brambles which her summers would be depending on for sustenance if those offerings ran dry. An old stone wall meandered through them, in places still knee-height after the world's death and all that had come since. Another kind of relic. Another kind of ghost.

Eventually the rutted dirt path tacked off at a steep incline into a narrow pass, where the rock turned reddish and scorchweed grew. She followed it, dragging the bad ankle now, into a little clearing on a high flat plate of rock, with the paved path of multicolored scavenge-glass, the tiny yellow-windowed house, the potted wild blueberry plant that fired up fresh shoots each spring only to be beaten into submission by the wind and rebel anew.

There was no lock on the door. She needed none. The people would eat their dead before they stole from her. She pushed it open and shut it softly behind, as though that incongruous cozy light was a living thing she could disturb.

The house had not burned. The lamp was lit. There was a fire in the hearth. The ghost was sitting in her only chair, surrounded by mismatched stacks of paper in various degrees of fire-damage, water-damage, unidentifiable staining, mildew, and general dissolution. It appeared to be reading her field notes.

"Get your boots off my table," she snapped, and did not quite squirm under the look it fixed her with, or under the ensuing silence as it went back to reading.

Force of habit, she found herself studying it. It was all she could do not to pull out her notebook and start sketching it on the spot. Its clothing was basic and dark, something like a uniform but not one she recognized from any ghost she'd seen before. The gun and sword were in its belt. The ghost turned pages with a trained precision, a spring-loaded sort of predatory grace in which no fraction of any movement went wasted. Between its person and its clothing there was no color to it anywhere; it was all pale and dark, with those gray eyes. Its face was sharp, guarded, possessed of an icy and immaculate calm. Its posture was miles better than hers. It hadn't moved its boots.

Usually Wasp didn't find silences awkward and felt no need to fill them with pointless chatter, but this, this was unendurable.

"I didn't know you could read," she said. She was cringing before she'd fully finished the sentence. "That didn't—I mean—because you're—look, forget it," she finished lamely.

Because you're dead, she'd wanted to say. *Because you're a ghost. Because the other ones I find are prize specimens if they can recall enough of themselves to give me clues to when and where and how they died. The way they're dressed. The way they talk, even though they can't say much of anything—usually their dying words, over and over. And that's a whole lot more than I get out of most of them. But you, whatever you are, by now I don't think there's anything you could do that would surprise me.*

What she heard herself saying instead was: "So, this other ghost. The one you need my help to find." Something passed over the ghost's face, gone before she could put a name to it. Whatever it was, it fascinated her. Her reflex was to try and bring it back, pin it down, write it up in her notes. To find a knife and twist it. "Dead friend of yours?"

A pause while the ghost squared papers, set them down. "A colleague."

Wasp, thinking of her own colleagues, found this the tiniest bit hard to believe. It must have shown on her face, because the ghost continued: "She was murdered. Tortured to death. By our—" its mouth twisted faintly "—employers."

Now this tallied more with her experience. Still, the idea of this ghost's search—of having something, someone, worth searching *for,* after however many centuries that must have passed since it'd died—it got under her skin and itched there, made her lash out in a way she didn't understand. "Well, maybe you should have thought of helping her while they were busy torturing her. You die that way, you're a long time dying. Plenty of chances to be *rescued.*" She spat the word like poison. "It's a little late now."

As the words left her mouth, she wondered if the leash of salt and blood would hold or if the ghost would stand up at her little table and shoot her dead. But it held, or something held, and the ghost didn't so much as favor her with a glare.

She busied herself by limping over to the hearth and plumping down before it, her hands held out to the fire. When her fingers had thawed enough to flex, she started on her shoes. Half-frozen mud and the cold sweat of injury had molded them to her feet, and she was braced for the flare of sick pain when she tugged the fractured ankle free, but as small as her wince was, it didn't escape the ghost's notice. She looked up, and it was already beside her. She hadn't even seen it get up.

It had a sort of device in its hand that was nothing like anything she recognized, in the field notes or out of them. It was a kind of metallic cylinder about the size of her thumb, one side covered with a glossy black film. The ghost set one fingertip to the film and it lit up.

"Stay still," said the ghost, and pressed the device, light-first, to the greenish swelling at her ankle. Nothing happened for a second, but then the device gave two little chirps and started humming in a way Wasp could not hear so much as feel: belly, scalp, and teeth. Whatever it was doing hurt worse than walking on the ankle, worse than busting it in the first place. This went on for a very long moment. She bit her lip and rode the pain the whole way down, and then, as suddenly as it had started, it was done, and the ghost was sitting its bootheels before her, watching her attempt at stoicism with thinly veiled amusement.

Then, too fast for her to pull away or do so much as yelp, it grabbed her ankle between both hands and turned it hard each way. She had a split second to remember how the ghost had attacked her on the ledge, a split second to make a grab for the knife, a split second to prepare for the pain to jolt its way up every nerve in her leg when the fracture snapped across for good. It never came. Even as she looked on, astonished, the angry color faded from her skin, and she could have sworn she saw the swelling begin to subside. The device, meantime, made three mournful little beeps and its light dulled and winked out. "There," the ghost said, and stuck it in a coat pocket as Wasp stared. "Now you should be able to walk."

"What," she said. "What did—what *is*—"

"Standard issue," said the ghost.

Her fingers itched to draw it. "Can I—"

"No."

She couldn't help herself. "So why didn't you use that thing on your—"

The ghost's fist shot sideways, sending a shelf of ancient glass jars to shatter on the floor. Wasp gaped in horror after them. Whatever she could learn from this ghost would have to be more or less priceless to make up for that.

Already the ghost's infuriating calm was restored, leaving only the mess to prove to her she'd broken through at all. "I *did*."

Wasp put on the Catchkeep-priest's gentling voice, which fit her badly. "And . . . and it didn't . . . ?"

"I don't want to talk about it," said the ghost, chafing at the salt. "Understand?"

There were times, Wasp knew, when *I don't want to talk about it* meant exactly the opposite. At least it did for her. She also knew that this was not one of those times. She could force it to talk. She could string it like a puppet and watch it dance. Maybe. But that was a last resort. If she was going to treat the dead the way the living treated her, she'd be no different from everything she was trying to escape. And the ghost *had* healed her ankle. It wasn't *quite* like she felt she owed it, but—

On the other hand, even pausing to consider her options was letting her guard down, and that was a slippery slope straight to nowhere good. She wouldn't be the first dead Archivist to underestimate a specimen.

Sitting here, watching this ghost seethe, Wasp felt the lack of the notebook like she'd feel the loss of a limb. No way could she let this thing walk.

Even so, something was prodding her gently at the back of her mind. It took her a moment to recognize it as her conscience.

She had to open her mouth and tell the ghost the truth before things got messy. She could say *So if you're so smart, and you already know that I hunt ghosts, then you already know how I do it. Which is how it's always been done. I'm not a tracker. Archivists, we just catch what we find. We don't go looking for specific ghosts. Nobody ever has. I don't think it's even possible. I can't promise you anything.*

But she didn't.

"In case you haven't noticed," Wasp said instead, "I'm not exactly in a high place to scatter favors from. I know what you want from me. I'm getting that loud and clear. I still haven't heard what you're offering in return."

After a moment, the ghost reached into a pocket and came out with the thing it'd healed Wasp's ankle with. "This."

Wasp eyed the device hungrily, and something huge turned over slowly in her mind, forcing her to ask herself hard questions.

Could she have bought her way free with what the ghost knew about the world Before? Would the Catchkeep-priest have *really* let her go?

The ghost might have told her exactly what had gone wrong with the world, and on whose watch, and how to keep it from going wrong again. It might even have told her what had come Well-Before, going back and back to the beginning of time. And none of that might *matter*.

Catchkeep might never let her go. The Catchkeep-priest, the upstarts—to say nothing of the townspeople, who would not be cheated out of her, the one they made offerings to so that the ghosts that thronged and jostled at their walls would leave them be.

But now, with this device, it wasn't up to them, wasn't up to anyone but her. Wasp wouldn't *have* to buy her way free. Wouldn't *have* to barter with the Catchkeep-priest. Wouldn't *have* to play by his rules, or Catchkeep's, anymore.

She was certain she could take the Catchkeep-priest in a fight, if it came down to it. What she hadn't been at all sure of, until this moment, was her ability to survive her wounds for long enough to enjoy more than a few feverish blood-poisoned hours of freedom.

And when she was out and gone from here, a normal person, a person with whom people did business, what *couldn't* she get in trade for this thing? It could keep her in real food and fresh water for years. It could buy her seeds and compost and planting soil, and she could feed herself for years to come. She could buy the offerings-cart and hack it into firewood, and never again be indebted to the people's *tolerance*.

Wasp swallowed. Her head was swimming with possibility. She almost had to lean against a wall.

Watch it, she thought at herself, quick and hard and fierce, like the pinch that tells you you're dreaming. *Don't you go carrying a last resort in both hands.*

Then she realized how silly it sounded. What was her Archivist-path paved with, if not last resorts?

What was sillier was that she just couldn't make herself speak up and seal the bargain, and she didn't like her guess as to why.

So maybe she felt more affinity with the dead than with the living. That wasn't news to her. *This* particular specimen, though, had come at her with a *sword*. No *way* was she going to let herself feel bad about deceiving it. Let it think she knew exactly how to find its missing ghost. Wasp reckoned the thing'd been dead some-thousand years already. A little false hope wouldn't hurt it.

The ghost was watching her closely, eyes narrowed like it could see through all the layers of her person to the self-serving, lying-by-omission, desperate bones beneath.

She built herself a blank face and stayed behind it. Wait this out.

"You're wondering why I'm here," the ghost was saying. "Why I came to you for help. After all, I don't know you. I have very little reason to trust you." For the first time, Wasp saw the faintest flicker of confusion in its face. "And yet I find I do, a little."

"Well?" she said. "Why?"

"First let me ask you the same."

Wasp blinked. A ghost was interrogating her. Oh, the Catchkeep-priest would love this. If by *love* she meant *probably whip her senseless if he found out about*. Well, he wasn't here. This was still her house. "Fine."

"I came to you. But you let me in, knowing I needed your help. Why?"

"You're avoiding the question. Weren't you reading my field notes? You see what most of them give me to work with. A few mindless words, if they've been at the blood long enough. A name. Or nothing. Sometimes I can guess how they died. If I see a ghost full of bullet holes, I write *shot*. If one's on fire, I write *burned*. If one's walking around carrying its *head* under its arm, I write—"

"Now who's avoiding the question?"

"You don't get it. I *had to*. I had to bind you. I had to bring you back here. Do you think I *chose* any of this?" She backhanded the air, a gesture that took in the entire tiny room. Dimly she was aware that with every word she spoke she was climbing out on a limb and sawing it off behind her. But she'd loosed her temper now, and it wasn't coming back when called. "I had to kill people to get here. I have to kill people to stay here. And I'll be stuck here until they figure out how to kill me. The door out of this place is my grave. You want to find a ghost? Here's ghosts." She tore the pin from her hair, shook out the black-brown-red-blond of it, and the room filled with a carrion stink that she may or may not have been imagining. "There's some more." She flung her hand toward the piles of paper that were her life's work and the life's work of all the Archivists before her, violently shortened lives though they'd been. "And out there in the dark? They go on forever. Why don't you go take your pick. You want my help? You tried to kill me. So you can just—"

"That," said the ghost, unperturbed, "was an accident."

"And *you*," Wasp retorted, "are a resource. Like water. Like firewood. Like dried dogshit, when the firewood's run out." She'd warmed to her own anger now. It swept on out before her and dragged her along behind. "There's a list of questions in that box that's been waiting four hundred years for a specimen like you to answer. I don't *have* to help you. I don't *have* to make any kind of deal with you. And I certainly don't *have* to risk my ass out there for you. Maybe instead I keep my head down and do the work, and you sit there and serve your purpose. Maybe we make a new bargain. You give me that thing, and I don't destroy you when I'm done with you."

The ghost's smile made her wish her faith in the harvesting-knife had carried on unbroken. "Try it."

This was one hole she wasn't going to dig any deeper. She'd had enough of her grand plans blowing up in her face. She could still see that upstart staring up at her from the reddened sand. The Catchkeep-priest's voice replayed in her head: *Do you know it took that poor girl four days to die of her wounds, raving of fever and thirst in the street?* She could have at least given the upstart a quick death, clean, with dignity. Everything she tried to fix only ended up breaking worse. She was done.

"You know what? Get out. I changed my mind." Wasp was on her feet, kicking the blood-salt current clear of the ghost's boots. Casting about for the harvesting-knife to finish slicing it free. "Maybe I thought this was different. Maybe I thought we could help each other." She could have punched herself in the face for how stupid that sounded. "I find your ghost. You give me that thing you fixed my ankle with, give me a fighting chance to get out of here. Well, I should have known better by now, shouldn't I. Like I should have known better when I tried to save—"

The words died in her mouth, unsaid. Her eyes stung. She stared at the floor. "Just get out of here."

A moment of fear as she paused, knife in hand, and wondered what the ghost would do, when she finished freeing it of the bindings. Kill her for ensnaring it? Flicker back into memories again, as it had on the ledge, and kill her because of whoever it had mistaken her for?

Well, she and her knife were as ready as they were going to get. Looking at her options, going down fighting a forbidden fight on her own terms was surely not the worst of them.

The silence was endless. Then:

"I came to you," said the ghost, "because there's a ghost I need to find, and I need a ghosthunter's help to do it. Because the dead speak highly of you. Find the girl with the knife in her belt and the scars on her face, they told me. She's different from the other girls who'd come before her, even though they'd carried the same knife, worn the same scars. She helps the dead, when she can, even when the living punish her for it. She probably will not want to be found. But she is worth finding."

This brought her up short. Her thoughts and feelings were all slagging together, mismatched, half-formed, inseparable.

Embarrassment: the ghost knew she'd disobeyed orders and let other ghosts go. She wasn't half bad at keeping that secret. The Catchkeep-priest had beaten her every time he'd found out, of course, but there'd been plenty of times he hadn't known about. And the Catchkeep-priest was cozy in his bed a mile downhill, sleeping the sleep of the innocent. Not here.

Pride: those ghosts had gotten away, gone back down to the ghost-place, because of her. She'd accomplished at least this one small rebellion on her own. The Catchkeep-priest couldn't whip that out of her.

Mostly, though, she was stunned. The other ghosts were *aware* that she'd let them go. They *knew who she was.* Here, aboveground, she was lucky if one in ten specimens could mindlessly spit out a couple meaningless words, totally oblivious of her scribbling them down—as if any of them had ever proven useful. But down in the ghost-place, they were *discussing her amongst themselves?*

Wasp stared, distantly aware that her jaw had dropped.

The ghost cut its eyes at her, pure scorn. "I see they were mistaken."

It dropped a mocking little bow before her and walked out, trailing what remaining bonds of salt and blood she'd not yet broken, which it had snapped at whim.

It was over.

It was over and she was out of ideas. Trying to force her way out had failed. Trying to win her way out had failed. Trying to break the cycle and free the upstart Aneko had failed. Trying to bargain her way out had failed. Her chance, slim as it had been, had passed her by. Leaving what? A cot in a closet of jars. A leaky roof. An old knife and a box of salt. The scared charity of the living and the worthless notice of the dead. All of which were hers by right, like it or not, until another year had passed. At which time she would either kill to keep it or be killed herself and leave a corpse for the upstarts to gloat over.

She pictured throwing her knife down in the sand. Letting them defeat her. Choosing to die. She pictured her ghost walking, a knife in its back, savaged by shrine-dogs, a green stone on her tongue as befit a dead Archivist. Dying all over again, with every step, of shame.

If Wasp were writing field notes on herself, they'd read:
plans attempted: 1000000
plans succeeded: 0
never learns. better off destroyed.

Her gaze fell on all those shattered jars. It wasn't that she was afraid to die, or afraid of pain. How many times had she drawn blood with the harvesting-knife to bind a ghost? How many wounds had she taken in combat and walked from? It couldn't hurt much worse, and if it did, she wouldn't notice for long. Already she could see the Catchkeep-priest's face when he found her on the floor, bled out and smiling. Let the upstarts fight over the knife and the saltlick and the rotting little house. Let the system dissolve altogether, and Catchkeep's stars tumble from the sky to burn this whole place down. She was done.

The harvesting-knife in her hand felt like an extension of her arm. She'd taken good care of it, kept it clean and polished and so, so sharp. It had drawn her blood countless times, and she could depend on it to cut clean. So clean that, for a few precious seconds, she knew she wouldn't feel a thing.

She set the blade longwise against the blue vein in her wrist, drew a steadying breath through gritted teeth—and stopped.

She probably will not want to be found. But she is worth finding.

The thought went rolling around her mind pleasantly, like a smooth stone. There was a certain agreeable novelty to having value attached to her actions. Not her actions as Archivist, as the puppet of a goddess, as Catchkeep's-bones-and-stars-Her-flesh, but *her* actions performed through *her* choice, *her* risk, *her* boldness.

In the face of it, sitting there, giving up, she felt foolish and ineffectual. What she was doing was no answer at all. She couldn't win this way. To make those long cuts up the insides of her arms was to do nothing but prove herself too weak to fight back. She looked at the jars and thought of her own ghost-self scrabbling at the walls of one of them, a stunted silverfish Wasp, caught by whatever upstart succeeded her, once the knife had changed hands and the blood had been mopped from the floor. She thought of bending her neck to the saltlick as the Catchkeep-priest looked on smiling. It made her sick with hate.

If she chose to help the ghost—Wasp didn't have a clear idea of what exactly that would involve. But if her bad luck finally caught her up out there, it would be the result of choices she had made. It wouldn't be for nothing. And it wouldn't be *here*.

And after that? Right now she wasn't sure. Her mood had either swung back into tentative hopefulness or hit rock bottom, where the only place to go, she'd heard, was up. She couldn't tell which. She'd learned they mostly feel the same.

Either way, for the moment, with the ghost's device escape seemed almost possible. So maybe Catchkeep would reach down out of the stars and slap her dead. But that would mean that Wasp had first succeeded in gutting the Catchkeep-priest like the pig he was, and run far and fast enough the upstarts hadn't caught her before their goddess did. And, in light of her alternatives, she found she was pretty much okay with that.

But this ghost's quest, meantime—whatever happened to her in the end, *this* might end up being the first plan she set her hand to that actually worked. Something to fix instead of break for once. Something she could weigh against that pile of failed escape attempts and dead upstarts and destroyed ghosts and wasted years. Something she could *do*.

She watched her hands, as if waiting to see what they would decide. She watched her fingers brush the sixteen stars arrayed along the blade, watched her thumbtip trace the razor edge, watched her hand close round the hilt. She held the knife in her fist a moment. Then she got up.

The ghost was sitting on the doorstep, drawing some kind of symbol in the dirt with a stick. Where the firelight hit it, it shone through.

The ghostgrass bundle was no longer hanging in the doorway, she only realized now. She'd been too distracted to replace it when she'd left. This specimen could get up and walk at any time. The fact that it still showed no inclination to was intriguing.

"If you try to attack me again," she said, "I'll put you down or I'll die trying. I have nothing to lose."

"Neither do I," said the ghost. "Not anymore."

"Then here's how this is going to play out. That thing you fixed my ankle with?" Wasp lifted her chin in the direction of its coat. Her voice was shaking, but she had ground to stand, and nobody was going to stand it for her. "The second we find this ghost of yours, that thing is mine. No shit, no later, no I-changed-my-mind. No more *accidents*. Mine. Or I'll end your ghost in front of you."

The stick stopped moving in the dirt.

"I would not have offered it in trade," the ghost said icily, "if I didn't intend to trade it. Apparently some of us hold our word in higher regard than others. I do not make empty promises. Or—" it eyed her—"empty threats."

Wasp drew breath to snap back, then stopped. She could engage with this, or she could get out of here tonight. There wasn't time for both. Right now, on winter's threshold, there were a dozen hours left before morning. Before her absence would be noticed. And the Catchkeep-priest's reach was long.

She stuck out her hand like a gambler sealing a bet. "So we have an understanding?"

The ghost looked at it a moment, then took it. Frostbite and vertigo, all over again, even through the glove.

"Okay then," Wasp said. "Let's go hunting."

Chapter Six

She packed as she had packed each time she'd run away: filling the backpack with such things as she imagined a person might take with herself on a journey, if a person found herself suddenly in a position for journeying. After binding the ghost earlier, she'd collected her ghost-destroying kit from the ledge. Now she removed the milk-vial, the notebook, and the charcoals, and left the other things in the pack, along with the apples slowly turning to mush at the bottom. She refilled her bottle from the last musty dregs of the water-jug and repacked that. Then added the handheld sharpening-stone for the harvesting-knife. Her last clean shirt, wadded into a ball. The end of the raisins. Unlike when she'd run away before, a jar. She was hunting a ghost, after all.

She deliberated a moment, then swallowed her pride, wrapped the upstart's blanket around her shoulders, and went outside with the backpack and a lamp to inspect the heaps of offerings she still hadn't brought indoors.

Most of it was random bits of salvage junk, intriguing at best, or food, rendered basically inedible by having spent so many days out in the air. A pouch of black walnuts and dried wild blueberries didn't smell rancid yet, so she took it. There was also a pair of knit mittens and a new set of laces for her shoes. She stuffed it all in the pack.

Her lamplight caught on something a few feet away, back on the path. Her knife. Not the harvesting-knife, the other one. The one she'd fought her Archivist-choosing fights with, murdered the better part of a dozen upstarts with. It lay where she'd dropped it yesterday, Aneko's blood still streaking the blade, staining the grip.

She stomped over and grabbed it, then stalked back to the house. Closed her fist around the hilt, drew back her arm and drove the blade an inch into the doorframe. Let the Catchkeep-priest find it there when she was gone. Let him chase her around with it forever. She wouldn't set her hand to it again.

On her way back in, she noticed a big old cookpot full of firewood. It might be of use to her later. She started to carry it in.

Standing in the doorway, with the knife just past her ear and the cookpot hugged in her arms, something snapped in her like a bone.

Later. It *might be of use to her later*. As if, deep down, beneath all her talk, she knew that what she was about to try would fail, as everything else she tried had failed, and then her life would go on as it had always done, pacing out the length of its leash, smashing into empty air at either end like a bird against a window. Take the knife out of the doorframe. Sweep the dust from the little house. Restock its jars with the useless dead.

For the first time, she was standing on the edge of something vast. She could back down, or she could jump.

She threw the pot to the floor. It slammed up against a wall, knocking down a teetering jar. The jar fell and shattered, and she flinched. The *sound* of it, though, she found deeply satisfying. It was like a drink of cold water after a day of trudging through dust and coming home emptyhanded. It was like the split second after waking, when she didn't yet remember who or where or what she was, and only drifted, nothing amid nothingness.

Experimentally, she swiped another jar off the nearest shelf. It broke. She felt it the whole way down her spine.

The rest of the shelf followed after. Then the next. From wall to wall she went, tiptoeing over shards of glass and clay, calmly, methodically knocking every jar down as the ghost sat at the table, chin on gloved fist, and watched.

For an instant she worried that Catchkeep Herself would materialize in the little house and strike her dead, but She did not. For another instant she worried at the colossal noise she was making. But the benefit to living ostracized from the rest of the town was that nobody was likely to hear her way out here, a mile up a hill of slag from anything.

She stood a moment, catching her breath. Whatever had snapped in her had not re-knit. She had moved beyond impulse and into purpose. She'd knock this whole place down.

What she really wanted was to set the house on fire, but she knew the smoke would carry across that mile, and anyone who looked up at the hill would run to the Catchkeep-priest, and he would be up there with a search party within an hour in daylight, two in the dark. The dogs would make it in less.

She compromised by cramming the hearth with as many armfuls of the field notes as it would hold and lighting them. Once the fire took, she fed it with a few logs from her supply, which would keep it sending its cheerful smoke up her chimney for some hours after she had gone. Another couple of trips from the table to the hearth and the notes were consumed.

Wasp took a step back to admire her handiwork. It was a bigger, cozier fire than she'd ever dared light for herself, firewood being so scarce and winter so long. Some small part of her wanted to curl up on the floor in front of it and sleep. Instead she rummaged around under her cot for one last thing.

The Archivist-coat came out in her hands, covered with dust and smelling as foul as the day she'd first stuffed it under there. It was given to her with the harvesting-knife and her name, and she would be divested of it along with the knife when she was replaced. She seldom wore it because she despised what it marked her as: predator and parasite, poisonous and holy, scapegoat and saint. Also because she still woke sometimes from nightmares in which it reached its mottled arms up from under the bed and kissed her to smothering with the mouth it had somehow grown in the place where, were she wearing it, her shoulder blades would go. Its breath was dogleather and gore and the smell of that daisy-chain of dead girls who had worn it before her, who would wear it after.

It was, however, the warmest thing she owned. And if it unnerved her somewhat that it fit as well as it did, causing her to suspect that dead Archivists of all shapes and sizes had marveled over that themselves—this was not the time for it. She slid her arms in, suppressing a shudder. Buttoned it up to her chin. Squared the backpack on her shoulders. Her ankle took the extra weight with no complaint.

She almost wished she'd be there to see the Catchkeep-priest's face when he realized she'd either taken or destroyed all the Archivist-tools. The knife, the coat, the jars, the field notes, the salt. She doubted it would break the cycle of bloody-handed Archivists and dead upstarts altogether. But she was certain it would slow it down.

"Ready?" said the ghost, waiting at the door.

"Always," she said.

Coat or no, the cold still took her breath away. Three steps out into it and any warmth she had thought to hoard from that roaring fire and bring with her had evaporated. And the path in the dark was a terrible thing. The ghost at her side gave off a dim silvery phosphorescence which she could only hope would be enough to keep her from breaking her neck.

Only one way to find out. She pulled the coat-hood up over her head and started walking. There was a certain rhythm to it, involving the ghost walking at a forward diagonal from her, so that she could see where her feet ought to go. After years as Archivist, it irked her unaccountably to rely on a ghost, but if that's what got her out of here in one piece, she'd do it and like it.

"How long before they realize you're gone?" the ghost asked.

Wasp shrugged invisibly in the dark. "If I'm lucky? Tomorrow. The upstarts get up early. The Catchkeep-priest sleeps late. He's the one to worry about." She couldn't orient herself well enough to know whether tomorrow was the day the cart would come up her hill with offerings. If it wasn't tomorrow, it was soon.

The ghost did not ask *And if you're unlucky?* She was glad of it.

"So what's your name, anyway?" she asked.

There was a pause. "I don't want to talk about it."

"You don't remember." It astounded her, given the ghost's strength, but there it was. "Do you."

Another pause, and then: "I remember hers."

Wasp waited. It wasn't forthcoming. Colleagues, she thought. Right. "So what's hers?"

"Foster," it said. "Catherine Foster." A third pause. "Kit."

They walked in silence, trying to oil up their rusty etiquettes.

"Mine's Wasp," said Wasp.

"Wasp," said the ghost. "What kind of name is that?"

"The one I was given," she said. "Because when it was my turn to fight the Archivist, I poisoned my blade and stabbed her full of holes. Then I became Archivist."

"Archivist."

"Yes."

"*You're* an archivist."

"Yes," said Wasp, getting testy now. Defensive of something she had no interest in defending. Which only made her angrier. "Why."

"Well," said the ghost.

"What."

It shook its head. "Nothing."

More silence. They were down into the orchard now, negotiating between wide-armed shapeless trees. Circling around would have been quicker in the dark but also took them much too close to town. Even in the cold, with nearly all of the fruit wintering in town cellars, the air smelled like applesauce. *Ghosts of apples*, thought Wasp.

The moon had fought free of the clouds now, making Wasp rather easier to spot if someone happened to be looking. It also released her from depending on the ghost's own light to see by, so she took a few long strides to come up alongside it and found she had to hurry to stay there. Still, it was easier to talk this way. Not that she really knew what to talk about. She mulled it over for a while and gave up.

"You don't look much like a wasp," the ghost said eventually.

Wasp nodded. "It's the wings, isn't it," she said.

The ghost didn't acknowledge her attempt at a joke. She couldn't really blame it.

"I would have expected someone a little more. I don't know. Willowy?"

This was not a word in Wasp's vocabulary.

"Smaller. Slighter. Less—" The ghost made a vague shape with its hands.

Wasp, who had earned her muscles, took this as a compliment.

Further silence. As they neared Execution Hill, the moon passed behind it, and they walked into its shadow. It occurred to her that the ghost hadn't actually told her where they were going. There were any number of places where she could count on ghosts to appear. There was the fallen well out back of town, the tiny meadow of suns-and-moons in the dark beneath the snapped spine of the oldest bridge, and the collapsed maze of white tunnels that branched like roots beneath the town of Sweetwater, stretching as far as the mountain of bricks and glass and tortured metal that marked one corner of the garden's perimeter fence, appearing to terminate somewhere down there, among the other roots, in the dark. And there were always ghosts who'd only show their faces during a thunderstorm, or a blizzard, or when those greenish lights would streak across the night sky like rain against a window, which made people say that Carrion Boy was crying, and lock their doors, and light their lamps. Maybe because she'd found this ghost up the Hill, it felt right to her to return there. At least this time, with neither ankle trying to murder her, the climb'd be easier. But the ghost was moving with a purpose, and that unsettled her. How did it know where to go?

"Back up to the ledge?" she asked. "It's pretty slow up there after dark. The bridge is better. Or," she glanced up, gauging the film of ash over the stars, "maybe the well. This is a waste of—"

"You'll see," said the ghost, and she stopped walking. She was about two seconds from telling the ghost she wasn't going into this blind, whatever it was, and she wasn't budging another inch without some details. She glanced at it, irritated, to find it measuring her with its eyes. She felt like a new puppy under the Catchkeep-priest's appraising gaze: how sharp might her teeth get, how long her claws, how much use might she be before she failed. "How high can you climb?"

"High enough," she said, and, fueled by spite, started up.

Half an hour later they made the ledge. Down from there was darkness, darkness and a few late distant lights from the town. Even from this height, if other towns cast other lights, off among the hills, she couldn't see them.

"We're here," she said. She'd been right. The ledge was deserted. Only the faintest gray light seeped from the crack in the rock. "What now?"

"I already know you can climb this high," said the ghost.
"I asked you *how* high you could climb."

"There's nothing higher. Just more rock."

"But you can get there."

"It's *just rock*. No ghosts. Nothing."

"It sounds perfect," said the ghost, already climbing.
Wasp hung back, torn between defiance and curiosity.
Eventually she started up, wondering if she could remember
the way she'd ascended the one time she'd managed it, gained
the peak, and stood there in a bleak wind and an emptiness,
expecting more.

It was a harder, sheerer climb from the ledge on up, often
with no approximation of a path, not even a broken one.
Handholds, footholds. Sometimes not even that much, and
she flailed and fumed and clung cursing to the wall like a tick
on a dog and the ghost reached back for her and hauled her
up in merciful silence.

When they reached the top, Wasp was sweated to
wringing inside the Archivist-coat, but taking it off in that
wind would be chasing the Chooser's cape and no question.
She stood on what little ledge there was, shivering and
miserable, willing herself not to look down, while the ghost
extracted something else from another pocket of its coat and
shook it out into what at first Wasp mistook for a spiderweb
the size of her quilt.

"Here," said the ghost, tossing it to her. She expected the
wind to rip it away before it reached her, but whatever it was,
when she caught it she found it was surprisingly substantial.

"Look," she said. "I'm tired. I'm hungry. I'm freezing. You
still haven't told me why the hell you're wasting my time up
here, and I'm—"

From somewhere in the valley, faint but unmistakable,
came the baying of a dog, and Wasp's veins ran ice. Possibly
closer, certainly not more distant, another took up the cry.

"Sounds like we'd better hurry," said the ghost.

"Hurry *where*? I've escaped up here before. They'll outlast me. They always—"

"Give me that."

Wasp was still staring down the Hill, straining her ears in the silence to gauge how far the search party had come. When the ghost pulled on the spiderweb-thing in her arms, she let go.

"Now lie down."

This got through. "*What*?"

"Listen. We don't have much time. You don't know me. You don't like me. But for five minutes you need to be quiet and trust me."

Wasp had no idea what would happen if she said yes. But she had a crystal-clear idea of what would happen if she said no and waited for that hunt to catch her up instead. There was no third option. By the time she made her way back down—*if* she made it down—it would be too late to evade the Catchkeep-priest and his dogs. She wouldn't even be able to antagonize them into killing her where she stood. They wouldn't let her off that easy.

She looked at the ghost. Then she looked out into the dark beneath the Hill.

She lay down.

"Curl up," said the ghost. "As small as you can." She crammed her knees up against her ribs, and the ghost draped the spiderweb-thing over her. "Try to stay calm. This will feel . . . a little strange." As the thing settled on her, the edges of it tucked themselves in around the edges of her, adhering to the rock where it touched, while the middle sank in places to snug itself to her shape. The ghost held it clear of her face, which she was glad of in a moment when she realized that the thing was actually pinning her to the rock on three sides, and the fourth side was busily and soundlessly questing for an anchor point.

"What the—" she gasped, exerting the whole of her will to keep from thrashing. "Get it off!"

"It hasn't been five minutes yet," said the ghost amicably. "And it's going to get worse before it gets better."

There was something in the ghost's free hand. Wasp was one for two in having excellent reason to dislike the objects that appeared there and was about to start fighting in earnest when another howl drifted up from somewhere among the apple trees. She went still.

"Now there are two ways we can do this," the ghost was saying. "Calmly or the other way."

It held up the thing in its hand, thumb-and-forefinger. In the bare light coming off of its hand itself, the object looked like a pebble, but probably was not, and the ghost was squinting at her doubtfully. "Are these even around anymore? Pills. You swallow them. Don't chew."

"I know what a damn pill is," Wasp said. "And you can shove—"

"It's this or them," said the ghost. "That's it. There's nothing else now."

Wasp eyed the pill. In the light, it might have been green.

"It won't hurt," said the ghost to her unasked question. "It makes you sleep. That," nodding to the spiderweb-thing, "is a cloaking device. Camouflage. In part." That dubious look again. "Do you—"

"I can make my own camouflage."

"Not like this you can't. With this they won't be able to find you. You'll be safe until we're back."

This was feeling wrong now, all wrong. "Back from where?"

"From where the ghosts are."

Wasp spluttered. "It's going to *kill* me?" As soon as the words were out, she wondered why she cared. Then wondered why she wondered.

"No no no. Nothing like that." A pause. "Not quite."

In the ghost's hand, the spiderweb-thing seemed for all the world to be trying to scrabble out of its grip. The ghost held it steady, but Wasp could feel the outmost edges of the thing tickling at her jawline, seeking purchase. She'd heard enough. "Let me—"

The noise of the dogs again. Voices, joining the hunt, close enough to hear.

"Shit," said Wasp. A moment passed. "Give it."

The ghost dropped the pill into her mouth. She dry-swallowed it and almost immediately fell back dizzied. "My head . . ."

"Feels strange. It will. And it's about to feel a whole lot stranger. I can leave you alone or talk you through it. But I have to close you up either way. The edges start oxidizing almost immediately if they're not anchored. They lose resilience. And we need them more or less airtight."

Whatever was in that pill had Wasp feeling like someone had unpacked her skull and stuffed it full of wet clay, but at *airtight*, alarm started slowly bubbling up.

"Wait," she said. "What?"

"Trust me," said the ghost, and let go.

Immediately the thing was upon her, fusing to her skin. So light, so seemingly immaterial, she could not tell at first how far it had spread over her face.

She willed herself not to scream—and screamed. Or thought she did.

No sound came out. And no breath came in. She tried to fill her chest with air, as if preparing for a dive, but her lungs kicked up against her ribs and would not cooperate. Still she could feel no pressure on her face. Her time was running out. The pill had congested her nose, but she tried to filter some air through it anyway. The first two breaths felt like inhaling through a mattress but the third breath failed her altogether. Her lungs pulled and pulled, got nothing.

Her eyes cast about and landed on the ghost. It was saying something, but she couldn't hear it. The spiderweb-thing must have already blocked up her ears. Darkness was sidling in on the periphery of her vision. Was it the thing's searching edge? Or was she blacking out? The ghost reached and gently thumbed her eyelids down, and a pale softness crawled inexorably over, and she was blind.

All there was left to her was the pounding of her heart, hard and fast, then slowing, slowing. There used to be a story the upstarts used to tell, up late, in the dark, trying to scare each other sleepless. Something about a person knocking at a door, hard and fast, then slowing, slowing, and his friend inside the house, in the dark, too afraid to answer until the knocking had already stopped. Whatever he found on the doorstep always changed, depending on the telling. His friend, his head staved in, his fists bloodied on the door. A monster, eating his friend, whose fists were bloodied on the door. His friend, become a monster, sharpening its bloodied claws against the door. Or nothing.

Wasp's heart gave those last few feeble taps and misfired, dropping her down into the dark. The story's wrong, she thought. Nobody answered after all.

Chapter Seven

Wasp was dreaming. She hated dreaming.

In her dream she was lying on a ledge on a mountaintop in a black wind, something pressed against her face. She couldn't move. She couldn't breathe. Someone was saying, over and over, soft and low: *it's going to be okay, it's going to be okay*. Then there came a silence in which nobody said anything, not even the wind, and she found she could get up, so she did.

The ghost was waiting. It looked different. The markers of its ghostliness were gone from it. The shattered salt-chains at its feet. The dark glow evaporating off of it. The way it flickered, sometimes, as the real world snagged at its edges and sent moonlight shining through it for a split second before it regained control.

She heard the dogs again, closer still. Above the din the Catchkeep-priest was singing out in high glee, sending a shiver up her spine: *Wasp, oh Wasp*. A merry chase.

"You don't need to worry about them," said the ghost. "They won't find you now." It had its hands on her shoulders. This was not designed to be comforting. It was designed to hold her in place. Reflexively she twisted free, tripped over something on the ground, and went over in a heap. The night sky swung wide above her in narrowing arcs as her head recalibrated. If she had ever been so disoriented before, she couldn't remember when.

That thing on the ground, though. It was all the no-colors of the rock of the Hill, shadowed as the moonlight would shadow such rock, and even actively looking for it, her eyes could barely pick it out from the ledge on which it lay. Still, she couldn't discern its outlines, its shape. Even stranger was the thread, fine as an eyelash and the color of lightning, which connected the thing on the ledge to her. She touched the place where it disappeared between her breasts. She had strangled upstarts with wire that felt like this thread. She backed a step and the thread unspooled from somewhere—within her? within the thing on the ledge?—to follow.

"I'd thought to ease you into it," the ghost was saying. "It's a shock, I realize." As an afterthought, "At least it worked. I wasn't sure it would."

Her brain was muzzy. A shock? What was? She remembered a pill, far smaller and far smoother than the midwife's herbal boluses, with a kick swifter and harder than anything she'd ever pilfered out the back of the distillery when the brew-mistress's back was turned. A pill, and then that awful dream of airlessness, and then—

All at once she began to laugh. "I'm a ghost?" She couldn't put her finger on exactly what was so funny, but once she had started laughing, she found it very hard to stop. Her laughter flew out over the valley, and down below in the dark, the dogs kept on with their snuffling and the Catchkeep-priest kept on with his hallooing and not a one of them was any bit the wiser. "I'm a ghost!"

"You still have your knife," said the ghost. In its tone was something Wasp took a minute to place as admiration. "I didn't expect that."

"I ought to stick you with it. Trust you. You said your pill and your whatever-it-is weren't going to—"

"And they didn't. Your body's systems have been slowed down dramatically, but you are exactly as alive as you were ten minutes ago. And with a considerably better chance of staying that way." The ghost paused, grasping after phrasing she would understand. "Sort of like a bear? In winter?"

"Bears are built to hibernate. I'm not."

"And that," it rejoined smoothly, "is why we don't have time to stand here talking."

Wasp squatted down beside herself, awkward in the Archivist-coat. That had come through along with the knife, and also the backpack. More nuisance than anything, she guessed, but kept them on. "I've never seen anything like it." She aimed an experimental poke at what she guessed was her shoulder and glanced up surprised. "It's cold."

"It provides camouflage in the infrared as well as the visual spectrum. Never mind. More importantly for you, those dogs shouldn't be able to smell you, either."

Wasp ran her hand lightly over the cloaking device she still thought of as a spiderweb, wondering how her previous escapes would have gone if she'd had this thing on her side then. Wondering where she might be right now if she had.

She clamped her mouth shut on the crazy laugh that threatened to tear its way back out of her. She could feel it boiling in her gut. Her blood had turned to lightning. The Catchkeep-priest, the shrine-dogs, all of them down in the orchard chasing their tails. Sniffing each others' asses too, maybe. She wished them joy of it, and gnawed her tongue to keep from giggling.

Killing pissant little upstarts, that was supposed to make her feel victorious. It never had. Until this moment, she never really knew what that even felt like.

"We don't have long," said the ghost. "We have to keep moving."

Wasp snapped out of it fast. "How long?"

The ghost shrugged. "Two days, maybe three, once you're through to where we're going. But that's weeks up here. Sometimes more."

"Sometimes?"

"Like I said. We have to keep moving."

"Moving. Sure." Wasp surveyed the ledge. "Moving where?"

"Back down." At the look on Wasp's face, which encompassed the baying of the shrine dogs and the Catchkeep-priest running along behind, the ghost clarified. "To the lower ledge. Where you go—" it paused to invest the next word with infinite disdain—"hunting."

Wasp didn't much like its tone of voice, but what could she do? She was in too deep now to turn back. The thread in her chest reeled out slack as they descended.

The ghost reached the ledge first. "There."

It was facing a wall of solid rock.

"Where?"

Arms folded, it tipped its chin. "There."

There was a crack in the wall the width of Wasp's shoe. She'd seen hundreds of ghosts change their size at will and disappear into it, but apparently being a ghost didn't confer that trick unto her automatically. Nor could she really imagine this particular ghost shrinking itself down to the size of a rat to wriggle in there.

"If it makes it easier," the ghost said, "imagine a door."

Wasp looked at the crack in the rock.

"Forget that. Look ahead of you. Always ahead."

Wasp looked ahead. Six feet to either side, rock. Dozens of yards above her head, rock. Where the ledge ran out, the drop. The ghost took two steps forward and disappeared, then reemerged. "Now you."

Wasp thought: *I am a ghost. I will pass straight through.*

She strode forward and smashed her face on the wall.

"Don't think: the rock is insubstantial. It isn't."

"Yeah, I kind of got tha—"

"Think: I am stronger than the rock."

She eyed the wall with deep misgivings. "Am I?"

"I don't know," said the ghost. "You tell me."

"I am stronger than the rock," she said, and smashed her face again.

The ghost made an exasperated sound. "It might help to close your eyes."

Wasp bristled. This, all of this, was moving way too fast, and not one crumb of it was anything she'd expected when she agreed to it. "I don't take orders from you."

"No. You don't. Why don't you wake yourself up and run back to the people you do take orders from. The pill will wear off in a couple of days. Get comfortable." Halfway through the wall, a parting shot. "I should have known you weren't up to this."

The ghost disappeared. Wasp waited, but this time it didn't return.

"You need me," Wasp shouted at the place where it had vanished. "I'm going to find your Ragpicker-taken dead friend for you, remember?" She kicked at the wall. In her semi-ghostly state, she found this profoundly unsatisfying. "Remember?"

Nothing. She crushed a rising panic down. She walked to the wall, pressed her hands against the rock and pushed. Feeling stupid, she shut her eyes and held her breath and tried to shrink herself down to squeeze through that crack at her feet, as she had seen so many ghosts do before her. Some minutes passed. All it gave her was a headache, which she didn't think should have been possible.

She thought about turning herself in to the hunting party. She thought about letting the pill wear off, climbing back into her body, and waiting on the ledge to freeze. She thought about risking an escape by foot, on land, among the living, with the shrine-dogs on her scent. And she thought about what would happen when she was found.

"Not this time," she said, and walked through the wall.

✝

There was a moment of disorientation as the fabric of her person interleaved with the fabric of the rock, but before she'd noticed she'd passed the point of smashing her face again she was already through. The ghost was waiting at the other side, in an almost perfect darkness. Before them, a wide path opened up in the raw rock of the Hill and curved gently down into the black, studded with luminescent fungi, or insects. They were too high up for her to tell. The light given off from them was feeble and flickering, shadowing more than it illuminated, the milky green of pus. And in it, the ghost nodded at her, evidently satisfied.

She could have punched it.

"That's it," she said. "No more tricks. If you're about to push me into a pile of shit, you tell me before I'm up to my neck in it. Make me believe that helping you is a better choice than going back where I came from. Or I walk."

"If I'd told you what you had to do to get here," the ghost said reasonably, "would you have come? I couldn't risk you staying behind. It seemed the most expedient way to convince you."

"What did? Making me think I couldn't do those things? Climb the Hill? Get through the wall? Live through that— whatever that *thing*—" The sensation returned to her, of the spiderweb-thing smoothing over her nose and mouth, her lungs kicking against nothing. Her skin crawled.

"And then make you realize you *could* do them," said the ghost, watching her levelly. "Yes. You were hardly going to take my word for it. You had to prove it to yourself."

"I—" Wasp began, then stopped. There was no tactic that would have fit her better, and she knew it. She didn't want to ask, but she had to. "How did—"

"You remind me a little of someone I used to know," it said. "Long ago."

"This ghost of yours, you mean?" Wasp asked. "Foster?"

It said nothing.

"So she was—"

"Stubborn?" The ghost's gaze slid over her, down the path, toward nothing Wasp could see. "Breathtakingly."

A pause. "We should keep moving." After a few steps it seemed to realize Wasp wasn't following. It stopped but did not turn.

"No more tricks," Wasp said to its back.

A moment of silence, and then it nodded. "No more tricks."

Wasp took a few steps toward the brightening farther down and stopped. What she wanted in her bones was to hang back and let the ghost negotiate the hall before her and encounter whatever was around the blind curve at the bottom first. So she put on a brave face and soldiered on.

The hall was longer than it looked from above, and steep enough that she had to curl her toes to grip the rock through her flimsy shoes. She couldn't tell whether, as she descended, the air grew warmer or colder, drier or damper; only that other, stranger smells than rock and autumn began to add themselves to it: spice and smoldering and chemicals, and a sweetish rotten smell that put her in mind of the Catchkeep-shrine, its carrion and flowers.

At the bottom, they found a door. The smell was stronger here.

Something had been nagging at Wasp since she'd passed through the wall, and this door, the hugeness and incongruity and somehow the *finality* of it, brought it to the forefront.

"If I die here. I mean, I *can't* die here. Can I?"

"A ghost can't, not by the strictest definition. But by the strictest definition you're also not a ghost."

"So . . . I won't?"

"So I'm not sure what will happen. So do your best not to find out."

"Yeah," said Wasp. "Thanks."

Its deadpan and her sarcasm sailed straight on past each other, strangers passing on a dark road in the night.

"You want to watch that," said the ghost, pointing to the thread emerging from Wasp's chest, disappearing back and back behind her. "Don't let it break."

Wasp immediately started fussing at it, gauging its strength. It was tensile and stronger at least than the hard tug she gave it. "What'll happen?"

"I don't know. I've never seen one before. My guess is that if something goes wrong, and it snaps, then you lose your way back."

Goes wrong, thought Wasp. *What part of this* hasn't *gone wrong?*

"Maybe you'll be stuck here," the ghost went on. "Maybe you'll disappear altogether. Like I said, you're not a ghost. You're in-between. You might just be—" here it made a gesture more eloquent than Wasp liked, an opening of one gloved fist like the ghost scattered something unseen to the wind: *all gone*—"undone."

"Right," she said, still fidgeting. "And if something happens to my body? Up there?"

"Again, I'm not sure. I imagine you'll know it if you see it."

"Great," said Wasp. Then something else hit her. "You said *stuck here.* You mean I die. I become a ghost. For real this time."

The ghost said nothing.

"This is *nothing* like in the stories. Down here, ghosts are supposed to be immortal."

"They are," said the ghost. "What they are not is invincible."

Wasp barked out a nervous laugh. "Doesn't look like it makes much difference from—"

"This is your last chance to turn back," it said. "I won't stop you. There are other exits, deeper in. But this door is not one of them. And I can't open it for you."

The door was a double door, its knockers fashioned of some dull no-colored metal. They were the exact perfect height for Wasp to reach, the exact perfect size for Wasp to grasp. They were neither overly warm nor overly cold to the touch.

The sound of her exhalation was louder than it should have been, in that space.

"Is it true?" she asked. She had not often looked the ghost square in the face, but she did now. "They—"

—*believe in me down here?* she thought.

"—talk about me down here?" she said.

"Yes," said the ghost. "No. Does it matter?"

"I don't know," said Wasp, and knocked.

Chapter Eight

For a long, long moment, nothing happened. Then, with a sound like someone's back breaking, the door split in half and began to slowly swing inward on silent hinges. Wasp, thinking of strange doors and the things that came through them in songs and stories—"Marryings and Buryings," "Catchkeep's Steeplechase," "Carrion Boy Feeds the Crows," "Off-map to Sweetwater"—leapt back and stayed there, white-knuckled on the knife-hilt, breathing fast and low.

From the corner of her eye she saw the ghost standing by the wall, its arms folded, its look pitying. It was this more than anything that terrified her.

What came through the door was herself.

Herself in miniature: maybe two years old, maybe less. Unrecognizable except for the fact that her parents were carrying her, and though she'd thought she'd long since forgotten them, she found that something rose up in her now, remembering. They were dressed in ragged lightweight work-clothes, though there was snow in their hair. The bones stood out in their faces, and the muscles had wasted on their frames. It was not lost on Wasp that the baby they carried was the only remotely well-fed one of the three.

They came through the door, walking the stilted, stuttering walk of ghosts, and stopped before her knifepoint and her stricken stare, not seeing either.

Behind them came the Catchkeep-priest, two shrine-dogs pulling a wagon full of food behind him. They stopped a few paces back, and the dogs lay down in their traces, surveying the Wasp-baby with glittering eyes.

All three of them, Catchkeep-priest and shrine-dogs alike, looked filthy, road-weary. Wasp thought of the times, once or twice a year unless combat or disease had made a particularly bad season for upstarts, when Catchkeep granted Her priest a vision of Her Archivist's new possible successors. He'd vanish for a week, nothing but threats of Catchkeep's retribution keeping the upstarts in line, and return with two or three scarred holy babies—larval upstarts, with no inkling of their holiness or of their doom.

It was very strange, seeing this happen to herself, but that was not the part that surprised her. The part that surprised her was the wagon full of food that the Catchkeep-priest was now unhitching and her parent-ghosts were clearly exerting a great deal of effort not to run to. Wasp narrowed her eyes. It looked for all the world like the Catchkeep-priest was *trading* food for—

That done, the Catchkeep-priest glided over and stood in a little triangle with her parents, the now-squalling lump of Wasp held with obvious reluctance out into the middle. She could not make out what they said, only that he was making comforting noises at them and they were making comforting noises at her. Then the lump that was Wasp passed hands and her parents took up the wagon full of food and made their faltering way back through the door with it.

The Catchkeep-priest watched them go. He was astonishingly young, maybe ten years older than Wasp was now. When they were gone, and the door had shut behind them, he folded the baby into the crook of his arm, tilting her into the light.

She didn't realize what was wrong about her face until he drew the knife, held the baby's head still, and sliced into her cheek the four long gashes that would in time heal over and thicken into the scar that Wasp now wore.

Catchkeep's mark.

Even now he was smearing some kind of sticky-looking black ointment on the wounds, and the bleeding stopped. This, too, Wasp had seen before, once when the Catchkeep-priest had driven his knife between the bones of her hand, pinning it to the wall. A festering had set into the wound, swelling her hand until it could no longer hold the harvesting-knife, and he had taken her aside, threatened her into silence, and smeared both sides of her hand with black goo. In an hour it was a scab. In three days it was a scar.

But this was impossible. The first thing any upstart ever learned about herself was that when she was still in her mother's womb, Catchkeep Herself had come to her and set Her claws tenderly to her unborn face. Every upstart was born with that mark, and Wasp was no exception. It branded them as Catchkeep's chosen, the raw unformed unproven stuff of Archivists. It was the basis and the justification for everything she and every Archivist before her had been put through in the performance of their duties. It was the chopping-block on which the life that should have been hers had died.

And, if her eyes were to be believed, every word of those stories, every minute of those lives, every inch of that mark was a lie.

The Wasp-baby squirmed, sobbing her outrage, and the Catchkeep-priest bounced her in his arms and sang soft songs into her tiny ear until she hushed. And this, at that moment, in Wasp's estimation, somehow above and beyond all else, was unforgivable.

A sound came out of her in a voice she didn't recognize and she drove the harvesting-knife to the hilt into the Catchkeep-priest's eye. From the blade outward he began to dissolve, still singing, and took the baby with him. The knife fell clattering. As the baby's face atomized to silver sparks, she was smiling.

Wasp slumped, all the fight run out of her.

"It shows you what you are," the ghost said softly.

"You could have *warned* me."

"I could have. And it wouldn't have made any difference."

Something in its tone got her attention. "When you went through. What did it show you?"

The ghost's face darkened. "Nothing I didn't know already." A pause. "We should continue."

They continued.

Through the door, the hall widened and spilled into a cavernous room. A sudden wall of sound and smell rolled out to meet her. The sound was voices, more voices than Wasp had ever heard in one place. More than on the busiest market-morning, more than in the celebrations before the bloodshed on the Archivist-choosing day. The smell was ghosts. Lots of ghosts. She entered the room and was abruptly surrounded. Unlike aboveground, here they looked like people, life-size, not silver. They had pigmentation, faces, clothing, mannerisms. Only the smell, like someone had left the window open on a clear March day, gave them away for what they were.

The door behind her opened again and a tired-looking old male ghost came through. It had not been there in the hall beneath the Hill.

"On the outside, the doors leading here are different," the ghost said to Wasp's confusion. "When they get here, they're the same."

Almost as soon as the door had shut behind the old male ghost it opened to admit a middle-aged female one, bled out to the color of milk, its arm having been bitten off to the shoulder. Still screaming *run* to nobody Wasp could see. Next came a male ghost, bloated blue with drowning, dressed in some shiny material Wasp didn't recognize. Then came two child-ghosts, walking hand in hand, nothing visible amiss with either of them.

Three years as Archivist had taught Wasp that a certain kind of death, especially the violent or untimely sort, will cause a ghost to imprint upon it, obsess over it, *become* it.

A certain kind of death or maybe a certain kind of ghost, she thought now, watching these. However each of the two child-ghosts had died, it hadn't been alone. They were not seeing death. They were seeing something else. Together, they had kept enough of themselves to bring with them, to light their way.

Beside Wasp, her own ghost was watching them, a terrible hunger in its eyes. She reached to touch its arm, thinking *this is what people do*, but then thought better of it and let her hand fall, halfway to its sleeve.

"Keep moving, right?" she said. Already in her head those words were taking on an almost ritualistic significance, like a rope she could pull herself along, hand over hand, when all else failed.

With a visible effort, the ghost dropped its gaze, smoothed its face to a blank.

"Right," it said. It lifted its chin toward something across the room. "Over there."

Over there was a second door, very like the first. It struck Wasp that there were no other structures to the room; just ghosts, and ghosts, and the door in, and the door out. One by one, ghosts approached that second door. Sometimes it opened. Sometimes it stayed shut. It began to dawn on her that a solid half of the ghosts in the room, maybe more, were milling around aimlessly, avoiding the queue for the door. Other ghosts, for whom the door didn't open, left the front of the queue to join them.

Wasp scrubbed her clammy palms dry on her coatsleeves and marched forward to take her place in line. The ghost went with her.

"Staring at the ground isn't going to find anyone," Wasp told it, mostly to keep her mind off her own apprehension.

"There's no one here I have any interest in finding," it replied.

Of course, thought Wasp. *These are the newly dead. But yours—*

"I guess older ghosts wouldn't, I don't know, come back up to give these ones a hand?" she asked. "They sort of look like they could use it."

From what Wasp had seen of ghosts in random groupings, she didn't really guess there was much by way of solidarity among the dead, and the only reason she could think of for having asked in the first place was that she'd been dragged down here on a hunt for the ghost of a centuries-old corpse she wouldn't recognize if it came up and kicked Wasp in the rear. She needed more to work with.

"I've never seen it," said the ghost. "But," after a moment, "as far as she's concerned, it wouldn't surprise me."

"Huh," said Wasp. In her mental field notes on her quarry she was underlining *stubborn*. Adding *reckless*. Adding *kind*.

The queue inched forward.

"Wouldn't it help if I knew what she looked like?"

"Of course," said the ghost, and then stood staring into space for a full minute, brow creased, to all appearances doing what the Catchkeep-priest called *waffling*. "She. She's."

Wasp felt her patience fraying. "Well, that's wonderful. You don't even—"

The look the ghost gave her was murderous. "I *remember*." It hesitated further, weighing something in its mind, and eventually removed a square of paper from a pocket and set about unfolding it with a care and delicacy, usually in Wasp's experience, reserved for a midwife's more complicated surgeries, or a scavenge-gang deactivating ancient bombs for parts. Wasp knew old paper, and unless she missed her guess, this one had been folded and unfolded countless times, crumpled and uncrumpled, thrown away more than once, but every time retrieved.

Unfolded, the sheet of paper was covered on one side with words written in a cramped and desperate penmanship, with a thick reddish smudge in a corner. Wasp only got the briefest glance at it, but one glimpse of the ghost's face told her, in no uncertain terms, not to ask. The other side had printed words, large ones above an image, smaller ones below. Age and wear had weathered the paper to felt along the creases and the words had all been lost, printed in something less indelible than whatever the words on the back had been scrawled in.

The image, too, was soft and grayed, but in it Wasp could see two figures standing, and she already recognized one. It—he—must have died shortly after the picture was taken. In front of the ghost, the image might as well have been a mirror. The same pale skin, the same dark hair, and due to the black-and-white nature of the image, even the same gray eyes. A mirror, right down to the meticulous mask of the face. Though, Wasp could see, the living man's mask was there to hide slightly different emotions than the ghost's was. She narrowed her eyes at it, intrigued.

In the image, he was standing in an obviously posed manner, shoulder-to-shoulder with a woman. Both had their weapons drawn. Both wore the same uniform, or nearly. The ruins of some building lay smoking behind them. *Colleagues,* thought Wasp. *I see.*

Wasp brought the paper up, inches from her nose, and squinted at the woman. Foster. The top of her head came about level with the man's eyes. Her eyes and skin were darker than his, and her hair was cropped shorter. Due either to the angle of the photo or to something else, her face took on a fierce, inquisitive cast, putting Wasp in mind of a predatory bird. She had one eyebrow lifted, one corner of her mouth quirked, as though issuing a challenge to Wasp across the centuries: *Find me, little girl-with-a-knife. Find me if you can.*

Wasp took in the sword and the gun, and the easy proficiency with which Foster held them, and into the mental field notes went *warrior*. Took in the eyes, quick and defiant, with a sorrowing edge. They were liar's eyes, and loyal eyes. She added *clever*. Also *dangerous*.

These traits were not all coming to right angles in her mind. The image was enough for Wasp to pick Foster's ghost out of a crowd—probably—but now she was worse off than before.

Now she was curious.

She made the slightest move to flip the paper over to the written side and the ghost seized her wrist and pulled the paper from her hand. Pure contrariness, she almost held onto the paper so that the ghost would have to tear it in half to get it free. But whatever the ghost had done to her wrist, she couldn't move her fingers, and the next thing she knew the paper was gone and her hand was beginning to burn and tingle as the blood rushed back in.

I deserved that, she thought, and said nothing of the kind.

Beside her the ghost was stewing in its own head, at the questionable mercy of thoughts she had no way of naming. If she'd had the materials to sketch it she would have tried. Catchkeep still rode her, even this far from home. It wouldn't end until she ended it.

Reach out, thought Wasp. *What people do.*

"She looks . . ." Wasp began, then found herself fumbling. Her mental field notes were rearranging themselves, condensing to a point, but if there was a word for what she found there, she didn't know it. "She looks . . . very . . . capable."

Something in the ghost's eyes lit and was suppressed. Pride. "She was."

"Is."

The ghost looked away.

"Well, she's down here somewhere," Wasp said. It was half a question.

"The dead can't die," said the ghost, "but they can be destroyed. You know that as well as anyone, don't you? Archivist."

Wasp literally backed a step at the sudden hate in its voice. "I didn't," she began, and then stopped, unable to finish the sentence with any certainty.

Yes, she'd freed many ghosts against the Catchkeep-priest's direct orders. But those orders had been to destroy them *all*—or at least all of the ones whose information she'd exhausted and transferred to her notes. A twice-caught ghost, according to the Catchkeep-priest, was as useless as a crapper with no hole in it. A thinned-out harvesting-field of ghosts, however, was not. How often had she obeyed? And how often had the Archivists before her?

The sheer weight of years was staggering. The ghost standing before her was older than her whole world and everything in it. It was a wink of the Chooser's good eye that it hadn't already been annihilated by her or by one like her, if any of them were strong enough to take it on. *The girl with the knife in her belt and the scars on her face.* Each of them the shadow of the one that came before. Each of them the same. And if what she'd seen at the door was true, and none of the upstarts were marked by Catchkeep in the first place, and none of them were special, and none of them were chosen . . .

She'd been lying to herself too long. She wasn't any different.

They stood the rest of the queue in silence. Eventually—a minute later, an hour, a day—Wasp's turn came. From a distance she hadn't been sure what to expect. A password, maybe. A lock. A trap. The door before her looked much like the one she'd entered through, except there was no knocker. Nor were there any knobs or handles or anything by which she could open it herself, if it refused her.

She took her place before the door and heard a voice inside her head. No, she thought later: not heard so much as felt, and not a voice so much as a compulsion. *Speak your name*, it said. *You have three chances.*

"Wasp," said Wasp.

Incorrect. That's one.

Her temper flashed up. "Ragpicker take you, you useless chunk of slag, my *name* is *Wasp.*"

That's two.

She stomped her anger down before it got her stuck here in some ghosts' waiting-room until Ember Girl burned the world and flung her free. Think. She had to think. Behind her, the queue was muttering already. It wasn't helping.

For years she'd been Wasp. It was who she was. Everything up until that point had been training to get there. She'd grown up as any upstart grew up: bounced back and forth between houses, cared for by the families of the town until she was old enough to begin her training, and each family had called her by whatever name it chose. She'd been called after a dead daughter, a runaway daughter, a daughter someone had never had. Then she'd moved to the shrine quarters, with its long table and its stone sleeping-alcoves, and by that time the false names had worn from her along with the true one, like an old coin too often handled. It had been so long since she'd even thought of what she'd been called before, and it sickened her that it had taken her until her third chance before the door to remember which name, under all of the false ones, was true.

"Isabel," she whispered, and the door swung open.

Chapter Nine

S
he stepped through—and was abruptly in a forest. It was unlike the orchard back home, unlike anywhere she'd ever been. She and the ghost had come out in a clearing ringed round with trees she'd never seen before and couldn't name, far taller and greener than the trees she knew. The grass of the clearing was dotted with flowers the size of her fingernail, blue enough to hurt her eyes. Overhead, the sky was bruise-colored and luminous. There was water, somewhere, near enough to smell.

The grass, the leaves, even the clouds stood still. Wasp felt the same tingle up her spine she used to get when entering the Catchkeep-shrine, long ago. Treading softly, so that whatever power slept in that place would not wake and find her there. There was no birdsong, no rummaging of mice in the underbrush. All was silent.

Until something crashed behind her, loud as summer thunder. She whirled, knife out—but it was only the door, shutting. A brief moment of panic: the thread that attached her to her body must be stuck now, in the door. But she pulled on it and found it spooling out of her, apparently endless, caught but unbroken.

The door stood there in the clearing, unattached to anything. Grass grew around it. Remembering her cooling body's camouflage, thinking of invisible walls, Wasp walked around the door. The clearing continued on all sides of it uninterrupted. She pushed it open. The clearing was through there too. At the boundary of the threshold, she could just make out the thread if she kept it directly in her sight, but the moment her eyes wavered from it, it seemed to vanish, and it was only after gasping and clutching at her chest that she reassured herself it was still attached.

Wherever she was, she was stuck there.

She glanced through the open door at the ghost. It seemed preoccupied, staring holes through the ground as though the grass and dirt of the clearing was reminding it of something it would rather forget.

Wasp cleared her throat, and the ghost snapped out of it.

"This way," it said. "We have to find the bridge."

It took off and Wasp followed.

Either the forest was tiny or the door was near its edge, because in a minute they'd come clear of the trees. Before them lay a river, black as tar and swift as thought, kicking up into whitewater. Among all that stillness, one thing that moved. Wasp saw no bridge, no boat, no crossing of any kind. The rushing water made no sound. Down it sailed a silvery clot of broken ghost-bodies, thrashing in silence but irreparable, having learned the hard way not to chance the river swimming.

They weren't too far from shore.

"I can reach them," Wasp breathed, and bolted toward the water with a branch.

Half a step from joining them, the ghost knocked her down onto the riverbank.

"You can't help them," it shouted in her face. "You *can't*."

"Oh, but I can help you?" Wasp snapped back, disengaging herself. "You and you only? That's convenient." She didn't think she'd heard it raise its voice before. Perhaps she'd finally shaken it. Still, deep down, she knew the ghost was right. She wasn't any use to anybody floating down a river, arms broken, leaking silver ichor from her head. And she wouldn't be much use to *herself* when she had finished here, if she cut off her way back to her body on the ledge.

Still, she wasn't about to admit a word of that to some specimen. And she sure as hell wasn't going to let it shove her around. It reached out a hand to help her up, and she ignored it.

"And you do not get to push me, get it?" Wasp stood, hand on the harvesting-knife. "I'll give you that one for free. You're going to pay for the next one."

Before the ghost could respond, a sound filled the air. A kind of rolling, keening howl, many-voiced, low and shrill and sonorous at once. The echo of it rebounded and faded, was taken up, elsewhere, again. In the silence since the door had shut, the sudden noise was huge. Worse, it was close.

Worse still, she knew it, in her blood and bones.

Catchkeep's hunt.

She'd forgotten all about it. It had been so long since she'd been a child small enough to be scared by fireside stories of the hunt, it hadn't occurred to her that she was going to the place where those stories were *real* and could do her actual harm.

No time to think about running. In the stories, once the hunt had locked on to a target, it could not be outrun. No time to guess what they'd do to her if the hunt tried to bring her down. Whether it would scent the Archivist in her first, or the interloper. In the stories the hunt had Catchkeep Herself at its head, and She was capricious and did what She liked. The hunt could send ghosts back to earth or annihilate them outright—or worse, it could be delicate, could break without destroying, and leave a ghost to try and make its way through eternity with whatever the hunt had left it.

As far as Wasp was concerned, none of these things was an option.

She squirmed out of the backpack and tossed it aside, back toward the woods. To her horror, she could see other ghosts making their way out from the door among the trees, following the path toward the river. "Stay back!" she shrieked at them, not knowing whether that would put them further from danger or closer. Hoping she and the ghost could draw the hunt, give them time to run or hide.

By the riverbank, the ghost was waiting, sword out, back to the water, eyes scanning the woods. There was something in its face and stance that made it look much more like the image of its dead self on the old paper than the ghost-self Wasp was coming to know. Its focus had changed. It was in its element. Well, that much she could understand.

She took her place beside it and drew the knife.

Later, it would unsettle her. Here she was, an Archivist, drawing weapons *with* someone rather than against. Fighting back-to-back with someone. Knowing that if she pulled through this, it would be in part because of the speed and skill and competence of someone other than herself. And if the ghost did, it would be in part because of hers. It wouldn't last, but at this moment, for the first time in her life, Wasp had an ally.

It was very, very strange. It was not wholly unpleasant.

"I make seven or eight by the sound," the ghost was saying. "And closing fast. That way." A tight little half-nod, over the woods. Back where she'd told the ghosts to stay. To keep them safe. Already, from the direction of the door, she could hear thin screams arising.

Wasp cursed, then broke and ran.

And something exploded out of the trees. She caught the briefest glimpse of it—vast, bright, snarling—and then she was on her back in the dirt with a weight on her shoulders and a stabbing pain in her chest where her air should be.

There was a little rhyme the children of Sweetwater would say, as they were tucked into bed and the snuffed lamps left them alone in the dark.

> *Catchkeep's lurchers, running free,*
> *Herding the souls out over the trees:*
> *Cold ghosts you are. Till ghost I be,*
> *You have no power over me.*

It did not begin to prepare her for the thing that loomed over her now.

It was like a dog, but not a dog. Its breath stank like a sickroom on fire, and its eyes glowed green. Its teeth were longer than her fingers. There was a silvery rag caught in its jaws. A silvery rag with eyeholes and a mouth. Over by the door in the clearing, the screaming had stopped.

No time. Wasp gripped the knife, gathered, and struck. The blade squelched in to the guard between two ribs, and she gasped. She must be hallucinating. There, for a second, she had faded out, lost consciousness, *something*—she had somehow *seen* a vision of Catchkeep's lurchers, several of them, stalking toward her dark-windowed little house on the hill. It jarred her. She faded back in just as she was pulling the knife free. If she had lost that second a moment earlier, a moment later—at any time but during the eyeblink of an opening following her blow—she would be dead, teeth in her throat, and knew it.

Would Catchkeep's holy knife harm one of Her own? It was a gamble on a guess. But the lurcher shrieked and lunged, and it took all Wasp's strength to wrench her head aside in time for the huge jaws to snap shut where her face had been.

The lurcher was clearly unused to missing targets. It swayed back, unbalanced, and Wasp got her foot up between them and pushed with all she had. The lurcher fell sideways a half step. It was all she needed. She dug her nails into the slime-slicked dogleather of the grip and dragged the blade free for a second strike even as she planted her foot in the lurcher's underbelly. It yelped like any kicked dog and swung back toward her snarling, but Wasp was out from under, crouched low behind the knife, counting seconds.

She didn't count many. The lurcher took another snap at her and she dropped her weight and shot up fast with the harvesting-knife, and the lurcher went down hard with the hilt sticking out of the soft of its throat and the point of the blade in whatever passed for its brain. She pulled the knife free as the lurcher began to melt into a kind of slurry, which disappeared into the ground with a smell of lilacs and a sound like eggs frying. The grass died in its outline, black and slimed. One down.

And then she saw the ghost. She had never seen anything like it in her life.

It had the death-stains of five lurchers arrayed around its boots and was working on a sixth. The lurcher leapt for the ghost's throat, and the ghost's sword got in the way. With no visible effort the ghost sidestepped, down came the teeth on the blade, the ghost gave what looked like a gentle push, and the top half of the lurcher's head came off and deliquesced as it fell. The rest of the lurcher, carried by its momentum, plunged into the river. The current bore it away, a skin of black goo on the black water.

Another sprang for Wasp, and the ghost, calm as ever, drew the gun in its off-hand and fired—and the bullet passed straight over the lurcher as it tumbled to the dirt at Wasp's feet, her flung knife in its eye.

With that, the silence returned.

"Looks like the last of them," she said, pulling the knife free. Suppressing a shudder at the feel of what she pulled it out of: meat, shadow, slime. Almost not registering the vision, dream-scrap, whatever, that zapped its way up the knife, through her arm, into her brain: a lurcher savaging what might have been a deer, facedown in its guts. She caught it in afterimage, blinked, and it was gone.

The ghost gave the woods one last once-over and holstered the gun. Still it kept its sword drawn, its eyes on the dark beyond the trees. Wasp cast a sidewise glance at it, finding herself suddenly, aggravatingly shy before this new aspect of it, this awful vicious elegance she'd only seen hinted at before.

To give herself something to do, she scrubbed the harvesting-knife on the grass. It didn't work as well as she'd have liked. "Do they come through here often?" she asked, squatting by the water to wash the blade in the shallows. "The lurchers. Catchkeep's hunt."

"Never," said the ghost. "I assumed they were after you."

This made no sense. Even tiny children knew about the Hunt. *Herding the souls out over the trees . . .* And this, where the ghosts walked, this was their hunting ground. Centuries down here, a ghost couldn't really help but notice. Either the ghost was lying or all the stories were. She thought of the scars on her cheek and wondered which was true.

Silent motion at her side as the ghost joined her. Its sword hadn't fared any better than her knife, and they were there for some minutes, saying nothing, letting the water do its work.

"You fight well," the ghost said after a time.

Wasp shrugged. "I don't have a choice. It's what I was made for." Something in the quality of the silence changed. She turned. The ghost's stare was unreadable. "So do you," she added hastily, looking away.

"It's what I was made for," said the ghost, so soft Wasp almost couldn't hear it, and now it was her turn to stare.

Despite the muddy riverbank, the ghost stood smoothly. "It's getting dark. We have to find the bridge."

"Bridge," said Wasp. "Right." Her questions could wait. She jumped up, dried the blade on her coat-sleeve, sheathed it. *The backpack.* She'd almost forgotten it. It was badly slime-splashed, and the fabric of it had corroded beneath the stains, disintegrated at a touch. Most everything in it was beyond hope of salvage. Only the saltlick, the jar, and the firestarter could be kept. She pocketed them.

Just as she didn't let herself ponder how the Archivist-coat somehow managed to fit all Archivists of whatever shape and size, she didn't think too long on how the pockets seemed to stretch to receive the box of salt and the jar. Not for the first time she resolved to burn the coat the first chance she could, and wondered whether this time she'd actually follow through.

Into the woods beyond where she had left the backpack, she could see a huddle of ghosts lingering by the door, gauging the safety of the path, muttering amongst themselves. Not looking at what lay ravaged at their feet.

She went to shout out to them, then thought better of it. She couldn't assure them of their safety. Not if she was, by her very presence, bringing the hunt down upon their heads. The best thing she could do for them was get gone. Fast.

The sky had deepened to violet, casting green-black shadows. She didn't see a bridge. "Which way—?"

"It doesn't stay in one place for long. Your guess is as good as mine."

Wasp blew air out of her mouth hard. "I don't know. Upriver."

They took off upriver.

"I mean, you're sure it's here somewhere, right? We're not going to just keep walking straight into another batch of those things?"

"I'm sure it's somewhere, yes."

"Funny. But the lurchers are out there, and they're looking for me, I guess, and you don't even seem to know how they got here to—"

"And if they find you, you'll handle it. You did as much already."

Wasp was not much used to having her abilities—not Catchkeep's puppet's but *hers*—spoken of favorably. She mumbled something incoherent under her breath and took a sudden keen interest in her surroundings.

Upriver was turning out to be much of the same. The woods were at her left shoulder now, and denser here. Here and there she could glimpse movement off in the dark: ghosts walking unknown paths among the trees. The same purple sky above, in which stars were now emerging, their constellations unfamiliar. Beneath her feet the dirt of the riverbank was red as berries and wet-looking, even beyond where the water reached. It gave off a metallic smell.

She mentioned as much to the ghost. "I know," it said. "We're getting close."

Some minutes later, it stopped. Wasp looked around. She saw nothing.

"Here," said the ghost.

"Here what?"

The ghost gave that slow half-nod toward something across the river. Wasp squinted in the almost-dark. A hundred yards of rushing water and a misty shore. A road beyond. The tall grass of a meadow. Lights, farther off: amber, sapphire, blackish red—and high up, like Wasp's town stacked on its own head thrice.

"Okay," said Wasp. "What?"

"Stand here. Where I'm standing." The ghost stepped aside, making room. "Now look."

Wasp stood, and looked.

And gasped. Because the bridge, suddenly, was there.

It had planes and angles and high graceful arches. It was dull, shining, black, white, transparent, many-colored. Short of Execution Hill and Lake Sweetwater, it was possibly the single biggest thing Wasp had ever seen on earth.

She took a step sideways and it vanished. Stepped back and it reappeared. She was beginning to understand what had driven that raft of broken ghosts to swimming.

Close up, the bridge was made of trash. Coins. Stones.

Shells. Keys. Birdskulls. Bits of glass. Bits of plastic. Bits of driftwood. Broken weapons. Dried flowers. Trinkets. Bullets. Leaves. Rings. And a thousand things Wasp didn't recognize. Some of it pristine, some of it eroded into nonsense. Most pieces no larger than the palm of her hand.

"The dead build it together," said the ghost. "From their pockets, from their coffins. From their mouths and eyes."

Wasp thought of all the dead Archivists, green stones on their tongues. How even the poorest dead of Sweetwater were buried with pebbles, pear-seeds, clay tokens. Something. How the townspeople thought it lucky to die in early summer, when the suns-and-moons could be picked from the fields and placed over each corpse's eyes: one yellow, one white.

She'd come with little and lost most of it already. What remained to her was a knife, a jar, a firestarter, and a half-empty box of salt. Her shoes, her clothes, a vaguely disturbing dogleather coat, the long curved pin holding up the burden of her hair.

Her hair. She felt silly even considering it. She felt like Ember Girl in the stories, who seemed to cut her hair off every time she embarked on an adventure. But it was there to leave, and she didn't have much else that she could spare, and it was nothing she would miss or need. And she liked the idea of laying all those murdered girls down to rest here after carrying them through the upper world so long.

She pulled the pin out, and her hair fell deadweight to her waist. As an almost-ghost, she felt she shouldn't have been able to still smell it, but the stink of death was still as strong on it as ever. It might have been her imagination, but she was sure that cutting into it only made the smell worse. As though it wasn't hair at all, but a rotten egg cracked open or a days-dead raccoon run over by a cart. And sawing through the mass of it, sharp as the harvesting-knife was, took much longer than she'd guessed.

As she worked, she explained to the ghost how for every upstart she had fought and killed, a large part of the dead girl's hair was cut off and interwoven into Wasp's. Three per year for three years, minus Aneko: undefeated. And some from the Archivist she had killed to get there. She explained how every year, after the fight, before she'd even recovered from her wounds, it all was unwoven, the new growth of her own hair trimmed, then everyone else's plaited back in and glued where the plaits didn't hold. How every year her head grew heavier, and if she were too successful for too long, the weight would blind her with migraines, slow her movements, level the field between her and the upstarts who would eventually tear her down.

"Why?" asked the ghost.

"It's how it's always been," said Wasp. Then, realizing how weak this answer must sound, realizing she had no better answer to give, started cutting faster. Where her hair left the knife it turned silvery, reduced to ghost-debris, like the tangle of broken limbs sailing down the river. Like the mask in the lurcher's mouth that was not a mask at all.

The ghost observed her, saying nothing, as around Wasp's feet the pile of braids and charms grew higher. Now that the fight with the lurchers was over, the ghost had reverted to that alert impassivity, precise and serene. When Wasp had said that she was made for fighting, it had been a bit of an exaggeration, meant to deflect an awkward compliment. But after what she had seen she had little difficulty believing that, for the ghost's part, it was literally true. It looked to her less like a person than like a weapon that had gone walking, out of a story and into the world, wearing a person's shape.

But what use would a weapon have for this search it was dragging her on, she wondered. What sort of person would a weapon call friend?

Another weapon, the answer came to her. *Another of the same.*

The whole mess made her think of stories, of Carrion Boy and His ally-enemy Ember Girl. Each quested across a hundred songs and stories searching for the other, but the reasons for these searches—to trick, to slay, to rescue, or something in between—depended on the story. The only constant was that each time They met, They met in collisions that broke one against the other. It was not Carrion Boy's fault, not Ember Girl's. It was simply what They were. And the next winter, and the winter after that, They'd get up and, unable to do otherwise, start again.

It was all well and good in bloodless stories about distant stars. Here, now, it made her uncomfortable on several levels, most of which she didn't want to examine closely enough to identify. *Another of the same* had hit her with hard enough of a pang already.

"What did you leave at the bridge?" she asked, knowing by now that she wouldn't get an answer. Only needing a stone, however small and ineffectual, to throw at her thoughts and make them scatter.

But the ghost surprised her. "A medal," it said, and the knife froze in Wasp's hand. She had hated so much for so long, but it paled to nothing beside the bitterness in the ghost's voice now. "The medal they gave me for turning her in."

Wasp swallowed. There was one right thing to say to something like this, she felt, and as the only one here, it was her job to say it, whatever it was. She kicked words around in her mind, all useless, all she had: *I am sure she was strong enough to forgive you. I hope she died well. They say the Ragpicker's favorite sweet is should-have-dones. Don't give Him yours.*

It was an easy choice between a wrong guess and a shut mouth, so she went with the shut mouth, and the ghost did, too.

The last strands of upstart-hair landed on the bridge. Wasp sheathed the harvesting-knife and stepped out of the pile, brushing off her sleeves.

The air was cool on the back of her neck. She felt so *light.* Almost unbalanced—she'd learned so long ago to move with this great ungainly weight strapped to her, and now it was gone. She half wanted the lurchers to return, so she could see how well she fought unrestricted. Whether her skill would match the ghost's. This ghost's or the vanished one's, Kit Foster's, trapped in that faded paper, testing her with its eyes.

Shut up, she thought. *Focus.*

She ran a hand through what was left of her hair. It was about fifty different lengths and stood out every whichaway, but everything that had belonged to the dead had been removed. What was left, as far as she could tell, was hers.

The bridge stretched out before her. She started walking.

Chapter Ten

A cross the bridge, a path led away amid grass as high as Wasp's head. After the door-attached-to-nothing and the nearly invisible death-token bridge, she expected something more than what she saw: a dirt road, straight and narrow, tamped smooth by countless feet.

The grass made her nervous. It could hide anything. Especially in the dark, which by now was virtually complete.

In the monotony of the meadow it was impossible for her to tell how far they walked, and it seemed the city in the distance grew no nearer. She didn't ask if that was where they were headed. She assumed it was. There was nothing else to see.

Ghosts passed them, from time to time, on other business. None of them was Foster. They kept their heads down, their mouths shut, their eyes averted, so Wasp did the same. A moon hung low in the sky, heavy and orange.

Wasp was getting tired, or thought she was. *Could* she be thirsty? Hungry? Footsore? Did she need to sleep, down here?

"A little farther," the ghost said, as if sensing her thoughts. "We can make up lost time in the morning."

Morning. Night. A moon. That these even existed in this place was a surprise to her. In hindsight she couldn't now picture what she'd thought of, before, when she thought of where the dead go when they die and Catchkeep brings their ghosts across. A long road, leading nowhere. An empty room in which to sit and wait for nothing. A field to wander, as the ghosts she caught aboveground must have wandered, bent beneath whatever quests still rode them. Or aimlessly. Well, she was in a field, anyway.

Yet again she found herself kicking questions around in her head. How was she to find Foster or anyone down here? Where was she even to begin to look? Could she catch ghosts with the saltlick down here? The idea seemed ridiculous. It was one thing when the ghosts she caught were faceless silver paper-doll cutouts the size of mice, and another when they seemed like ordinary people, as big and real looking as her. And—if this ghost had been searching for hundreds of years already, what on earth did it think she could do that it hadn't already tried? It wasn't going to be happy when it realized that Wasp's only ghosthunting experience involved sitting around waiting for specimens to come to her salt.

And then there were the questions she wasn't sure she wanted answers to. Was what the door had shown her—that the Catchkeep-priest had marked her for service himself—true? If the basis for choosing upstarts was a lie, what else was? And if Catchkeep's hunt was not a fixture of the ghosts' land as the stories told, then had she fought Catchkeep's hunt at all, or something else? How had it found her? Would it find her again?

Would she survive it if it did?

"Here," the ghost said, and it took Wasp's legs a second to remember how to stop walking. They had stopped in the middle of the path, nothing of note before them or behind. Off in the distance, rising up above the tall grass, Wasp could just make out by moonlight a roof, a chimney. Smoke.

"Someone's there," said Wasp, but the ghost was already tacking off through the grass toward the house. Moonlight caught on its sword. *Quieter than the gun*, thought Wasp, and, sparing a glance up and down the road for lurchers on her tail, drew her own blade and followed. Tiny bright things chirped and trilled at her from the grass as she brushed by. They didn't look like any insects that she knew.

From the way it was approaching the door, Wasp thought the ghost would kick it in. But it stopped at the last minute and tried the latch. Not locked. The door swung into the room, and the ghost slipped around it without a sound. Wasp snuck in after, blade ready, and the door clicked shut behind.

There was nobody there. A fire in the hearth, a bed stacked with quilts, a table piled high with food and drink. Wasp, whose cradle-tongue was stories, eyed these warily. "What is this place?"

"A waypoint," said the ghost. "Of a kind."

"A what?"

"It tells you where you are. Sets out a small place in a bigger one."

"A map."

"Like a marker on a map," said the ghost. "Also like a door. Also sometimes like the room behind the door. Sometimes not like that at all." It crossed the room and took a seat: elbow on table, booted heel on knee. "You wanted to rest. Now you can."

Out the windows, there was nothing. Grass grew flush against the walls, sighed and fretted at the panes. They could be anywhere.

Wasp was eyeing the bed yearningly. It looked soft. It looked like a trap.

"What's the point of all this? Ghosts don't need to eat. They don't need to sleep." She paused, unsure. "Do they?"

"You tell me." It gave the neighboring chair a kick, sending it skidding across the floor to rock to a stop before her. "Sit down before you fall down."

Wasp sat. The chair did not eat her. It did not wrap wooden arms around her and burn her alive. That at least was something. She picked it up, carried it to the table, and parked it next to the ghost's.

There was a drinking-bowl of water at her elbow. It looked safe enough, and she was so thirsty. She sniffed at it, then took a sip. It tasted like drinking out of cupped hands from a clear brook in high summer. She drained the bowl dry, then returned it to the table. When she glanced at it again, it was full.

What with the weight off her feet and the coziness of the fire, it was going to take some doing for her to not start snoring then and there, her face on the tabletop. But there were grapes there, a basket of them, and not the stunted, wild sort that ran riot through the orchard-rows, a hundred to a handful. They were the size of her eye, the color of the river she had crossed. She could smell them from where she sat. They smelled untrustworthy.

The look of longing on her face must have been obvious, because the ghost picked a couple of grapes from the basket, ate one, shrugged a little, then tossed her the other. She caught it. Rolled it in her hand. It wasn't poison that worried her. It was doing something that would let this place lay claim to her. She set it down.

"Something strange happened today," she heard herself murmuring.

"You don't say."

"When I stabbed the lurchers. I—I saw things." It sounded stupid any way she cut it. "Things that weren't there. It—"

"Go on."

"I saw them in the other world. The real one. They were heading toward my house. They were scenting for something. They hadn't found it yet."

The ghost was watching her closely, eyes narrowed. "When you stabbed the creature."

"The lurcher," said Wasp. Pure reflex, pure rote, the childhood rhyme was on her tongue. She swallowed it. "Yes."

"With that blade?"

She nodded.

"Let me see."

Wasp unsheathed. Firelight glittered on the sixteen stars. Not for the first time it came to her: sixteen stars in Catchkeep's up-self, one per year that Wasp had wasted in Her name. She flipped the long knife and caught it by the point. Even as she offered the ghost the hilt she chastised herself: *and since when have you been a show-off, hmm?*

The ghost took the knife, evidently unmoved. "You're sure this happened when you stabbed it."

Wasp thought back. The lurcher, leaning over her. Her arm, drawing back to strike. The feel of the knife going in. Her vision, cutting away with the abruptness of a scene change in a dream. "I'm sure."

The ghost nodded. For a long time it said nothing. Then: "It's an interesting piece. It looks old."

"The first Archivist carried it," said Wasp, despite it all feeling a small upsurge of pride, probably misplaced. "Four hundred years ago."

"Not everyone who fights with a blade knows how to care for it. They train you well." The ghost was turning the harvesting-knife over and over in its hands. The question it asked next did not look to be the question it was thinking. "Where did this first Archivist find it?"

"It fell from the sky." The upstarts learned this story first of all of them. With no effort on Wasp's part, it came flooding back. "Catchkeep fought the Chooser for dominion over the land of the dead and won, sort of, but the last star was knocked loose from the tip of Her tail and fell, and the first Catchkeep-priest found it in a ruin deep underground, and gave it to the first Archivist, who realized that it could—"

She stopped talking, disgusted at how she sounded. As though she were once again a wide-eyed nursery brat, dreaming of a day when she could fight and kill to make that holy knife her own.

It was giving her second thoughts about that damn grape anyway. She popped it in her mouth. It was delicious.

"These inclusions of darker metal," the ghost was saying, still studying the knife. "What do they signify?"

"Catchkeep's up-self," Wasp said, chewing. "Stars."

The ghost tilted the pattern into the light. "I remember this constellation."

"Yeah? I noticed the stars are different down here. That memory must go way back. But . . ." She paused, realizing what the ghost was saying. "Catchkeep should still be—"

"People used to call it Ursa Major." It hefted the long knife a couple of times, thoughtfully. "A bear."

It threw her, that Catchkeep was not always Catchkeep. Where Wasp came from, Catchkeep drank whole rivers, bit mountains from the sky, herded ghosts back and forth between the worlds of the living and the dead. The earth itself was Her first litter's afterbirth. She was the beginning, and, when She finally caught the sun and ate it, She would be the end.

Everything Wasp had been told since she left her body on that ledge had only confused her further. Her whole world felt like a spinning plate that someone had applied the lightest of touches to, beginning imperceptibly but unstoppably to teeter toward the wobbling that would knock it flat.

"And this knife is the main part of your equipment," the ghost was saying. "For the hunting of ghosts."

"It cuts them free," said Wasp, though the words were crumbling in her mouth, losing all meaning. She would rather have explained this yesterday.

"So that you can trap them."

"So I can *observe* them."

The ghost had an expression she was getting used to, a narrowing of the eyes in thought, but quickly smoothed over, as if it had been caught out giving a secret away. It did this now.

"It's not a weapon," Wasp said. "It's—I don't even know what it is anymore. Yesterday I thought I knew. Today, I might as well have been harvesting ghosts with a fish-gutting knife, if it's all a lie at the bottom of it any—" She blinked. "What are you doing?"

What it was doing was removing the glove from its off-hand, then drawing the blade along the palm so that silver blood leaked out. It held the blade there a moment. Nothing seemed to happen. The ghost made an aggravated sound and let go of the blade. The edges of the cut were silvering, curling up like paper.

It started to hand the harvesting-knife back, then stopped. It wrapped its cut palm back around the knife, blood to blade, and held the hilt to Wasp.

She folded her arms. "What."

"I just want to see what'll happen."

"What exactly do you *think* is going to happen?"

"You cut a ghost with this knife and you saw something. Yes?"

What she had left out of that recounting was how the visions had left her dizzy, woozy, just shy of retching. She was covetous enough of her dignity that the idea of hurling on the ghost's boots gave her pause. "Twice," she said. Not reaching for the knife.

"It might not mean anything," said the ghost. "If it happens again, it might. We won't know until we try."

It was true. She knew it was true. Besides, she'd come down here to do the work, and this was the work. It wasn't like she had much in her to throw up anyway. "Fine," she said. "But this is ridiculous."

Wasp took the hilt—and the room vanished around her.

She was standing in a gap between high buildings in a city so alien-looking to her she thought she must be dreaming.

The ghost stood a few feet away. So did the woman from the picture, Foster. Even if she hadn't worn the uniform, the sword and gun, Wasp would have recognized her from her stance, from the calculating tilt to her head, from the set of her jaw and the light in her eyes. They weren't much older here than Wasp, eighteen or so at most.

The alley behind them was packed wall to wall with people, as far back as Wasp could see. These ones wore no uniforms. Some were armed. Most were not. Many were visibly injured. Most looked like they hadn't seen a bed or a hot meal or a bath in some days. Wasp could hear at least three different babies screaming.

Foster stood in conference with two men and a woman at the front of the crowd. As she spoke she was holding a device like the one the ghost had fixed Wasp's ankle with, and the crowd was sending forth its injured.

The ghost—though not a ghost, not here, not yet—stood apart, watching the street through half-lidded eyes. He and Foster were each flanked by a semicircle of staring children. He suffered their awed pinching of his sleeves and coat-hem in silence.

From the distance came shouts, explosions, bursts of gunfire. The ground trembled a little under the approach of something large and slow, but Wasp couldn't tell which direction it was coming from. The noise of it was monstrous.

"One of those goddamn things took out our complex," one of the men was telling Foster. "Came out of nowhere. Took about ten seconds. Think it was aiming for the barricade." He gestured toward the crowd. "We're what's left."

Foster gave the crowd a once-over. "Sixty?"

"Sixty-two," said the woman. "Eighty to start. It's been a rough few days."

Foster nodded grimly, her device pressed to a teenage boy's shattered knee. After a moment it beeped three times and powered down. She cursed a streak, and the ghost—Wasp didn't know what else to call him—took an identical device out of his pocket and tossed it to her wordlessly. Foster caught it and addressed the queue waiting to be healed. "If you can walk, get out of line and bring me somebody who can't," she said. "Fast. Then get ready to get the hell out of here."

She lowered her voice to keep what she said next from spreading. "You're in the wrong place at the wrong time, and things are about to get pretty hot where you're sitting, believe me," she said to the men and woman beside her. "And you need medical attention. More than we can give. But we can clear a path."

The ghost raised one eyebrow at her. "Hospital's still standing, last I knew," Foster told them, shooting him a complicated look as she spoke. It was clear from his face what he thought of playing medics and escorts, but after a moment he swept his gaze over the assembled crowd and nodded. "Food and blankets," Foster continued. "Worst soup you ever ate, but plenty of it."

The noise of whatever Wasp had heard approaching suddenly changed pitch and got much louder. The ghost drew his sword. "You just ran out of time."

Foster didn't look up. "How many?"

"Enough."

The crowd started rustling, drawing guns, adults herding children back behind them. Foster stood between them and the mouth of the alley, hand on her sword-hilt, warning them with her eyes. "Heads down," she said. "No heroes. I mean it."

"Thank God they sent you in for us," said one of the men. "We never hoped—"

Foster, halfway into the street, shot back a look over her shoulder like she'd swallowed a bug. "They didn't," she said, and left. The ghost went with her. Wasp found she had no choice but to follow.

Immediately she realized what had been making that horrific noise, though she had no idea what to call them. They were shaped almost like people, though were made entirely of metal and stood several times her height. There were three of them, coming down the street in a V formation. They ran on two legs in a slickly gliding gait, with gun barrels the diameter of a tree where their hands would be.

"Best of three?" Foster said.

"Why bother?" he replied. "You never win."

Her eyes glinted. "Neither do you."

Blue fire sparked in one of the gun-arms. Without any further warning, the street exploded at their feet, at Wasp's a few feet away.

If the Ragpicker were dangling Wasp headfirst over His maw, she might not have been this terrified. She threw herself toward the nearest wall and crouched there as Foster picked up a piece of rubble the size of her head and hurled it down the street toward the machines. It was an impossible throw, but it cleared its hundred-odd feet and lodged in one of the gun-arms in the split second before it fired. There came the sound of a muffled detonation, then a larger, less muffled one, and the machine collapsed in flames.

The other two advanced, and suddenly Foster was dashing up the front of the fallen one, leaping off, catching the gun-arm of another, swinging herself up onto it, then dropping to the street as the third one, aiming for her, shot off the gun-arm instead. As Foster fell, she threw her arms out, fingers laced, making a step for the ghost as he launched himself off the street, off the falling gun-arm, off Foster's push, high enough to grab some sort of handhold far up on the machine and hang on one-handed. The other hand drew the sword and plunged it into a crack in the thing's armor. Someone inside it screamed, and as the machine fell to its knees the ghost landed lightly beside it.

Running, they were much faster than the shrine-dogs in full chase. Wasp had nothing to compare their apparent strength to that would suffice. She gaped. *Who* are *you people?*

There was one machine left. While the ghost was drawing its fire away from the people huddled in the alley, Foster took off toward a vast pile of rubble in the street that looked like it used to be a wall, if walls were made out of garbage. Something in it seemed to have caught her eye, and a few seconds later she emerged with a looped length of cable over one shoulder.

In the distance Wasp became aware of the drone of something low and fast approaching from the air. She squinted against the sun and saw nothing. She looked down, and a small group of people had broken from the alley and were standing ground in the street, small arms blazing uselessly at the oncoming machine.

Shouting, Foster flung herself down the street toward them, dropping the cable as she ran. The ghost walked to it, picked it up, drew his gun, tied it into the end of the cable. Waited a second, listening. Threw that weighted end of the cable high up into the air, as some kind of flying vehicle banked around the blind corner of a building, guns strafing the street before him.

The cable wrapped around the vehicle's tail and caught, yanking the vehicle into an about-face. He dug his bootheels in and pulled hard on the cable, whipping the vehicle from the air and straight into the path of the machine, which by now was a half-dozen stomps behind him. The vehicle slammed into it, and as the machine toppled back, its gun-arm fired. The shot went wide, a ball of blue fire slicing silently past him by a few feet to smash through a building half a block away.

The ghost walked back up the street to join Foster in the alley. Behind him, the machine exploded, shattering windows on buildings both sides of the street in a rain of glass.

"I was just going to try to tangle its legs," said Foster. She was sitting with her back to a wall in the mouth of the alley, still using the healing device on the queue of wounded. She worked one-handed, because one of the men was binding her shoulder where one of the flying vehicle's bullets had gone in. As he tied off the bandage, she winced, then grinned. "But that works, too."

"There'll be more," said the ghost. "Soon."

"No rest for the wicked," said Foster, getting up. "Okay, everybody, on your feet. We'll have a roof over your heads by sundown, but you have to do *exactly* as we say."

Chapter Eleven

And, with that, the city was gone. Wasp was back in the little cabin. Chair, table, basket, bowl. Her head was muzzy. It took her a second to realize where she was.

The ghost was watching her the way a person would look at a water pail if he were on fire. Not really holding out hope, but hoping anyway.

She winced as the nausea barreled into her. "How long was I—" *Dreaming,* she was about to say, though she'd never had a dream so vivid, so unreal. Then she realized the ghost was still holding the blade of her knife, and it all came back.

"Two or three seconds," said the ghost. "What did you," it began, and stopped. She ducked her chin, but the ghost caught it, held it up to see her eyes, which she allowed.

She pulled free, and it let her. "You saw something. Just now."

It was hard, this flickering out and in. The room was spinning. She burped and tasted bile. Those machines were going to show up in her nightmares, no question.

Her eyes fell on the thread. It looked finer. Must be a trick of the light.

"No rest for the wicked," she murmured, staring at her hands to make the room stay still.

The ghost looked like she'd slapped it. "You saw her."

"I don't know. I saw *something*."

Wasp wasn't sure it was even listening to her. "She used to say that," it said to itself. "I'd forgotten."

It rounded on Wasp. "You have to go back in."

It did not sound like a question.

"Not happening." Her ears were still ringing from the explosions. "Not a chance." She paused. Shut her eyes. She was going to regret this later. "Why?"

The ghost's impatience was palpable. "Because you can see her and I can't. Because there might be some clue in whatever you saw that tells us where she's gone. Because if there were any other option, I would have taken it."

"That doesn't make any sense. You were *there*. I saw you *there*. What could I possibly have seen that you—"

The ghost gave her the bleakest look she'd ever seen. "Do you know what it is to be dead?"

"Not really, but I have a feeling you're about to—"

"When you're trying to remember something that's slipped your mind," it said, "and you can't, but you know that eventually, if you stop thinking about it, look the other way, it'll surface and you'll catch it. Except that you won't, and after a while you realize that, once half the things you used to know have been pulled out of you by this place, and the half you remember keep you wondering about the half you've lost. And you're left with maybe one or two relics of it to anchor you." Unconsciously its hand brushed the pocket where the folded paper was kept. "Until you lose those, too."

Wasp could picture it, freshly dead, its memories hammering and blazing away inside it in a swarm. Those memories, one by one, going silent, going dark, leaving the fading fabric of its life more holes than weave. She decided not to ask.

"But you know all this already, ghosthunter," it went on. Suddenly it looked very weary. "You and your salt and your notebooks, you prey on it."

Wasp didn't think she'd ever heard the ghost say so much at once. It made her think of water forgotten in the catchment bins at either side of winter when the rains were good. Freezing and thawing, expanding and contracting, until the bin cracked under the pressure and the next melt sent all the water rushing out.

And it still wasn't done.

"Down here, you die alone, you walk alone. Unless you find the ones you walked with, up there in the world, and keep moving, and keep reminding each other, and when this place pulls on your mind you pull back harder. That's really all you can do. Or you end up like those ones in the river, so far gone you think water's for walking on." It shook its head very slightly, wonder or contempt. "I think that must be better than this."

"Well, then I'm doomed," Wasp said. She was half joking, or at least thought she was. Her tone was artificially bright. She hardly recognized it. "No family, no friends. *My* colleagues all want me dead." She shrugged. "I have myself. It's enough to get me through."

"It won't be," said the ghost.

"Yeah," she whispered. Then, louder, shaking off what had settled on her: "Well, we'll see."

But she took the knife, and she went back in.

She was standing at the crossing of two wide streets in the middle of a city. It looked like a different section of the same city she'd seen before. Now that nothing was shooting at her, she had a better chance to get a look at it.

By Wasp's standards it was ancient. The streets were straight and regular, and the buildings, swords of glass and steel, stabbed into the sky. Some of the largest buildings didn't even touch the ground, but stood on vast concrete pillars, so that the streets ran along underneath. Behind some of the windows Wasp saw trees, misted by gentle sprays of water, heavy with fruit. Behind one she thought she saw corn growing.

The streets showed signs of a recent skirmish—bloodstains, bullet-holes, shouts and screams; the front wall of a nearby building had blown out, beds and rugs and water-pipes dangling over the street—but like a summer storm it had drifted off, leaving echoes. Wasp could hear gunfire but not locate its source. Small arms fire, panicked hollering, and then the retort of a gun much larger. Wasp thought of those stalking metal monsters and shivered. A second of perfect silence, and then the screaming resumed, fresher and more vivid. From down a blind side-street an oily black smoke went up, smudging the walls it rose along.

In the middle of the crossroads stood Foster. She was a little older here than in the other memory, but not by much.

At least a dozen bodies in uniform lay prone around her feet. Wasp couldn't tell if they were breathing. If they bled, she couldn't see it.

Three men and two women were still standing, aiming their guns at her. They wore the same uniforms as the bodies on the ground, which bore a slight resemblance to Foster's, to the ghost's. They looked afraid. At some unseen signal they fired.

And Foster moved, too fast for Wasp to track her with her eyes, and within seconds their bodies had joined the pile on the street.

She hadn't drawn her weapons. She wasn't even out of breath. Wherever those bullets had gone, they weren't in her.

Foster sighed, gazing down at the pile as though it troubled her. At least a couple of the bodies, Wasp could see if she squinted, were breathing. Foster dropped into a crouch to set two fingers to the pulse-point in a neck and nodded slightly to herself. Stood, brushing her palms off on her legs. Turned, vaulted the pile of bodies easily, landed without a sound, and started running.

And the ghost—though not a ghost—stepped out of nowhere and collared her, swinging her out of her own momentum and up into the air.

"Start talking," it—he—told her.

Wasp froze, remembering the rock wall at her back, the air going out of her, her feet dangling. *So this is it,* she thought. *This is the moment you can't move past.*

Foster chopped her hands down hard on the ghost's wrists. He let go and she landed clean. "This isn't what it looks like."

He narrowed his eyes at her, but stayed put. "Clarify."

"I will. I promise I will. But first I—there's something I have to do."

His laugh had no humor in it. "Defection? Treason? This isn't one of your games. These are our men you—"

"Don't ask if you don't want to know. Anyway, they're fine. I didn't hurt them."

"And somehow that matters? From here you look like a traitor and a spy. You look like an experiment gone wrong. Where's that expensive brain of yours? You know what they'll do to—"

"I don't care what they think I am," she spat. "I know what they are, and that's worse. *Do* to me? What can they do to me that they haven't done already? Answer me that." A quick glance over a shoulder as she heard something Wasp could not. She started talking faster. "I'm done with it. I'm done with all of it. I'm gone."

"You're out of your mind. They'll find you."

She grinned, half nerves, half mischief. "Come with me." It sounded like something she'd been meaning to say for a while.

"And do what?"

"Whatever we want! For the first time in our lives we will do whatever the hell we want. All this time they've been doing all the choosing. Take us. Change us. Make us into, I don't know. Monsters. Superheroes. Whichever. And then stick us in uniforms and give us guns like everyone who actually signed up to fight, and assume we'll shoot where they point. Well, now it's our turn to choose. They won't let us go? Then we let *ourselves* go. Be our own superheroes. Our own monsters. Whichever. Neither. Both."

Even raised in a house of professional zealots, Wasp had never seen anyone so on fire with an idea. It practically shone out her eyes. "There's not a thing they can do to stop us if we don't let them," Foster went on, softer now. "Somebody told me that once. A long time ago."

Her hand went to her sword. Suddenly her eyes were hard. "I'm leaving now. I don't want to fight you. But you have to decide which side you're on."

He stared at her, expressionless.

"Give me fifteen minutes," Foster said, and toed the nearest body with a boot. "Keep these guys safe 'til they wake up. Think it over. I'll be back. And then we can put all of this—" her gesture took in the bodies, the crossroads, the city—"behind us. For good." Her face was alight with a fury of hope. "Can you even imagine."

"Idiot," he said, and looked away. Foster laughed, though her eyes did not, and took off running.

Wasp dropped the knife. The room came back to her with a start. This time she did puke. The floor wicked it away.

The ghost looked about ready to seize her and start throttling some answers out, but by some colossal force of will it passed her the bowl of water and gave her a minute. The nervous energy coming off of it was immense. It was like a thrown knife quivering in a wall.

How to say what she'd seen? She didn't even understand it. She was beginning to suspect, however, that she was in over her head. She cleared her throat, mentally framing charitable lies. *She looked happy. You did the right thing. I'm sure she's at peace.*

What came out of her mouth, though, was: "You didn't go with her."

The ghost went very still. Wasp half-expected it to leap at her with her own knife, but its rage didn't seem to be directed at her. "Now *that* I remember," it said softly. There came a pause so long that Wasp thought the ghost had forgotten her there. "I never told her I trusted her."

What does that *matter?* Wasp thought, exasperated, but realized she already understood. The closest she ever really came to trusting anyone was the upstarts, when she trusted them not to try and kill her, three hundred sixty-four days of the year. Or the Catchkeep-priest, who was forbidden from trying to kill her at all, so she trusted him not to try—though he was free to use any other methods to make her life miserable, and did.

She thought back on the fight with the lurchers on the riverbank, shoulder-to-shoulder with the ghost. It'd had her back, and hadn't stabbed her in it. It was, to her, impossibly bizarre and impossibly beautiful in equal measure that such an arrangement could exist in the world.

She understood, all right. Probably better than she wanted to.

"Okay, so," she said, half to change the subject. "There was a city. I saw it twice. I *think* it was the same one both times. There were . . ." She trailed off, trying to push words together in the shape of those impossible machines. Came up empty. "Foster, she . . . she helped some people. You both did. A lot of people. I saw that first. Then she attacked some other people, but I don't think she killed them. Then—"

The ghost was eyeing her stonily. She spread her hands. "Maybe if we can see more of where she *used* to be, it might help us narrow down where she is *now*."

Even as she said it, she didn't see how, although the longer she thought about it the more it started to itch in her mind. If a ghost was strong enough, when it appeared above it looked more or less as it did in life. In that case, at least in part, she guessed that what a ghost's aboveground strength must be truly measuring was the potency of its—

"Memories," she said. The nausea was wearing off now, nudged aside by the cautious elation of a new-hatched plan. She knew full well that by now she should know better, but there it was. "This whole place is built of memories. All the ghosts coming into that huge room, they were all wearing their deaths on them so clearly, like uniforms. The doors going in and out of that room. My name, my past. More memories. Even the stuff the bridge was made of. Maybe even this—" She looked up at the ceiling of the cabin, hazy in the moonlight filtered through that tall, tall grass. "This place. The food, the bed. This all *belonged* to someone."

It hit her with a jolt. "The city out there in the field. Is that—?"

"Your guess is as good as mine, Archivist," said the ghost. "Didn't you notice? We could go out there and walk toward it for days and it wouldn't get any nearer."

Wasp was on her feet before she knew it. She was thinking about all those ghosts milling around in the waiting room below the Hill, stuck there until they remembered their names. If they ever did. And if they didn't—

"Yeah, but don't you get it? Maybe it's another test, and you can't get there *because* it's important to you and *you don't remember it.* Maybe, just now, me seeing the memories you can't see anymore, maybe we just found the back door in."

The ghost did not appear to share her enthusiasm. In fact it looked downright hesitant.

She went for the direct approach. "These memories I see. I seem to be seeing them in pieces. You need to fill in the blanks for me." Wasp thought how she'd react if someone posed this to her, and it made her add: "You can't keep secrets. I need to know everything."

The ghost said nothing. Its silence was starting to pique her. "Look, if being down here by yourself is so unbearable—"

"Nothing is unbearable," it said, too quickly, and would not look at her, as though she'd caught it out in a lie. But she'd said nothing.

Wasp was just tired enough to let it slide. "Fine. So." She pictured Foster running off, down that city street, toward a destination Wasp could not begin to guess at. "We'll start from the top. Foster left you there for fifteen minutes in the crossroads. Didn't she come back?"

"Oh, she came *back*," the ghost spat, glowering. It didn't seem to want to elaborate. Instead it put the glove back on its cut hand, wiped Wasp's blade and passed it over, then stood, swept its chair over to the door, stabbed its sword into the floorboards beside it, and sat. "Get some rest. I'll keep watch."

She couldn't argue. Whatever had happened with the harvesting-knife had drained what little had been left of her energy. She might well fall asleep walking over to the bed. "Okay. You want to split the night or take it in shifts?"

The ghost, in silhouette against the fire, might have been a statue. "Don't worry about it."

"I guess you don't have to sleep anyway," said Wasp. Starting to kick off her shoes, then thinking better of it. They might have to make a quick escape. Mournfully she pulled her aching feet up under the quilt. "I guess that means I don't have to either."

Be that as it may, she was fading fast. She'd lost count of all her unasked questions, and at the moment she just plain didn't care. She slid the knife beneath her pillow. Just like home. Except that this pillow was softer.

"Don't worry," she heard herself say, sleepily. "We'll find her." The last thing she remembered was the ghost glancing over at her in surprise.

Chapter Twelve

When she woke, it was still full dark. Moonlight flooded through the windows where the grass had grown roof-high before, casting the whole room in blue. She blinked, disoriented. The windows had been blind when they'd come in.

"There was a hostage," the ghost said. Somehow sensing that Wasp was awake, though she was sure she hadn't moved a muscle. "A child. Foster's orders were to take him to the rendezvous point for extraction, where he'd be . . ." It trailed off, eyes narrowed, and decided on a different tack. "Where she said she had to go, what she said she had to do, that day—she was letting him go. Against orders. Dereliction of duty to help some useless idiot she didn't even know. It was . . . a stupid thing to do. It was the sort of stupid thing she *would* do."

"How do you remember all this?" Wasp asked. "If you can't remember anything."

The ghost's silhouette went very still, then turned its profile an inch toward her. "I can see glimpses here and there," it said slowly. "Like trying to remember a dream. I have had a great deal of time to try and connect the dots between them. Recalling where the lines should be drawn . . . requires effort."

At this Wasp found herself unsure whether the ghost had really realized she was awake before she spoke, or whether the monologue she'd interrupted was a discipline the ghost put itself through, from time to time, every night for all she knew, a litany to keep the memories it had fought to save from fading.

Wasp stared at the quilt. In that weird blue light, the gridlike pattern on it could have been tall buildings on regular streets, seen from above. Maybe, if she squinted hard enough, in one of those pale intersections, she might find monsters quarreling. *Or superheroes*, Wasp thought idly, like a child parroting words it did not know. *Whichever.*

"You were in a war."

"A civil war." Its glance at Wasp was probably not designed to make her feel stupid, but did. "Do you know what that is?"

"Yes," Wasp lied.

"It went on for a long time," the ghost said. "A long time."

"And she was in your . . ." Wasp fumbled for a word she'd heard from ghosts now and again. Ghosts who, almost invariably, looked to have died deaths that were messy, though not necessarily without their dignity. Shot up, blown up, shouting for their ". . . unit."

That same hollow laugh that Wasp had heard in her vision. "In my unit. She *was* my unit. There were supposed to be a dozen of us. Nobody else made it out of development. Only her. And me."

Development. Not *training.* Wasp chewed this over. "They weren't good enough to fight with you?"

"Evidently not, because the treatment killed them." A pause. "They didn't die well."

Wasp sat up and waited, but it didn't say more. Conversing with the thing was an exercise in tiptoeing and balancing. Any wrong move would upset or offend it back into that sullen silence.

She wouldn't get anywhere at that rate. It was time to push on through.

"Who *are* you people?"

The ghost gave her a long look, then shrugged. "This is going to sound ridiculous, but the most accurate thing I can say that you'll understand is that we were developed to be weapons."

Actually, thought Wasp, *that explains a lot.* Somewhere in her head something tiny was clicking into place. It felt like the edge of something bigger. "You said she had an expensive brain."

The ghost made a disgusted sound. "For all the good it did her."

"So wait a minute." This was giving her a headache. "Let's start from the beginning. Somebody . . . *made* you?"

"Yes," said the ghost. "And no. Our genetic material is human." Again that pause as it searched for phrasing she could parse. "Is mostly human. We were born, like you." Again the shrug. "They took us, as children. Orphans. Clean slates. They called it the Latchkey Project. Highly classified. We lived in the labs. We saw nobody outside. They—" It took a moment, visibly choosing words and discarding them, eventually settling on: "—changed us. Made us stronger. Faster. Smarter. At first in weapons training they gave us guns, like everyone else. Then they realized we were fast enough and strong enough that we'd be more efficient in close combat with swords, so they had some made. It was like a bad joke. Bringing a sword to a firefight. But nobody was laughing for long."

Wasp nodded. The pile of bodies. The astonishing speed with which Foster moved. The way the ghost had torn into the lurchers, like a streak of lightning given human shape.

"At the bottom of it, we're not so different from you," the ghost continued, as Wasp's eyes flew wide, then away. "You Archivists. Am I wrong?"

"I guess," Wasp said, or tried to say. No sound came out.

"They were going to do the same to the hostage. He was the son of, well, of an important woman. In the war. A very important woman. They could have ordered us in to deal with her, but they wanted to send a message. So they went after her son instead. They thought if they took him, and changed him the way they changed us, and sent him back to his family, he'd—"

Wasp saw. "Do their work for them."

"After what happened to the Latchkey unit in development, and it was determined that the treatment couldn't be survived, and we survived it anyway, our people were afraid of us. But they were more afraid of losing the war. They kept us on, but Latchkey was disbanded. Its methods were too expensive, its success rate too low. Its funding was cut, and no new subjects were recruited for treatment. Last-ditch effort or not, a four percent long-term survival rate was insupportable."

"Wait. Four percent? You said there were supposed to be a dozen of—"

"In the final phase of development," said the ghost, its gaze fixed on something just past her head, "there were." It paused for a moment, shook off something unseen. "Eventually it came out that they were still working to accelerate the process. They thought they were getting somewhere. The hostage would have been a test run. What took years to fine-tune in us might have taken months or less in him. Apparently the idea looked good on paper, anyway. Good enough to send us out to fetch him."

"If he lived through treatment," said Wasp.

"If he lived through the treatment."

"And didn't decide to light up this whole Latchkey place instead."

The ghost shut its eyes, held up one finger. "I never said it was a good idea. But it wasn't our decision to make." Wasp didn't argue, so it continued. "And Foster—as far as we knew up until those orders came down, Latchkey was dead in the ground. She put her life on the line to keep it there." The ghost looked almost miserable. "The war ended soon after she freed the hostage. She saved a lot of lives."

"Your side won?"

A sort of smile, a twisted triumph somewhere in it. "We lost. Or I should say they did. They tried to make it our war. It didn't take. And they couldn't win it without our help. She showed them, in the end, that there was more to us than what they'd made. But it was the last—"

A shadow cut through the blue at the window, knife-sharp, there and gone. *Another wandering ghost, come for the waypoint,* Wasp thought blearily, contemplating fighting whoever it was for the bed.

The ghost stood up, sword in hand, just as both windows blew in.

Wasp threw an arm up to protect her face from flying shards of glass, and when she lowered it there were two lurchers in the room. She grabbed the knife, thinking *Oh good, only two.* Thinking, *How did they fit through the windows?*

The question was in the midst of answering itself. Rolling through the windows was a kind of fog, the color of a struck spark, the color of a coal, and where it gathered near the floor it began to coalesce: bodies, heads, legs.

The lurchers didn't even bother snarling before they lunged. One for the ghost, who spun on its heel and cut it from the air, and one for Wasp, who threw the quilt at it as it leapt, lost her balance, and half-jumped half-fell off the bed. The lurcher came down tangled, flailing, snapping at her with a jaw the size of her whole head. Every moment of terror from every failed escape attempt came back to her at once and she stabbed at the quilt and the thing inside it, over and over, until both had gone still and the one had melted to slop inside the other.

Each stab brought another vision, as when she'd fought the lurchers at the riverbank. She saw a shrine-dog standing guard in the snow, a shrine-dog eating table-scraps from an upstart's hand, a shrine-dog being kicked at by a man dressed like the Catchkeep-priest, whom Wasp did not recognize.

She pushed it from her mind and came to her feet in time to help the ghost dispatch four more newly formed lurchers in the middle of the room.

Abruptly, Wasp found herself back-to-back with the ghost, each facing a broken window through which fog was still spilling.

"Still don't believe the hunt is real?" Wasp shouted. She was having trouble modulating her voice. Her teeth were chattering too hard. She had never been so tired.

"We bring our own monsters with us," said the ghost. "It looks like these are yours."

New lurchers were still taking shape from the fog, but she wasn't waiting. She sliced into a half-formed mass, connected with nothing, and the momentum of the failed swing almost tripped her. "The eyes," the ghost said behind her. "Wait for the eyes."

Those few breaths of waiting were one of the hardest things she'd ever had to do. She held her ground, breathing faster than she ought, stalking her opening. There were six lurchers before her and she had no idea how many behind. She was frantically trying to calculate whether they would attack her at exactly the same time or whether she'd have a fraction of a second to evade at least one. They stood nearly as high as she did, and at least as wide, and pound for pound were several times as strong. Any three of their teeth together were the length of the harvesting-knife, and until the fog let up, those teeth went on forever.

"We can't outlast them," she whispered.

"We have to," said the ghost, and the next lurcher sprang. Midway to her throat, its eyes came in.

She ducked and slashed out at its legs. It gave one cry, cut off by Wasp's knife in its heart.

Out of nowhere it came to her that she and the ghost were standing in a way that was almost identical to the way it and Foster had stood in the image on that folded piece of paper. Foster's smile, like a slap to the face. *Come with me.* It was a thing that Wasp had never been in a position to ask of anyone. Two alone against the world. And she had grown so used to being one.

Even making the comparison in the privacy of her mind felt like something she had to earn. She tore the knife free, tossed it lightly, grabbed it backhand, and struck out with all she had, opening a throat. Dragged it down, lengthening the wound, changing her grip faster than the deadweight lurcher could pull the knife away.

Showing off had opened her up much too wide. She didn't even see the next one before its jaws closed around her forearm. Mentally she thanked the One Who Got Away that it was not her knife hand as she sank the blade into the lurcher's gut and emptied it onto the floor. And thanked Him/Her again that the lurcher's teeth themselves were melting and she wouldn't have to figure out how to break them from its jaw to pry them out of her arm.

Still, though, they came on, endless. Wasp's burst of spite was wearing off. Now she was hurtling toward complete exhaustion. "Where are they coming from?"

The ghost shook its head in reply. Its sword was black slime to the guard, and it was beginning to look mildly annoyed. No matter how hard the damn thing fought, though, Wasp never saw it out of breath. She wondered if this was a trait of its ghostliness or of its person.

So many lurchers. Wasp was fighting now on instinct, ducking and slashing, swinging wide and sloppy like an upstart with a short straw she never wanted. Fully aware that her strength was winding slowly, surely down to nothing. The door was blocked. The windows. The lurchers were coming in faster than Wasp, faster even than the ghost, could mow them down.

Wake up, she shouted at herself. *Think.*

She couldn't begin to count the lurchers now. Each of them looked slightly different, though they all shared some traits in common. Their coats, pure black except for the gray star between the eyes. The ears that all came up in points. The back-curved wolfish plumes of the tails. The silence, except for that eerie howl they'd volley back and forth, sounding closing distances on a common target. Her.

All in all they looked a great deal like the shrine-dogs back home. That made sense enough to her, as the shrine-dogs were bred to those traits carefully, being the earthly counterparts to Catchkeep's hunt, as Archivists were the earthly counterparts of Catchkeep Herself. The process involved much trying and erring and countless rejects being drowned in the lake and put in the stew, but—

We bring our own monsters with us.

The vision of the lurchers, stalking those darkened windows. One of them had seemed downright familiar, and now she realized why. It was a dead ringer for one of the shrine-dogs from her first year as Archivist. It had even borne the scars she'd left on it from the three escapes it had dragged her back from personally, before it succumbed to the poison she'd left in its food as soon as she could limp out of bed.

It looks like these are yours.

"Weren't lurchers," she whispered.

Out loud it sounded crazy, but she was out of better ideas.

When the next lurcher fell, she dropped with it. She had to see. Another tried to rush her from behind, but she feinted sideways and the lurcher sailed over her shoulder to land, claws skittering on the floor. It wheeled on her, bewildered, furious, though neither for long, because the ghost's sword came down to skewer its head to the floor. The blade came back out with a sound that put Wasp uncomfortably in mind of biting into an overripe pear.

She only had a second or two before her lurcher melted into slime. She looked and there it was: on the big muscle of the outer thigh, where the lurcher's hair ran short, a faded gold tattoo. The flesh beneath it was beginning to disintegrate, but she could still make it out clear enough, especially as now she knew what she was looking for. An arrow, and a target, under a disembodied crown of sixteen stars.

Catchkeep's hunt, she thought, and a strange mad laugh bubbled up in her. She bit it back, twisting to kick out at another lurcher who'd thought to come down jaws-first on her bent neck.

It was as if the ghost had heard the laugh she hadn't made. "What."

Wasp was already fighting her way over to the hearth and the table beside it. "I know how to beat them," she shouted. Then, under her breath: "I think." To the ghost again: "Cover me."

"On it," said the ghost, already there.

Wasp thought about doing this one-handed, keeping the knife in her knife-hand where it belonged. To do otherwise would mean trusting the ghost. Putting her life, for a moment, completely in its hands.

A second passed while she considered the ghost, slaughtering lurchers with more skill and grace than she could hope to match with a lifetime of training. Shook her head. Cursed under her breath.

Then she sheathed the knife, turned her back on the fight, and went to the table.

Water. That was there already. Fire in the hearth. Milk, she needed milk. There was a wheel of soft cheese on the table. It would have to do. Blood—she glanced at her arm where the lurcher's teeth had gone in. Whatever was in the slime of its death-stain had cauterized most of the wound and left a spray of chemical burn around it, but blood still welled up from near her elbow where the slime hadn't reached. If that wasn't enough, she could always count on the knife to get her more.

She sprinkled the water around her in a circle and smeared the cheese on the floor in a circle over the top of that. Pinched at the open wound in her arm until she had enough blood to dip her finger in, and traced the circle again. Dumped the grapes out of their basket and stuck the basket in the flames of the hearth until it caught, then dragged it, scattering sparks, in the same circle again. The floor began smoking. This would have to work fast.

She reached one hand out past the circle's edge.

"Grab on," she told the ghost. "I should be able to pull you across. You don't want to be outside this circle when it blows."

Wasp had barely seen it move when she felt that frostbite-and-vertigo sensation again, and grabbed on tight. "Don't let your feet touch the circle," she shouted, and pulled.

The ghost shimmered a little as it crossed the layered lines of the circle, and for a horrible instant Wasp was sure it'd flickered back into some memory, was about to attack her again, and she was about to have to figure out how to bind it within the confines of a circle four feet across. But it came through clean, let go, and took its place behind her without her even having to say.

The lurchers lunged and slammed up against the edge of the circle as though they'd hit an unseen wall. They fell back snarling, pacing, throwing themselves against it again and again, until they were singed from the fire, bloodied from whatever invisible barrier they'd struck.

Wasp resisted the urge to taunt them. Instead she drew the knife with her off-hand and pitched her breaking voice to carry.

"I am the Archivist. Catchkeep's emissary, ambassador, and avatar on earth. Her bones and stars my flesh; my flesh and bones Her stars. I am She who bears you, She who sustains you, She to whom your dust returns. You have lived well. You have died well. I release you. Do not ghost my way."

She knelt and plunged the point of the harvesting-knife through the circle's nearest edge. Fire singed her fingers, but she held on. The holy metal sank through all four of the rings she had drawn, into the floorboards below, and light sheeted out from the circle in all directions. It rattled the door, threw the bed and table up against the walls, snuffed the hearth-fire, would have blown out the windows if they'd had any glass left in them to break. It flew screeching out the open windows and was gone, leaving a smell of ozone behind it.

The whole room seemed to waver a little, like the air above a fire, and all at once the lurchers were extinguished—candles blown out by no wind at all.

Their death stains vanished into the floor. The rings Wasp had drawn disappeared likewise. The fire left the circle and began to spread. The moon was very blue.

The ghost caught her as she fell.

Chapter Thirteen

Wasp was dreaming. She still hated dreaming.

This time she saw the shrine-dogs. It was a strange mix of images, all tossed together. She saw them as puppies tumbling in the straw, squabbling over their mothers' milk, sleeping in a twitching pile. She saw them being sorted by the Catchkeep-priest: those who would be tattooed for service at the shrine, those who did not make the cut. The ones kept back for the shrine whined and fidgeted on their new leads, struggling to join the others being bundled together into a sack weighted with smooth stones. The ones in the sack wriggled happily, ready for a game. Wasp saw full-grown tattooed shrine-dogs pacing Catchkeep's shrine, standing guard. She saw a group of them heading up the hill, through the narrow passes, skulking in silence toward her house. One nosed open the door and they filed in sniffing. On the floor, one of them found something interesting. It was the Archivist-coat, still bloodstained from the fight that had made Wasp an Archivist, discarded in disgust and defiance the first time she'd attempted escape. One by one, the shrine-dogs sniffed at it and snarled so far back in their throats it didn't even register on Wasp's ear as noise so much as a vibration, an itch in her head. Then they padded noiselessly back out the door and were lost to view.

The dream jumped scenes. She was looking at a long dark room lit by small running lights of such pure high vibrant colors that they hurt her eyes. In the middle of the room were twelve small white beds, placed in a double row, all the feet pointed inward. Wasp could make out unaccountable scuff marks on the floor to some distance either side of the rows, as though many other beds had been dragged in or out of there at some point in the recent past.

At the head of each bed was a panel, smooth and black, covered in numbers and strange bright moving lines that marched up and down in peaks and valleys from left to right across the screen. Beside each bed was a kind of tall narrow metal rack from which an array of multicolored bags of fluid hung. Tubes snaked from these bags down toward the beds themselves.

Each of the beds held a sleeping child, six or seven years old, buckled to the mattress with heavy straps across the hips and wrists and ribs. From the ceiling a device was suspended, emitting just enough bluegreen light to see by. To Wasp's amazement, it was singing. It was running through a loop of three children's sleep-songs, approximated in tonal beeps. Even Wasp, who knew what a lullaby sounded like, knew that they were songs meant for babies, or toddlers, not children the age of the ones sleeping here.

Still, it might have been working. Several of the children had the tracks of dried tears on their cheeks, and Wasp saw at least a few who'd gnawed their lips or fingernails to scabs, but in sleep they looked almost at peace.

After a moment a woman in a white coat arrived and walked the perimeter of the field of beds, scanning the panels. At one child's bed she stopped and sighed, then removed a device from her pocket and spoke into it. Before she left, she tapped that bed's panel until it went black, then reached down to thumb the child's eyelids shut. Her hand came away red. When she pulled the sheet over the child's head, it soaked through where it settled, and Wasp, death's chronicler, found herself wondering what exactly had done that child in. The sheet below the child's chin stayed white.

As the woman's footsteps faded, another child opened her eyes. It looked as though she hadn't been asleep in some time. She lay there a moment, perfectly still, staring at the ceiling. After a moment she furrowed her brow, as though sensing something Wasp could not, and began struggling out of her restraints in complete silence. Once she got one wrist free, it was only a matter of seconds before she sat up, threw off her sheet, and stood. She brought the rack of bags of fluid with her, careful to keep enough slack in the bundle of tubes so that they didn't dislodge from their feed at the crook of her elbow.

In the bed opposite hers a boy appeared to be sleeping. She reached with her free hand to poke him awake, but just before her finger reached his shoulder, he opened his eyes. He didn't look surprised to see her there. It wasn't clear to Wasp whether the girl had picked the boy because he was the nearest, because she'd sensed he was the only other one pretending to sleep, or neither, or both.

Without a word between them, the girl reached down to unbuckle one of the boy's wrists. He permitted this, but didn't move to undo the rest of his restraints. They regarded each other without expression in that hazy underwater-colored light.

"Another one," said the girl, sticking out her tongue, clutching her throat, rolling her eyes back in her head. She smoothed her face and stared at him expectantly. She leaned in. "You do it."

"Another one," said the boy, mirroring her parody of death, if somewhat less dramatically.

He didn't ask who it had been, and she didn't say. Neither seemed much disturbed. Wasp recognized the neutrality in their faces and voices, even as one of their own lay hemorrhaged two beds down. They were like tiny upstarts, far less intimate with the notion of camaraderie than with the notion of death.

"Not you," said the girl, and reached down to punch him on the arm, playful, grave.

He eyed her quizzically. She shot him a pointed look. He got the idea.

"Not you," said the boy, and reached up to punch her on the arm opposite.

"Not me," said the girl, and spat on the floor to one side.

"Not me," said the boy, and raised his head to spit on the floor to the other.

"Not ever," said the girl, and held one hand, palm-out, at arms-length in front of her.

"Not ever," said the boy, and set his hand against hers, where it overlapped perfectly.

Then, the call-and-response apparently over, the boy lowered his arm and the girl refastened it before returning to her bed to redo as many of her own restraints as she could. Both children stared at the ceiling a moment, then scrunched their eyes shut and waited for sleep to take them. Above, the musical beeping stopped, kicked over in its loop, and began again.

Wasp came to, her knife-hand sticky with silver. She had been gripping the harvesting-knife in her sleep, her fingers on the blade. She sat up fast, not knowing where she was, and lightheadedness made her regret it instantly. She dropped back on her elbows until her vision cleared.

She was lying on a mossy slope tending down toward a black pit of a pond around which gory-looking lilies grew. A breeze blew up from the water, smelling of copper, limes, and carrion. A lonely pale willow overhung the pond, and the breeze set its fronds clicking together. Closer, Wasp would find that they weren't made of leaves at all, but whiplike plaits of tiny bones.

Morning dew was damp against her back. The bite-wound in her arm was bound, as were the blistering fingers of her off-hand. Above, crouching on the willow, the sun looked like a ragged hole blown in a lavender sky. It cast no reflection in the water.

Her gaze fell on the thread. It wasn't a trick of the light. It really did look frailer, finer. Less silver. More gray. What was it the ghost had said? She'd be stuck down here or vanish. Be *undone*. It wouldn't be long now.

Nothing for it. The only way out was through.

The dreams. The dreams that were not dreams. The first one must have come from the lurchers' blood against her blade, but the second—

"You're hurt," she croaked.

The ghost was kneeling beside her, sword on the moss between them. "I'm dead."

Wasp, formulating a response to this, suddenly caught a smell on the air above and beyond the stink coming off the pond. It smelled like a warn-fire. With some effort she turned her head. Higher on the slope, behind a tumble of bluish rocks, she could see the cabin's chimney, standing alone and naked in the air. The rest of the cabin was gone.

"I burned it," she whispered, aghast. For some reason she felt a worse pang at destroying the cabin than she had at the prospect of destroying her house, although her memory of the cozy cabin full of bloodthirsty lurchers wasn't vastly more pleasant.

"It'll grow back. They always do." The ghost narrowed shrewd eyes at her, piecing together Wasp's deduction. "What did you see?"

"First tell me how you managed to get cut on my knife."

"Well, I'm not sure how you envision you got out of there," it said drily, "but you're heavy. And awkward. And the only way to get that knife out of your hand would have been to break your fingers." It tipped its chin at her. "What did you see."

"You carried me out?"

"You weren't in any position to carry yourself."

"How did we get here?" The wall of grass around the cabin. Then the moonlight pouring through where the grass had been. Now this. What had happened while she slept? "The cabin . . . *brought* us here?" She pictured it, stumping through that tall grass, the rising plume of its chimney-smoke following along behind.

"Not in the way you're thinking," said the ghost. "Now. What. Did you. See."

"Not much," she said, stalling. She hadn't fully understood what she'd seen, but it felt like something buried too deep for too long for her to dig up and air out comfortably. "Mostly it's lurcher blood on there. I don't think we'll be seeing them again. If there are even any left after that." She paused, running the extermination of the lurchers over in her mind. An idea gone right instead of wrong for once. It pleased her. "Anyway, I saw where they're coming from. I was right. They're the ghosts of the shrine-dogs. Scenting a live Archivist down here, I guess. The coat, the knife. Something. Catchkeep's hunt, indeed." She snorted. "It's like the scars. Just a story. It's only real now because of *me*."

The ghost fixed her with a look. "Those things' blood didn't tell you about the cut on my hand."

"Then I saw some kids. Asleep." Wasp shrugged, all innocence. "There was a." *Dead kid, bleeding out every hole in its head.* "A song."

"Oh," said the ghost. It blinked, or flinched. "*Oh.*"

Suddenly, Wasp was desperate for a change of subject. And what with all this talk of visions, she didn't have to look far before she found one. She thought of the lurchers scenting her, tracking her. After all, the shrine-dogs were bred to obedience and trained from birth to keep Archivists obedient as well, and now a live Archivist had appeared among them, in a place where the living did not go. Who knew what they must be thinking. What joy in their dead hearts.

Maybe she could do the same.

"So I was thinking. If I." Her mind was going along faster than her mouth and it was telling her that she wouldn't like the new subject any better than the old one, but there it was. "Okay. I have no idea how the harvesting-knife reads the blood, but it does. It reads lurcher blood. It reads your blood. It might." She swallowed. "Read Foster's blood. If we had any."

She looked over at the ghost, who was as still as a carving, its face about as readable. *Just say it*, she told herself. *It's not like it's going to get easier.*

She breathed deep and pushed the words out before she came to her senses. "There's blood on that paper you carry around. I saw it when you showed me before. At least I think it's blood. It *looks* like blood. If it's hers . . . maybe we could use it. I mean. To find her. It might show me some memory you weren't in. Something you didn't see. Something I can't learn from anyone but her. It's a tiny bit but I don't know, it might be enough."

There was a long, long pause. Then the ghost sighed, reached into a pocket, and brought out the little square of paper. It unfolded it, print side up, and flipped it over.

The page was exactly as Wasp remembered. The words packed top to bottom, side to side. The handwriting like a handful of fishhooks. Here and there words leapt out from the jumble: *letter, time, fight, Latchkey, together, help, nothing, understand.* And there, in the corner, a red-brown smear. The ghost was staring at it, jaw clenched. "It's hers."

"Okay," said Wasp, aware she could hear her pulse hammering at her ears. She was no good at swaggering, so she couldn't bring herself to say *It'll work. It'll definitely work. Give me that thing and let's go find the person who wrote it* And she couldn't think of a smart way to tell the truth, which was more along the lines of *I still have no idea what I'm doing. I never said I did. I'll probably destroy that paper, whatever it is, for nothing.*

There was a tearing sound.

"Here," said the ghost, holding out a scrap. She took it. It was about the length and width of three of her fingers held together. The stain overlapped fragments of a few lines of text, which had been torn out with it, preserving as much of the blood as possible.

. . . don't want to have died for nothing . . .

. . . think you understand . . .

. . . fun while it lasted. See you around.

Wasp's throat was suddenly very dry.

"Okay," she said again. "Okay."

The ghost said nothing, and suddenly Wasp couldn't hold it in anymore. "You said she was tortured to death," she blurted. "This is—"

"When there were twelve of us left, they partnered us up," the ghost said quietly. "Not to help each other. To inform on each other. Who was getting sicker. Who was turning dangerous. After she . . ." It trailed off. When it spoke again there was actual defiance in its voice, defiance and pride. "It didn't work out quite the way they wanted. But then everyone else was dying and it didn't matter. The whole time, though, we'd been covering for each other, just . . . taking turns saving each other. That," it said, eyes on the bloodstain, "was her turn. Her last turn." It folded the remainder of the paper along those worn creases and pocketed it. "Now it's mine."

Wasp sat, harvesting-knife in one hand, bloodstained paper-scrap in the other. This time she had arranged her position so that if she reflexively dropped the knife again, or collapsed again, both the knife and she would land safely in the moss. She trusted the ghost would see to it that the knife did not land under her.

It wasn't ghost blood, her specimen. At least, it wasn't at the time it was spilled. The knife might well not be able to read it. Wasp took a deep breath. Only one way to find out.

She steadied the harvesting-knife in one hand and carefully wrapped the paper around it, blood to blade. She shut her eyes and waited.

Nothing happened.

She blew her breath out sharply: exasperation and relief. *Relief?*

Then she realized where it came from. Of course she wanted to find Foster, solve the puzzle, beat the clock before she was stuck down here for good and Foster lost forever, but that was the kind of wish she'd have to sell her eyes to the Ragpicker for, because no way was she landing it on her own.

But say she did. Say she did find Foster. Her prospects afterward weren't promising. She could fight her way free of the Catchkeep-priest and flee out into the Waste until she found some other crappy town to hide in, or else starve. It was all she could hope for.

In the meantime, though, the Catchkeep-priest was not here. The Waste was not here. Crappy towns and probable starvation were not here. The world above, held next to the world below, seemed dull and faded, the less real of the two.

And, hopeless as she knew this search was, for the first time in as long as she could remember, she was enjoying herself.

"It's not working," the ghost observed.

"Yeah," said Wasp. "I can see that." Holding the paper to the knife one-handed, she pushed herself up off the damp moss. "Well, here." Reaching to unwrap the paper from the blade. *So much for ideas gone right.* Embarrassed and disgusted. If this was the best she could do—

Her off-hand touched the bloodstain and she jumped.

The high driving whine of a motor, small arms fire, and over that, Foster's voice. Laughing. "They think they're being clever. All right, we'll play it their way." *The whine of the motor changed pitch, and another sound joined it, which Wasp couldn't identify.* "Engaging."

Wasp pulled away and the sounds disappeared.

She blinked and poked the paper again.

A boy's voice, ten or so years old. Wasp, having seen the room of twelve beds, recognized it. "What're you staring at up there?"

"Not staring," *said a girl. Wasp recognized her voice, too.* "Wishing. Shut up a second."

"You do this much?" *All scorn.* "Wishing?"

"You care?" *A pause might have been him shrugging, or her, because then she said,* "Since they brought us here. Same wish, same stars." *Another pause might have been her pointing.* "There. And then, you draw a line up through those two, you get the North Star. My mom taught me. Before she died. People used to—"

"What'd you wish for?"

There was a grin in Foster's voice, fierce and sad. "Like I'll tell."

And it was gone. Wasp looked from her moss-dampened hand to the bloodstain and back, then up to the ghost, her eyes narrowed. As gently as she could, she adjusted the paper wrapping on the blade, then licked one fingertip and pressed it to the stain.

"They're betting on us," *Foster said. She sounded a little older here, thirteen at most. She had her voice pitched like she wanted it to carry, but there was some undercurrent it kept breaking on, rage or horror.* "Who pulls through this sickness. Who doesn't. They have it all written up. I saw it."

Several other children's voices, muttering together. Wondering whether to believe her. Wanting to know their odds. Someone among them had a nasty cough. "*Now Foster,*" *came a woman's voice,* "*you have been told time and time again about these fabrications of—*"

"*The Director lost a thousand on Salazar last week,*" Foster shouted over her, and Wasp knew the silence that curdled after. It was the silence following the mention of a death it was forbidden to mourn. "*And Sorensen, let's just say she's* really *not happy about that cough.*"

"*Catherine,*" said the woman, all concern, "*it's clear you're upset. Are you tired? Hungry? Did you have a bad—*"

"*We're not special,*" Foster was yelling. "*No matter what they say. Martinez was special. Tanaka was special. Salazar was special. You know what we are? We're* just *the ones who didn't die.*"

Wasp surfaced, nauseous, shaken, pulse pounding at her ears. Looking anywhere but at the ghost. Thinking about the dead little kid she'd seen, earlier, strapped into those white sheets, bled out—she hoped—in its sleep. Thinking also about the gamblers on the Archivist-choosing day, how they'd grabbed at her for spoiling their show, and Catchkeep had not struck them down.

Both spoke at once.

"Tell me," it said.

"Water," she said.

Momentarily, the ghost looked bewildered. "Could you possibly be a bit less cryptic?" There was an edge of fear in its voice, low and broken, as it struggled to remember what it could not.

"No," said Wasp. "I didn't mean . . ." She made an exasperated sound and began again. "The blood's too dry. It's just voices without it. It—" She inspected the paper scrap, already so old and so worn, beginning to disintegrate where the moisture had touched. She forced herself to meet the ghost's eyes and hold them. "I think it will only work once."

"But you're confident it *will* work."

Wasp shut her eyes, exhaling. It was all too easy to put herself in the ghost's position. It was stuck down here for eternity. Only a matter of time before its paper was destroyed, its gun lost, its sword shattered, and all that would be left to it was a memory that was already doing its best to betray it.

She wondered what it must be like to be so ruthlessly *competent*—except where it was needed most. As soon as she thought it, it felt like something she could relate to.

The least she could do was tell it the truth.

But she couldn't back down now. She needed that device.

"Yeah," she said. "I'm sure."

The ghost gave one tight nod. "Do it." It looked away. "It's only an old paper anyway. I've been carrying it long enough."

There were many things that Wasp could say to this, but she kept them to herself and began making her way down to the pond.

The wet moss against the steep rock hill was slipperier than she'd guessed. By the time she reached the bottom she'd nearly fallen twice. She found a spot at the water's edge as far from the ominous lilies as she could, near a likely stone. There she suffered a sudden attack of honesty. "Last chance to back out."

The ghost folded its arms and answered her with a stare.

"All right," said Wasp. "This is it."

She flattened the paper against the pond-dampened stone, and set the harvesting-knife down beside it. Moisture began leaching up into the bloodstain immediately. She had to be careful. Too little water and she'd have to try again, and she knew what risk she took of damaging the paper with every new attempt. Too much water and it would dissolve.

When the stain had darkened sufficiently, she eased the paper up and draped it over the blade. It stuck and tore, but the dampness of the paper adhered it to the blade and to itself, at least for the moment she required.

For a second she paused, knife-hand hovering over the hilt. It was hopelessly gummed and filthy with gore from the ghosts of the dogs whose leather had gone to wrap its grip. She took a steadying breath and exhaled it slowly. "Going in."

Chapter Fourteen

"—phase of your learning," the woman at the head of the room was saying. Her voice was rich and bright. Her shoes sounded crisp on the floor. She looked very, very tired.

Eleven children sat at desks before her. Their eyes tracked her, four steps and turn. There were wires attached to their temples, running down into the collars of their shirts. They might have been seven years old. "But before we begin. Who can tell me how a garden works?"

A couple of tentative hands went up.

"Ayres," said the woman.

A boy lowered his hand and spoke. "You plant seeds and water them. They need dirt—and sun—"

"Very good, Ayres." The woman beamed. "You plant *lots* of seeds, right?"

A few nods.

"But they can't all thrive, so you have to thin them out. Do you know what that means?"

Wasp thought of the ghost, saying *four percent survival rate*. She thought of the sea of scuff marks on the floor around those dozen little beds.

"You remove the failing, weaker seedlings for the good of the healthier ones," the woman said. "They get more nutrients, more light. They get stronger. Taller. Brighter. A beautiful garden." She turned the full force of her smile on them. They smiled back, a few of them, but Wasp saw distrust in their eyes. She began to wonder whether the *thinning* of those beds was gradual or all at once, leaving the occupants of the remaining dozen to find their way to sleep in a room full of sudden echoes, like a cave.

"What's sad about a garden," the woman continued, "is that even then, despite the gardener's best efforts, some of the plants will die. But do you think this makes the plants sad?"

"No?" said a girl. The woman looked at her, and she flinched.

"No is right, Martinez," said the woman. "They do not care. They *cannot* care. They only concern themselves with their own survival. If they didn't, they would die, too. Now." That smile again. "I want you all to close your eyes and listen."

"Yes, Director," they all chorused. Some eyes shut immediately, but many hesitated.

"You aren't fooling me," the woman sang out. "All the way closed. And don't scrunch them. Relax. Listen." She dialed up the soothing voice, which sounded enough like the Catchkeep-priest's gentling voice to make Wasp shudder.

"You aren't just ordinary children anymore. You are special. You are irreplaceable. When we're done with you, you're going to be *superheroes*. Would you like that?"

"Yes, Director," they said, with varying degrees of enthusiasm.

"You will be given important jobs to do—jobs that nobody else, not even grownup soldiers, can do. Some of these jobs will be dangerous, and you may see each other in trouble. When this happens, you will be like those plants we talked about. If you see someone in trouble, you will not help them unless you are told to. You will do whatever you can to stay safe. Remember that you are special. You cannot be replaced. It is better to lose one than risk two. Say it."

They said it.

"Again."

They did.

"Now open your eyes."

They opened, and the woman was holding a kind of panel, similar to the ones Wasp had seen above the children's beds. This one was the size of Wasp's palm, the thickness of a few pages of field notes, set with a number of buttons. She ran her gaze over the desks. A finger followed it, tapping at the air above each head. Where it stopped, she crooked it gently.

Trembling visibly, a boy approached. At the front of the room, the woman bent down before him, setting her hands on his shoulders to look him straight in the eye. "I want you to know," she said, "that I do not enjoy this."

And she pulled his head back by a handful of his hair and punched him square in the face, five times in an instant, before she let him fall. He lay there, stunned, bleeding from the nose and lip, the corner of an eye. He tried to get up and failed.

Eight of the other ten children were on their feet. Four of those were staring in mute shock, but the other four were screaming at the woman to stop. Three of those were running toward the front of the room. The woman glanced them over, pressed eight buttons on her panel, and those eight children dropped deadweight to writhe on the ground, clawing at the wires on their heads, choking on their cries.

The woman pressed a button, and whatever was happening to them stopped. "Salazar and Tanaka," she said, smiling at the two children who had remained in their seats. She sounded slightly out of breath. "Well done. You have each earned a cookie. The rest of you—" She reached down, set the boy swaying on his feet, raked her gaze across the children, struck him back down with a fist to the hollow of his throat. He toppled, retching for air.

Five of the eight children knew well enough this time to stay put. The other three joined them swiftly. One boy hit his head on a desk corner on his way to the floor. This time the woman let them lie there kicking for a solid half minute. Where their feet hit the floor, it cracked.

The next time, only one stood. She was tiny, but Wasp recognized her from the white beds, the singing room. She had bitten her tongue, or her lip. Blood ran out her mouth. There was no rage in her eyes, only cold determination. The ghost's voice in Wasp's head: *When there were twelve of us left, they partnered us up. It didn't work out quite the way they wanted.*

"You disappoint me, Foster," the woman said, with genuine sadness, and lay one soft finger on the button.

Foster had her head down, her shoulders set, charging as if into a strong wind. She got two steps before she dropped. In her convulsions she puked and thrashed facefirst into it. None came to her aid. Wasp lost track of how long the woman left her there, spluttering, unable to roll clear.

"This is what happens," the woman told the children. "This is what happens when you lose sight of what is most important." She switched Foster off. Foster did not move. Neither did the boy. The other children were hauling themselves back up into their desks, moving like old people in miniature. They kept their eyes averted from the two left on the floor.

The woman's sigh came up from deep within her. "Pretend this was a real mission," she said. "One of those dangerous jobs we talked about. Now instead of one dead—" leveling a finger at the boy—"we have two. Two we can't replace. It is better to lose one than risk two. *Say it.* It is better to—"

—and the vision stuttered and resumed, changed. Wasp was back in the city, at the same intersection of wide streets.

"Give me fifteen minutes," Foster said, and toed the nearest body with a boot. "Keep these guys safe 'til they wake up. Think it over. I'll be back. And then we can put all of this—" her gesture took in the bodies, the crossroads, the city—"behind us. For good." Her face was alight with a fury of hope. "Can you even imagine."

"Idiot," he said, and looked away. Foster laughed, though her eyes did not, and took off running.

She darted down a side street, where tall buildings to either side walled off the sun. She followed it along until she came to a failed old barricade made of big gray bricks, shop signs, trash, mattresses, and the carcasses of wheeled vehicles, which, despite having burned to black iron bones at some point, still looked a hundred times better than the fossil-like traces of them that Wasp had seen, on occasion, a lifetime ago at home. The Archivist in Wasp, taker of field notes, solver of history's mysteries, caught herself gawking.

Foster was crouching in the ruins of the barricade. It was huge. It spanned the alley and had probably stood yards thick, and twice her height, before it fell. She cast a quick glance up and down the alley, then removed a tiny flat rectangle from the collar of her coat and pressed her fingertip to it. It glowed faintly, chimed a few soft tones in quick succession, sprouted a propeller, and levered up lightly off of her palm. She followed its tiny hovering glow and its repeating three-note signal farther into the wreckage, where the notes sped up increasingly until the thing alighted on a mass of garbage from an overturned plastic bin.

"Rise and shine," she whispered to the mass of garbage, then knelt and lifted part of it away in her arms. As she picked it up, it stopped looking so much like an armload of trash and started looking more like a cocoon roughly the size and shape of a child curled on its side. It looked like the spiderweb-camouflaged body Wasp had left atop Execution Hill, though much smaller. It must have weighed at least a third what

Foster did, but she one-armed it like it was a feather pillow. *The hostage,* Wasp thought.

Farther back, the device was perched on a tumble of scorched bricks and trilling its impatience. When Foster clicked her tongue at it, it hopped up her arm and nestled back into her collar. Meantime, she was squatting to feel around the bricks at ground level. After a second she got her fingers under the edge of something and tugged. There was a faint whooshing sound as the air went out of the something, and part of the fall of bricks turned whitish. She whisked her arms sideways, and another of the spiderweb-things came up in her hands. It crumpled to nothing in a palm and she pocketed it.

Underneath was a vehicle unlike anything Wasp had ever seen, back at home or here in this strange old city. It had no wheels. It had no obvious steering controls. It was the exact right size for Foster, seated, and the hostage slung over before her. She bent forward to stare into a blinking red strip of light for a three-count, and the vehicle hummed to life beneath her, floating six inches off the street.

Running lights appeared around a sort of palm-sized dome, which she set her hand to, her fingertips fitting into little grooves set around its perimeter. She shifted her hand slightly and the vehicle shot off down the alley in total silence, dodging debris—

—Wasp was in a strange room, as big and empty and echoing as one of the town storehouses at the backdoor of a bad winter. Eight children stood along one wall, still and silent beside a uniformed man. Six of the children were visibly in varying degrees of illness, slouched and glassy-eyed and clammy, but stood to attention as best they could.

The man read from a handheld panel. "Salazar, Foster," he said. "Floor's yours."

Two girls stepped forward. One of them Wasp thought she'd have recognized as Foster even had the man not said her name. The other one, Salazar, had olive skin and dark patchy hair. A raised open lesion covered most of one cheek and several smaller ones tracked down that side of her neck. Her eyes shone with fever. Both girls walked to a metal rack, took down wooden training swords, and faced off in the center of the room.

Wasp was put uncomfortably in mind of the dueling in the sand on the Archivist-choosing day. The only differences seemed to be that these children were about twelve years old, she saw boys and girls alike, and there was no blood on the floor.

Salazar stood behind her training sword, swaying slightly but glaring hard, her mouth pressed into a line. Her grip on the sword was iffy, due to a calcified-looking growth that had come up between the fingers of her right hand, nearly fusing them together in places. Someone had tried to cut it away at least once, from the look of it, but it'd grown back. Small noises leaked from her throat from the cough she was suppressing. Foster was furrowing her brow at Salazar in interest or concern.

The uniformed man blew a whistle and Salazar rushed Foster. Fast, so fast, but not quite fast enough. Foster sidestepped neatly, leaving Salazar wide open—and made no counterattack. Salazar stumbled, cursing, and the cough she had been suppressing came out. It sounded wet. It lasted for the better part of a minute. She took a tissue from her pocket and spat into it, keeping her hand close to her lips and tucking the tissue away instantly. But Wasp could still see the clots of blackish red caught in the corner of her mouth.

Foster saw them, too. She stuck the training sword in her belt and stood with hands raised, a gesture that even Wasp from centuries later could read. "Mia, you need to see the medic," she said gently.

"No way," said Salazar. "If you can fight, I can fight. You're not better than me."

Without taking her eyes from Salazar, Foster raised her voice to address the uniformed man by the wall. "Sir, Operative Salazar requires immediate medical attention." To Wasp it sounded strange, such crisp phrasing in such a distraught tone. *Operative.* Either of the girls might have come up to Wasp's shoulder. "Give her the point. I forfeit the match." She turned and headed off the floor.

"Oh no you don't," Salazar shouted, and ran at her again, swinging the training sword high for Foster's head, low for Foster's knees, thrusting the point at Foster's throat and belly. Foster dodged it all. Salazar kept shouting, her voice thick with anger, her attacks losing focus and accuracy until she was three beats behind Foster and hacking with the training sword like she was chopping firewood at face-height in midair.

"You don't even get it! Look at us! Look at this!" Salazar threw her training sword aside to tug at a hank of her own hair. It came away easily in her hand. She threw it at Foster. "Look at *this!*" She held up her hands so that Foster could see where three of her fingernails had fallen out, the empty nail-beds oozing pinkish serum. Another coughing fit took her and she doubled over, gagging, drooling gore, as the uniformed man began shouting into his panel for the medic.

Foster ran to hold her up. Salazar shoved her away with the last of her strength and fell backwards, scooting away from Foster along the floor, her scrabbling feet smearing a black-red trail before her. Foster grabbed her anyway, grabbed and held on while Salazar batted at her weakly.

"What *are* you?" Salazar was saying. Her voice was softer now, garbled and sodden, as though there was a wet sponge caught in her throat. Tears stood in her eyes, but she didn't let them fall. "We're dead. We're all dead. We all know it. So why are you okay? You and that other one over there." She glared at something along the wall. "Why aren't you like us? Are you even human? Why isn't it killing *you*?" Her breath hitched and hitched until she had enough to shriek with. "*Why isn't it killing—*"

The third coughing fit was the worst yet. It seized her in its teeth and shook her, the way a dog shakes a rat, and when the medics loaded her onto the stretcher her lips were blue from lack of oxygen and her eyes were red from the capillaries she had burst in coughing.

Foster sat staring at the smear on the floor where she'd been. "I don't know," she whispered to it, wide-eyed, one perfect red palm-print on her cheek—

—and Foster sat at a table. On it was a smallish black box and a stack of papers that looked much like the front of the one the ghost carried: big pictures, words printed above and below. Two men stood near her. They wore dark suits. Wasp hadn't seen them before.

Foster was cuffed at the wrists, elbows, ankles, and knees to her chair, with wide straps across her chest, waist, and the tops of her thighs. The chair, in turn, was bolted into the floor.

"Wish you'd reconsider," said one of the men. "I hear they dial down the pain receptors on you Latchkey freaks. Makes you harder to . . . question . . . effectively. Never did know if that was true. Well. Learn something new every day."

"Come on, Catherine," said the other. "I can call you Catherine? Look, we're giving you an out here. Take it. Give us something to work with. Listen, we read your file. We know what they did to you in Latchkey. Hell of a thing. Forty-four failures, two successes. Two *survivors*. That kind of thing, you know, it pushes people together. Makes 'em hard to break back apart."

"Can the soap opera, will you?" said the first man. "Let's just get her cracked and get out of here. This is starting to eat into my lunch break."

"Shut up a minute," said the second. His tone became urgent, sympathetic. He took a seat to get her at eye level. "You have to put yourself in our shoes, Catherine. You have to see how hard it is for us to believe that those two survivors showing up in a pile of their own incapacitated subordinates is a coincidence." He gave her a moment to think this over. "If he's working with you, protecting him will only get you killed. But if he is—and you put that on the record—"

"Have you *met* him?" Foster laughed bitterly. "Working with me. He gave me to you! Somehow that's supposed to inspire such friendly feelings in me that I'd sit through this circus of yours to *protect* him? He's made it very clear to me whose side he's on." She snorted. "Guess his obedience training or whatever you call it took better than mine, huh? That son of a bitch is one hundred percent incorruptible. You think he gives a shit about—"

"We should bring him in here," he said. "Let him see what you've been reduced to."

Foster's hands went white-knuckled on the chair-arms. The chair-arms, solid steel, crumpled like paper in her grip. When she noticed it, she stopped squeezing.

He chuckled. "You should see yourself." He stood, shaking his head. "I'm done here. It's your show now."

The first man was standing in a corner, sleeves rolled up, his jacket slung across the back of a chair. He had a shiny glove on one hand and he was slowly wrapping a strange-looking chain around it, the thickness of two fingers. When he came to stand in front of Foster he gave his wrist a turn so that a couple feet of chain fell slack. Then he did something to the wrapped part of the chain and the whole thing hummed to life, blue with electricity.

Foster glanced from it to him, unimpressed, then away. Her gaze fell on the stack of papers on the table. Wasp's followed it, and her eyes widened when she recognized the topmost one. Foster stared at the photo on the paper a moment, something hardening in her face, then tore her gaze from it. "Look, I *told* you—"

The chain tore whistling through the air to connect across the side of her head, rocking her sideways in the chair. Both Wasp and Foster cried out, once, and clamped down on it—Wasp biting her lip and staring, Foster drawing huge shuddering breaths through her teeth.

"Guess they don't dial 'em down *that* far," said the man. "Gonna be home for dinner after all."

Wasp lost count of the blows before his partner interceded.

He squatted down before Foster, gave her a moment to gather herself before he spoke. She swallowed wetly and raised her head. One side of her face was a wash of blood from the flap of skin that had unpeeled from her forehead to hang in one eye. She regarded him evenly out of the other one, already swollen to a slit though it was.

Wasp had seen someone hit by lightning once. The mass of burns on Foster's face looked like that. There was a cooked smell coming off of her.

"You're incredible," he said, true respect in his voice. "We knew you would be. You're Latchkey. You're a machine." He produced a handkerchief and began dabbing gently at the oozing ruin of her head. She spat a tooth at him. "Look at you," he said, delighted. "You take a shitkicking to the face and you *just don't care*. Look at her," he told his partner. "That's discipline. We're pushing buttons that aren't there. Now," rounding back to Foster, "you know, it got me thinking. If I were you, Catherine, which is to say if I had nothing in the world past the grounds of this building to call my own, nothing but a cot and a locker and the admittedly extremely impressive ability to swing an extremely expensive sword . . . *where would my buttons be?*"

Wasp looked at Foster, and the bottom went out of her stomach. It had shown in her face a split second, no more, but it was there. Wasp saw it.

Foster knew what was coming next, and whatever it was, it scared her.

The man saw it, too. Now he stood, smiling. "Let's take a look at those famous hands, shall we—"

"—to me, Foster," the ghost was saying. His tone was the one Wasp had heard the midwife use when a bleeder had to calm down and shut up before her heart wrung itself out onto the floor. "Foster. Can you hear me?"

The room was the one where Wasp had seen the children training with wooden swords. It looked the same, except that Salazar's blood had been cleaned from it, and apart from these two, it was empty. Foster had backed into a corner, wide-eyed, screaming incoherently at nothing Wasp could see. Whatever it was, it was about five feet taller than Wasp, if the angle of Foster's stare was any indication.

The ghost knelt beside her, sword across his knees. They were Wasp's age, give or take.

"It isn't real," he was hissing at her. "It's the fever. You're burning up. Whatever you're seeing *isn't real.*"

As he spoke, he was slitting the back of his left hand open on the swordpoint, running the blade carefully up between the tendons, breathing hard through gritted teeth as he dug deeper, revealed, lost sight of, then unearthed a hard silvery chip the size and thickness of a fingernail. Wasp looked on, amazed, unable to fathom how difficult it must be for a person of such absurd strength to do such delicate work.

When it was finished he took Foster's hand. She didn't
seem to notice. "Try to stay still," he said, then pinned her
hand palm-down to the floor and started cutting. She tried
to leap to her feet, spraying blood, one fingernail catching
and peeling back too easily. Glare fixed on something near
the ceiling. With some effort, he pulled her down. It looked
to be taking all the strength he had to keep her there. Eyes
narrowed at the wound in the back of her hand where Wasp
could see silver glinting. He kicked away the sword and dug
in with a fingertip. Still talking, for all the good it was doing.

"Foster, you're sick. You're hallucinating." She flailed free
of him, slick with her blood and his, but the chip was out.
He fished blind in a pocket for the device he'd healed Wasp's
ankle with and sealed up Foster's hand, then his. He stacked
both chips on the ground and crushed them underfoot, then
retrieved his sword. "We can't stay here."

Foster was starting to holler again. "Sorry," he told her,
and touched the base of her neck, and everything went dark.

She awoke in a different room—tiny, windowless, bare
but for heavy steel shelves bolted into the walls. It was colder
here, damper, felt much deeper underground. The ghost was
setting her down, locking the door. He took both guns and
both swords and put them on the highest, farthest shelf.

She lapsed into awareness and stared at him, her skin
papery and lucent with heat. "Get out," she rasped. Her throat
was shot to hell. How long, Wasp wondered, had she been
screaming? "Find you." Her voice went monotonous, her eyes
glassy. "It is better to lose one than—"

He shook her. "Stay with me. *Listen*. I got through the
sickness, remember? Martinez came close. You can do this.
But they can't—"

Foster barked a sudden bitter laugh, splitting her dry lips
to bleeding. Fading out again, Wasp suspected. "They sent
you after me again. Keep me out of trouble. Well, you can run
on back and tell the Director she can—"

"No," he said vehemently, and shook his head for emphasis. "Not this time. They can't ever find out about this." He sighed. "When they paired us up they showed me your file. Told me what to watch for. I should have told you sooner. They said you were a difficult case. That someday you'd be more trouble than you're worth. If they see you're sick . . . it'll be bad, Foster, really bad."

Foster opened her mouth to speak, then went still. She looked down toward her lap. Set a hand to her belly, took it away, and stared at the palm, an unaccountable horror dawning in her face. "What the hell—"

"Foster. Foster, *no*." Alarm blossoming in his voice. Trying, and failing, to tamp it down. "It's in your head. I'm looking right at you and there's nothing th—"

But she'd lapsed back out and now lunged at him in deadly silence, trying to get through him to her weapons. He tackled her down, and she struck out. The first kick pulverized a chunk of a cinderblock wall. The second unmoored the steel shelving from its anchors and brought it down on top of them both. In the chaos she twisted free and leapt for her sword. He got between her and it and without breaking stride she jumped up lightly and slammed both feet into his chest, torquing her body to spring off and up toward her sword as he fell.

He flew back into the wall—but he'd grabbed onto her ankles and took her with him. Through the wall they went, on into a stretch of dank-smelling darkened hallway, the walls furred with fungus, moisture warping the ceiling.

He was done talking now. It was taking all his concentration to try and keep her still, but Foster was having none of it. She threw him off and dove back through the broken wall, but he managed to catch her at the last second and sling her down, cracking the tile, and at that point she'd had enough. She sprang up into the darkness, plunged her hands through the rotten ceiling, grabbed a steel beam, and swung her legs out hard, giving the ghost both boots in the side of the head. As he staggered back she let go of the beam, backflipping neatly, and then he was under her with two fistfuls of her uniform and tore her from the air.

After some minutes he got her pinned and held her. She thrashed hard, and Wasp heard bones break, though whether hers or his she couldn't tell, and she didn't stop fighting, and he wasn't letting go. "Shut up, Foster," he was repeating, over and over, like a litany, "shut up, it's going to be okay, it's going to be okay."

Wasp had no idea how long she waited. The quality of the light did not change.

At times she could hear footsteps off elsewhere, echoing down and down to however deep they were, but nobody came to forcibly return them. Looking at the hallway it was easy enough for Wasp to guess Latchkey's motive: an expedition and all-out assault would bring the whole place down around their ears. The halls probably dead-ended deeper down. Like the shrine-dogs treeing Wasp up Execution Hill, they'd wait Foster out.

At times Foster slept, but the ghost did not. He stayed awake like he was holding a vigil for the dead, and while she slept there was an almost constant chirping and whirring as he healed their injuries, first with his own device and then with Foster's when his gave its three beeps and died, finally healing only Foster when her device was on its way out, too.

At other times Foster cried out and tried to fight her way free, and the ghost talked her down, or tried to, and maybe Wasp would hear another broken bone or dislocated shoulder, and maybe a bit more of the ceiling would fall in, and when Foster'd worn herself out, the hallway would be that much closer to caving in entirely, and the rotten ceiling-crumbs and groundwater and the spores from crushed fungi settled on them as she calmed.

At last Foster opened her eyes, and blinked, and the fever had gone its way, returning her to herself. She took the situation in at a glance.

"Where—" she said. She sounded like she'd been eating grit. She looked awful, but the ghost looked worse. Unless Wasp missed her guess, he was nursing at least a concussion. He drew her slowly into focus. "Hey," she said. "Whatever happens up there—" eyes to the ceiling, what was left of it— "for now, you saved my ass. Seriously. I owe you. How long was I—" She had a device on one wrist, which she worked one arm free to consult. Then turned back to the ghost, incredulous. "Three *days*?"

—city. Streets crossing. Bodies in a ring. Whatever Foster had done to them, they were still out cold but breathing shallowly. She was standing in the middle of their circle again, her sword drawn, both hands on the hilt, the point braced against the street.

"I need you to break my sword," she was saying.

He practically recoiled. "What."

Foster spoke fast and low, not much above a whisper. "You had to apprehend me. We fought. You broke my sword. You took me into custody. You brought me back to headquarters. You turned me in."

"I've got a better idea."

"This is the only way. They're going to be here any second. There's no time. I'm not going to drag you into this."

"So all that talk of running was only that. Talk."

"I guess I decided I didn't want to leave on my own." She gave a little smile, defiant and sad. "Out there we're just monsters anyway. But here, at least—"

There came a sound of many booted footsteps approaching fast. Over that, another sound, which it took Wasp a second to place as the humming of the kind of floating vehicle Foster had taken the hostage away on. There had to be at least ten of them. Close and closing.

Foster's eyes widened. She cursed and set her boot against the blade. There was no doubt in Wasp's mind that Foster could have broken the sword with her foot, with her bare hands, with her teeth if it came to it, but it seemed to be proving difficult in a way that had nothing to do with physical ability. She glared at him. "Are you really going to make me do this myself?" She caught sight of one of the floating vehicles speeding toward them down an alley and she cursed again, softer and more elaborately. Down other sidestreets, more approached.

"Too late," she whispered. Her hand tightened on the hilt. "Defend yourself."

In one motion she unfolded from her crouch, got her boot planted, and sprang up slashing. He leaned slightly to the side, and her blade hissed through the air half a centimeter from his ear. He looked down his nose at her, utterly unruffled. "I'm not fighting you, idiot."

Her miss lost her no momentum, gave no opening. Nor did it really look like a miss. She simply seemed to somehow pause in mid-whirl for a fraction of a second and then whiplash back the way she came. The tip of the blade took him across the cheek, light as a snowflake falling. "Then I'll make you."

The next swing came out of nowhere, and he caught the blade in one gloved hand right above the guard. He glanced at the vehicles. He looked to be counting them. Wasp couldn't quite name the thoughts warring in his face. His expression shifted like water over stones, then to stone and nothing more. At odds with it, his voice was strained.

"Run," he said.

But a kick was already on its way to his head, and as her leg swung up she dipped her whole upper body toward the ground, hauled on the hilt with all the force of her momentum behind it, then let go suddenly, unbalancing him just enough for a solid connect. It wasn't enough to knock him over, but it was enough to stagger him.

It gave her the second she needed.

"Not today," she replied softly, and as the vehicles touched down, guns out, she flung herself to the ground, bloodying her face on the street. Leaving him bleeding from one hand, standing over her in a circle of bodies with her own sword as the approaching footsteps caught up with the vehicles and a hundred guns sighted on them at once.

He hauled her up by one arm, and she started shouting.

"I surrender. Don't shoot. They're alive. They're all alive."

There was a second as the uniformed men and women pointing their guns toward that circle of bodies processed the scene before them. Wasp noticed that they were all dressed exactly like the bodies themselves. In that pause Foster started whispering, hardly moving her lips, so fast and quiet that Wasp, lacking their enhanced senses, could barely hear it even from so nearby.

"I owed you three days, remember? Looks like this is where I pay up. I'm going to show them you had no part in this. Then if you decide you want out, we get out. If you want to stay—if I don't screw this up—you'll be able to."

"I've decided," he said.

Foster sighed, though whether it was the sigh of a person laying down a heavy burden or picking up a new one, Wasp couldn't quite tell. "You haven't."

Chapter Fifteen

It felt like waking from a nightmare. Wasp's heart was pounding and she was in a cold sweat head to toe. The paper-scrap was pink pulp around her blade. She must have been out for hours—except the position of the sun hadn't changed. The ghost was sitting as it had been when she'd left. She herself was kneeling on a rock by a pond, but the lack of cold and pain in her knees assured her she hadn't been there for more than a minute or two.

All that was different now was that she found she was shaking with rage. She jumped to her feet, knife still out before her.

Now, Wasp understood being different. She understood being an outcast, an efficient monster, respected and feared in almost equal measure. She understood what it was like to be a tool fashioned by, and wielded by, the hand of powers not her own. She understood having nothing else beyond the life that had been shaped for her: no family, no friends, no past, and probably no future.

So she understood, even if she had never experienced, the desire—the *need*—to stick with the one person in the world who was exactly the same, even if it ended in disaster: like Carrion Boy and Ember Girl, endlessly drawn together, endlessly colliding, two against the world.

And while she certainly understood wanting to escape, she also understood that it was easy enough for *her*, having no Carrion Boy and no Ember Girl of her own to turn her back on and walk away from. What she did not understand was—

"You just *gave her to them?* After all you'd been through, you *gave* her to them so you—" The notion was too freakish for her to process and say at the same time. She gaped a moment, dumbstruck "—could *stay?*"

The ghost looked up at her, and despite her fury she backed a step, almost landing in the pond. She tightened her grip on the harvesting-knife. "Have you ever seen a wasp?" it asked her. "A live one?"

Still with that unbearable tranquility. She wanted to cut that studied mildness from its eyes. "Get to the point."

"The namesake fits. Good with a stinger. Useless otherwise."

Wasp laughed, utterly irate. "Really." She stepped down off the rock. "Well then. I'll be on my way."

She started walking. Ten steps uphill, the ghost spoke to her back.

"What you said a minute ago. That I gave them to her so I could stay."

She stopped.

"It wasn't like that," it went on. "But by all means, berate me over what you know nothing about. You could have stood there shouting for a thousand years and never told me anything I haven't told myself already."

Its unending calm was about to make her head explode. Well, she knew now where to find the knife to twist. In what wound it remained.

What the ghost hadn't seen.

"I was there when they tortured her," she murmured.

Part of her regretted the words as they were leaving her mouth, but part of her was watching the ghost's face with a perverse satisfaction. That part won out. "Don't you dare look at me like that," she spat. "Isn't that the wall you've been beating your head against all this time? At least, oh, I don't know, hundreds of years? Thousands? That's a long time to wonder and imagine exactly what they did to her. What you *let them* do to her."

Something had lit in her, and she couldn't shut it down. "If I—"

The sentence died on her tongue, half-formed. The mental glimpse she caught of what it might have been mortified her. She scrambled to cover her tracks. "No wonder she doesn't want you to find her."

The ghost had that look about it again, like it was holding something vast and dangerous inside it precariously in check. Wasp thought of it fighting those machines with Foster in the city, flinging however many tons of fast-moving metal out of its original trajectory with no more effort than it would take Wasp to pick her teeth. Wasp thought of what sort of force of will it must take, keeping a lid on that kind of strength if it wanted out. She was acutely aware that the only reason the ghost hadn't reduced her to a grease-spot on the ground was probably because its anger at her, no matter how hard she tried to rile it, paled to nothing beside its anger at itself.

"They couldn't have stopped her if she tried to leave," it said. "Neither of us figured they would risk damaging us, not after all the effort they . . ." A pause. "We figured wrong. We were young and we were stupid and we . . . we were brought up to think we were special. If we survived development, we had to be invincible. She . . . we used to break their rules. It was like a contest. Who could push the hardest."

Wasp had a pretty good guess as to which one of them made up that contest, and which one tended to win. She bit her lip, but the ghost caught the smirk she hadn't made.

"She was better at it," it admitted. "They pushed back, and it was a day in solitary, or a few missed meals, or they'd send us out with incinerator carts to clear the rubble and bodies from the streets. She got too comfortable. She grossly overestimated the thickness of the ice she was standing on, and she grossly underestimated what was waiting for her beneath. It was only a matter of time before they decided to cut her funding permanently." It took Wasp a moment to realize that this was the ghost's idea of a joke. "Well, she finally went too far. She sabotaged a hostage transfer. Nothing was going to convince them that she wasn't trying to switch sides. That she hadn't gone turncoat. That all she wanted was for it to be over so she could get out. They assumed she'd turned double agent. And they treated her accordingly."

It stared into the black water of the pond. Something flicked and seethed below the surface of that water, and it did not look like fish.

"Still, any twenty of them were no match for her. She could have gotten away whenever she wanted. But she didn't even *try*. So I thought . . . I thought she was safe. Three days, she said. I trusted her. I thought she had the situation under control." The ghost made a contemptuous sound. "She did. Only . . . not in the way I was expecting."

Under the weight of the ghost's words, Wasp's rage had smothered to a smoldering. In its absence she felt dizzy and sick. Foster was still there in her head, the ghost of her ghost, laughing in the last bloody light of the sun. Two against the world.

"No. You're wrong. She didn't want to die. I saw her in there. She wanted to live."

The ghost's face contorted. It was slight, but it was real anger. Real anger, slipping out from behind the mask. When it spoke, however, its voice was still calm as a stone. "Is that right. Then explain to me why she sat there and let them cut into her. Explain to me why I dug a grave and put her in it."

It stood. "We're going to find her. And when we do, if she wants me to walk away, I'll walk away. But first I need to talk to her. One last time."

Of course you do, Wasp thought. *You're a ghost. You need answers. You need closure. You need them like the*

*living need air to breathe. You think it's just you, but from
what I've seen, most of us die without getting either.*

*And maybe that's all a ghost is, in the end. Regret, grown
legs, gone walking.*

But Wasp was still no closer to finding her.

Whatever was in the water was still moving. Absently the
ghost drew its sword and stabbed it down into the center of
the commotion. Pulled it out and there was the upper half
of a tattered old ghost stuck to it, silvery and worn. It was
unguessable how long it had stayed stuck down there, alive
but immobile, clawing toward the surface.

The ghost considered it for a long moment, then slung
it down off the blade onto the grass, cut it into pieces, and
kicked it back into the water. Sheathed its sword and started
walking toward whatever lay behind the willow. It might have
been a path.

After a few steps it stopped.

"Has her blood given you any more ideas about where she
might be?"

Wasp pondered this.

—incredible. We knew you would

—going to fight you, idiot.

—lose one than risk two.

—not going to drag you into this.

—up, it's going to be okay.

—was only that. Talk.

—ones who didn't die.

—monsters anyway. But here, at least

Thanks to Foster's blood, Wasp was more overwhelmed
than before. It must have showed in her face, because the
ghost sighed. "I didn't think so. Well, this way might take
us closer to the city. If there's anyone left who's seen her,
chances are they'll be there. Who knows." It gave a sardonic,
bitter little laugh. "Maybe today we'll be lucky."

Without waiting for a response the ghost set off again
down the path, leaving Wasp staring at the ground, ashamed.

She had been underestimated before. It had won her fights more than once. Having been overestimated, and falling short—this was new. She liked it rather less.

"Wait."

The ghost took a few more steps, but slowed to a halt. "Yes?"

"What about everyone else who was involved in this Latchkey Project? And whoever you worked for? And the people who . . ." *Tortured her,* she thought. "Questioned her," she said. "They must be down here somewhere, too. If we find *their* ghosts, we might . . ." The ghost was looking at her over its shoulder, and she trailed off when she saw its face. "What."

"Oh, *those* ones I found," it said. "Long ago. We won't be finding them again."

"You killed them."

It was not quite a smile. "Eventually."

Wasp shut her eyes. Wondering which would come first. Her thread snapping or the ghost realizing that she'd lied and calling off the bargain. She could do nothing about the thread. But she stood some tiny chance of bluffing her way out of the other thing. Buying some time.

"Fine. Fine. Let's go to this city and start knocking on doors and hope she's behind one of them, because I'm all out of ideas that you haven't sabotaged." She went storming around the pond's edge, circling the willow, avoiding the plaits of bone that reminded her altogether too much of the plaits of dead upstarts' hair she'd cut away in tribute to the bridge, and headed toward the path. "You blew up every road that might lead us back to her. Every single road. And your memories are useless, and her memories are useless, and I'm going to run out of time and get stuck here or disappear any minute and what am I supposed to do then? What *exactly* am I supposed to—"

Suddenly the ghost was before her, staring at her with such intensity that she shut up and stood there, her mouth hanging open.

"Keep moving forward," it said. "Even if it doesn't get you anywhere. You stop long enough for this place to catch up with you, it'll trample straight over."

"It's pretty much the same up there," Wasp muttered, pointedly shading her eyes against the sun to get her bearings. Anything to get away from that stare.

Behind her and to her left was the fall of mossy rocks where the cabin had appeared. To her right was that path tacking off through a grove of fruiting trees. Past the pond, the earth sank in a series of declining swells toward a broad meadow, yellow with tall grass, a black river slicing through it. Off in the distance, Wasp could make out the city they had seen the night before.

"Down there," she said. "Looks like we can walk it. It doesn't seem too steep, but I can't gauge the distance. Might take the day, but—"

"No," said the ghost. "Not that way."

Wasp pointed. "But it's right—"

"Haven't you figured out by now that that isn't how it works down here?"

"Isn't how *what*—"

The ghost turned on its heel and took off down the path without her. Wasp swept one last dubious glance from the city in the meadow to the path heading off in the opposite direction, then sighed and followed.

"Think how we got here," the ghost was saying. "How we found the bridge. You don't travel in straight lines in this place. You want to get somewhere, you see it out of the corner of your eye, you keep it there. You look at it head on, it'll disappear. What we're after is another waypoint. Hope it gets us closer than the last one."

"Another cabin?" Wasp asked, squinting through the trees.

The ghost shook its head. "I'll know it when I see it."

"How long did it take you to figure all this out, anyway?"

The scornful sound the ghost made was not, Wasp

thought, directed at her. "If I'd figured it all out," it said, "I wouldn't be here."

The path curved gently, tending upward between rows of trees. The trees themselves were about the size of apple trees, though their fruit looked more like blueberries, if blueberries were white as snow, with thorns the length of Wasp's little finger. Unappetizing though they looked, they reminded her that she hadn't been hungry or tired since the night in the cabin, despite having slept little and eaten less while there. Maybe she was getting used to this place. Or maybe it was because the thread connecting her to her body was weakening, slackening, and would soon wear through, stranding her here or else returning her to Execution Hill. She pushed it from her mind.

It was getting on for midday, and they had passed beyond the grove and onto a rocky plain, scorched and desolate, when the ghost stopped. "There."

At first she took it for a heap of rocks. Nearer, it was a well. A big well. It had to be eight feet in diameter, and a rope ladder disappeared down the inside into the dark. From the surrounding terrain, there wasn't likely to be any water in miles. From the stone Wasp dropped down the hole, there wasn't any here either.

"Because it's out of place?" Wasp asked. "That's how you know?"

"That's part," said the ghost, jumping neatly up onto the rim. It didn't bother with the ladder. It vanished down the well, and Wasp counted seconds until she heard its boots hit bottom.

At ten she was still counting.

At twelve she heard the lurchers.

She spun, drawing the knife. They weren't in sight yet, but they would be soon. Could they follow her down the well?

It was anybody's guess, but between in there and out here she knew where she'd feel safer. Backing toward the well, ready to throw a leg over and feel for the ladder with her foot, something caught her eye, and it wasn't lurchers.

Three ghosts were sprinting up from thirty or so yards away, keeping close to a tumble of rocks as they ran. She couldn't make out their faces at this distance, but all three wore the wide-legged long pants, wide-sleeved shirts, and cloth shoes that, with their abundance of costly fabric, marked the holiness of upstarts.

As they closed, and their scars and faces became visible, she still didn't recognize two of them. The third, the one in the forefront, she did. It stopped and stood defiantly, old blood staining its pantlegs from the arteries in its thighs it had slashed when Wasp had drawn the short straw instead of her.

"Becca," she whispered.

Another howl, closer this time, and the upstart-ghosts all drew their pairs of little knives and stood in a triangle, back-to-back, blades out.

Working together. They were ghosts now, but they were upstarts first, and they were working together. Wasp felt like Carrion Boy in the Sinkhole of Gentle Deceits for as much sense as this place was making. Hell, even like in the story, there was a part of her brain whispering, louder as she pressed on: How bad would it be if she stayed? At least here there was one lousy person she could count on. Dead though that person might be.

Gentle deceits indeed.

The lurchers topped a rise and suddenly were there. Wasp had taken many dozens of them out at the cabin, but there were at least another fifteen here.

Five per upstart. Those were Chooser's odds, and Wasp didn't like them. She looked at the lurchers, then at the well, then at the upstarts. She broke into a run.

And the ghost of Becca shook its head. Pointed to the well with its favorite knife, the little whalebone shiv that had been her death. "Get out of here," it called. Watching the lurchers instead of her. Bouncing on its toes in sheer excitement. "I still hate you, Archivist. But I hate *them* the tiniest bit more." It grinned. "When you're dead for real, I'll find you, count on it. You still owe me a fight. For now I've got no time for you."

As the lurchers neared, the ghost of Becca flipped both little knives and caught them, then broke into a run, trailing both knife-hands loosely behind. The other two upstarts followed.

Wasp started running after them—and stopped. Whatever waypoint the ghost had gone through, down the well. She had no way of knowing how long it would last before, like the cabin, it moved on without her. She couldn't wait.

She took a deep breath, pocketed a couple more stones, and swung her legs over onto the ladder. It appeared sturdy enough. Down she went, hand over hand, for several minutes. When the opening had dwindled to a pale dot in the darkness the size of a coin, she dropped another stone. She couldn't hear it land. A couple more minutes' descent and she dropped a third.

Nothing. She looked up.

The mouth of the well was like a full moon in a starless sky. It hadn't changed.

Well, if the ghost could do it, so could she. She took a moment to scan back through the memories she'd seen, first in the ghost's blood, then in Foster's. The city reappeared most, so she fixed her mind on that. The razor-straight crossroads, the stilt-legged buildings. In the middle of the crossroads, a ring of bodies, and Foster in the middle of that. Wasp locked her mind on it. If that instant, that choice, was the moment Foster's ghost couldn't move past, she might be there still, trapped and waiting.

She cast a little thought, not quite a prayer, toward the One Who Got Away, and let go.

Chapter Sixteen

She landed in a drift of dry leaves. The first thing she did was look up, straining her ears for some clue as to how the fight above, between the lurchers and upstarts, was going. But the bottom of the well, where she'd mostly expected to land, was no longer there.

Neither was the ghost.

She thought of calling out to it, and stopped, her mouth half-open. What would she say? *Ghost? Here, ghost!* She was a long way off from that desperate.

And she couldn't get the upstarts out of her mind. *A wink of the Chooser's good eye to you, Becca,* she thought, and touched her fingers to the scar on her cheek, and raised that hand to the empty air. Then, because she knew she could do nothing to help them now, she got up and looked around.

She did not know a name for the thing she found herself in. Certainly it wasn't the crossroads with Foster in it, which would have disappointed her more if she'd been at all confident that her idea of navigating the waypoints with memories would work.

There were long walls to three sides of her, higher than her head, higher than the ghost's, but made of bushes or low wide trees: some flowering, some fruiting, some evergreen, some bare. She couldn't begin to guess at the season.

The walls still kept some of their shape, though not much. It looked like someone used to maintain them, trimming back the branches, but hadn't done so in some time. The fallen leaves were everywhere, half a foot deep in places, and when she kicked some away she found a floor beneath, the stones of it arranged in a simple pattern of dark and light, alternating.

If she set her eye to a gap in the bare branches she could peek through. Beyond she could see a wall of what looked to be part blackberry bushes, part holly. Marking the corner of that wall was a massive evergreen bush that had been cut into the shape of some sort of towering animal, long since overgrown so that extra limbs jutted out from its sides, strange appendages from its head. It reared up on its hind legs, higher than the surrounding walls. It reminded her partly of a bear with antlers, partly of Catchkeep Herself. But there was something else about it. Something that snagged at her mind, made her itch to examine it closer.

In front of her a path opened out, walled in brambles on the left side, yellow flowers on the right. Off in the distance she could make out objects caught in the brambles, though she couldn't tell what they were.

She started down the path toward them, hating how much noise her feet made in the leaves, hoping she would find the ghost before something else found her. She reached the brambles and the things caught in them were pieces of ghosts. Hundreds of pieces of ghosts, silvery and fluttering, fastened tight to the brambles as though someone had pinned them there lovingly. The bodies from which they'd been subtracted were nowhere to be seen. Many of the pieces were hands, with or without partial arms attached, and they seemed to wave at Wasp as she hurried by.

In the wall of yellow flowers opposite, a low gap appeared, mostly overgrown, and she ducked through it. To her left and front, more paths branched off. She could see gaps through the walls even from here. Behind her, on the other side of the gap she'd ducked into, she could sense the ghost-hands fluttering their fingers. She shivered. Trying not to connect *missing ghost* with *ghost pieces pinned to thorns.* Wondering if she had any way of recognizing any of those pieces, silver and identical, if she wanted to get closer and try. Which she didn't.

She'd wandered maybe five more minutes when she heard a crashing sound off behind her. She thought of that animal-shape carved out of a tree, overgrown into something unrecognizable. She thought of the ghost-faces, breeze catching their mouths so it looked like they were about to speak.

Whatever was making that noise, she wasn't about to give it the satisfaction of dragging her out of some hiding place in the bushes, kicking and screaming. If it wanted her, it was going to have to earn her.

Wasp drew her knife. "I'm here," she shouted. "Let's get this over with."

"And lucky to be here," came a voice, behind her. Close behind. Wasp spun, slashing with the harvesting-knife, and her blade had struck the blade of the ghost's sword before she saw who'd spoken. "If you'd waited any longer to jump down that well," it continued, "who knows where you'd have ended up."

"I was delayed," she said, fighting down annoyance—but also a small upsurge of pride. She'd made the ghost draw its sword to block her. She wasn't going to dwell on how it had gotten so close without her noticing.

"This way," the ghost said, halfway through a gap in the wall. "I think I found our exit."

"Yeah, about that," she said, hanging back as the ghost returned through the gap. "There's something I saw back there. It looked, I don't know. Weird. Like a monster cut out of a tree." She stuck a thumb over her shoulder. "Back that way."

The ghost glanced toward where she was pointing, then back at her. Wasp bristled under its look. "I thought we were looking for things that were out of place," she said. Knowing she sounded defensive. Not caring.

"We are and aren't," said the ghost. "Show me."

She led it back through a series of guesses at turns toward where she'd seen the bear-thing through the gap in the wall, hoping with everything she had that she wouldn't make a wrong turn and run them into real trouble. Or, at the very least, make her look like a fool. So far, she wasn't exactly feeling any closer to getting her hands on that healing device. Chooser knew how, but she was going to have to seriously step up her game here.

After a minute they stood at the base of the thing, looking up at it. It was even taller than she'd thought, seeing it from a distance. It had to reach five feet above her head.

"Here," Wasp said.

"This?" said the ghost.

She nodded.

"This isn't anything."

Wasp reached up a hand and touched the bear-thing's flank. Somehow it was hard for her to turn and leave without investigating further. The ghost narrowed its eyes at her. "You think this is a door."

"I don't know. I just have a. A feeling. I guess."

"How does this feeling propose we get in?"

"I don't *know*. Cut through it? Climb it? Maybe there's something hidden—shit."

She bent to retrieve the harvesting-knife, which had somehow managed to fall out of its sheath to land with a soft crunch in the leaves at the bear-thing's feet. "Stupid," she said to it, or to herself, replacing it at her belt. A fine time for it to start coming unsheathed. Her one weapon and her one way to access the clues that might eventually lead her to Foster. If she lost it down here she was cooked.

Wasp started circling around the bear-thing, peering at the drifted leaves in its shadow.

She got most of the way around the back when she stopped, feeling a strange tugging in her chest. She turned, and the ghost was holding her thread, thumb-and-forefinger.

She nearly gasped. Without a doubt the thread was dissolving fast. She stared at it, shaken. Her mind raced. The change in it had not been as gradual as she'd expected. She'd first noticed it weakening in the cabin where she'd first read the ghost's blood. Then again as she lay in the moss outside the cabin. And now. Each time it had been fainter than the last, and this time the change was especially distinct. It looked like if she breathed on it it would break. But as far as she could tell, she'd only been gone one night.

At last she made the connection. Not only the first time, but *each* time she noticed a change in the thread was after she'd read the blood. If she hadn't been so furious the last time she'd surfaced to reality, she suspected she'd have noticed it sooner.

The good news was that if she'd already seen what she needed to see, and she didn't need to read any more blood, she might well get out of this alive. But if she hadn't—

When the ghost had her attention, it let go. "As you can see, we don't have all day."

Wasp gave the bear-thing one last once-over but saw nothing of note. She wasn't even sure why she had this feeling, or where it had come from, or how to put it into words beyond the vaguest possible surmise. And certainly not how to put it into action. And of the two of them, she wasn't the one who'd been down here, navigating waypoints, for longer than she could begin to guess at.

"Fine," she said, and followed the ghost as it began cutting its way straight through the walls of the maze to a clearing where a lonely stone fountain stood. A pedestal rose from the center of the basin, terminating in an upright stone ring a little over a yard across. Whatever used to be in the center of the ring had fallen or been knocked out, leaving jagged teeth of stone around the ring's inner edge, like the glass around the frame of a broken window. Without it, the fountain's water couldn't spray. It trickled down the sides of the pedestal to collect in the basin, black and cold.

Yellow leaves floated on that black water. Coins glinted, silver and copper, farther down. Each of the leaves had something written on it, many in alphabets Wasp didn't recognize. She picked up a few. What was written on them was names. Not even sure what she was looking at, Wasp skimmed the surface of the basin with her eyes, scanning for one that said *Foster*. She didn't find it.

"Up we go," said the ghost, and Wasp stood eyeing the pedestal and the ring doubtfully.

"That's the door?" she asked.

"One way to find out," said the ghost, and by the time Wasp had climbed up onto the basin's edge, the ghost was already on top of the pedestal. Its boots didn't even look wet.

"I hate you," she said.

It squatted down, holding out a hand. It crooked two fingers at her. "Jump."

She jumped and caught, and got her other hand up on the edge of the pedestal, and pulled herself up. "See you on the other side," the ghost said, then stepped through the ring and disappeared.

Wasp paused, feeling stupid, glad the ghost was not there to witness what she did next.

She went down flat on her belly, reaching with the knife until she'd hooked one of the yellow leaves from the water's surface. Whatever it had used to say was now obliterate. She cast about for one futile moment for something to write with, then cut into her fingertip—to her relief, touching her own blood to the knife showed her nothing—and began to scrawl out *kit foster* on that wet leaf as best she could.

"City," she said. "Crossroads. Bodies in a ring. She didn't
kill them. She wants to run and can't. Three days, she said.
I need to find her." She paused. If she felt stupid before, she
felt beyond absurd now. She shut her eyes. "Please take me
to her."

She dropped the leaf back into the water and waited until
it touched down.

Halfway through the ring, she felt a strange prickling at
the back of her neck. For a second she was convinced that
if she turned, she would find the bear-thing padding silently
up behind her, ghost-shreds caught in its claws from the last
victim it had pinned to the bramble-hedge.

She turned. Of course, there was nothing there.

At first she thought she'd come out on the high ledge of
Execution Hill. The same dark rock, the same long drop.

The ghost was half-sitting half-leaning on an outcropping,
arms folded, staring out at a paste-colored sky. It was unclear
to Wasp how long it had been waiting. Below them was a
snowfield, pocked with pits and trenches of what looked to be
greenish fire. The city in its meadow was nowhere to be seen.
Neither was the maze they'd left, or the rocky plain with the
well in it, or anywhere else Wasp might have recognized.

So the one idea up her sleeve was going the way of every
other idea she'd ever pulled out of there before. It didn't need
to surprise her to disappoint her. Or to piss her off.

"What," she said, "so we keep bouncing back and forth
through these things until one of them randomly drops us
where we want to go? *That's* how you've been trying to find
her?"

"When you arrive at a better idea," said the ghost placidly,
"I'll be delighted to hear it. Until then—"

Wasp's patience was patchy to begin with, but between
her encounter with the upstarts, the ghost's dismissal of

her efforts, her failure to get through to Foster, her failure to bargain for the one thing that would let her escape the Catchkeep-priest, and now this, her temper stretched to snapping. "What do you call that back there? I *had* an idea."

"You had a feeling."

"You didn't have a better one."

"I got us through."

"Through to *what*?" Wasp waved at the drifted expanse below. "If she's down there, I hope she's got a nice warm coat, because if she wasn't *completely buried in snow* we would see her." She cupped her hands to her mouth and started shouting. "Catherine Foster! Are you there? Stand up and start waving if you can hear me, because your friend here is about to get me killed looking for you, and I'd really rather not die down here in this ditch of a place, okay?"

She set a cupped hand to her ear with a flourish. "No? Not here, you say? Huh. Interesting. Maybe next time your friend wants someone's help, your friend might try *listening to that someone's ideas.*"

Wasp turned to the ghost. "What about those ghosts that told you to find me? Trusting *them* but not the person they pointed you to seems pretty stupid."

She was getting used to reading the ghost's silences. This one stopped her cold.

"There weren't any ghosts telling you to find me," she said dully. "Were there."

A moment passed.

"Oh, I don't *believe* this. You're a real piece of work, you know that? You—I could—" She wanted to walk. Right there, just turn and walk, and don't look back. How low she had sunk, to be lied to by a specimen and have to stand there and take it because their bargain was the last straw she had to clutch at. She could walk, but only so far without that thing to heal her.

In the memories she'd seen, the ghost's and then Foster's, those devices had had limited power. Foster healing the people in the alley. The ghost healing Foster in the rotting tunnel. Both times, one device had died and been exchanged for another. Both times, Wasp hadn't really gotten a great sense of how much healing they had done before they made those sad little three beeps and powered down, so it was a matter of blind hope that this one had enough juice left in it to fix her up from whatever damage her next and final escape would leave on her after—

That sound. That weird sad little sound those devices made when they died. She'd heard it before. In her house, before the fire, as the swelling faded from her ankle.

For a long moment there wasn't enough room in her for words and rage together and she stood there trembling with the effort not to attack the ghost right then and there.

She'd wanted to trust it. She'd *needed* to trust it. She'd fought down every instinct she had to *not* trust it, and all that had earned her was the novelty of an emotion she'd never before been in a position to feel.

Betrayal.

"Show me that thing you healed me with," she said, her voice thick. "You know. That thing you said you'd trade me if I helped you."

The ghost's eyes widened slightly. For a second the assurance fell from its face and it was nearly unrecognizable. "No need," it said, recovering itself smoothly. "It's secure where it is. Think about what you're saying. Do you really want to risk me losing it in the snow just so you can reassure yourself I haven't lost it alrea—"

Wasp held up the arm the lurcher had bitten, the ghost had bandaged. "Why not heal this?" she said. "Don't you need me in peak condition if I'm going to live long enough to hunt Foster down for you? In fact." Unwrapping the bandage. Hurling it at the ghost's feet. "I think it's getting infected. Maybe you should do it now. Just to be safe."

"Later," said the ghost. "We're too exposed out here. This isn't the time or place for—"

Wasp folded her arms and stared at the ghost, its all-wrong voice, its wary eyes, and she could feel her rage rolling back from her, leaving an icy certainty in which rage would do no good, because all at once she knew that there was nothing left to her future worth raging for.

"You know what the worst part is?" she said softly. "The worst part is that I *was* starting to trust you. I thought that this—this ridiculous search you've dragged me into—was somehow better than what I came from. Like down here I could be different, I wouldn't just fuck up everything I try to fix. Guess I was wrong."

Wasp took a few steps from the ghost, then swung back around. "Actually, no. The worst part is you're an asshole. And I'm stuck down here with you. And you don't for *one second* deserve my help."

The ghost's hand was on its sword-hilt. Wasp didn't know why until she noticed the harvesting-knife in her hand. She wasn't entirely sure yet what it was doing there.

She looked at the knife. Then she looked at the thread. Then she looked at the ghost.

"Truth is, compared to what I'm used to, this place isn't so bad. I'm not starving. I don't have to look at the Catchkeep-priest's stupid ugly face every day. Nobody's plotting to slit my throat and put my head on a wall. Do you know, I saw dead upstarts back there and they were working together. They pulled fifteen lurchers off me. Up above, they would have tried to kill me. And I would have been supposed to try to kill them back. Maybe I cut this thread and I go join them. Maybe I just disappear. Wherever I go, the Catchkeep-priest won't be there, and neither will *you*. Doesn't sound so bad to me."

The ghost's mouth opened slightly, then shut. It eyed her. "You're not bluffing."

"You have no idea," she said, "how right you are."

She slid the knife in under the thread. She could see the dark stones of the blade through it. She swallowed.

"Wait," said the ghost.

"Nothing to wait for," she said. "Deal's off. Go back to wandering around down here with your head up your ass for another thousand years. Oh, and you can keep that piece of garbage. I hope it keeps you great company for the rest of forever. I mean, look at it this way. At least you have one thing in common. You're both already broken."

A second from cutting the thread, one last stray thought surfaced for the others she'd tried to help and failed—the four-days-to-die upstart, the child-ghost whose parents had looked upon her with such hate, and all the rest.

One more on that list would make no difference. She would die with that curse on her head all the same. Let the Ragpicker gorge Himself on her should-have-dones. She hoped He choked.

And then she paused.

Something she'd said. *I wouldn't just fuck up everything I try to fix.*

From the look of everything she'd seen lately, that curse wasn't on her head alone. It was the exact same misfortune that had gotten Foster killed.

Even if she'd known she could cut and run, and survive it, there was no way she could leave now.

Now it was personal.

"You're right," the ghost was saying. It took a step closer to her, palms out. She knew that stance. She leapt back.

The ghost shook its head. "I'm not trying to disarm you," it said. "I'm trying to tell you the truth."

"You're no better than anything I left up there," Wasp spat at it. "You all just feed me some story so I'll do whatever you say, laugh behind my back when I fall for it. *Catchkeep chose you, Wasp. Kill some upstarts for Her, Wasp. Go live in some freezing little hut with no friends. Oh, help me find my poor lost lonesome ghost, Wasp, I've been searching for you special. What? You want to escape your shitty life? I*

*have just the thing to help you fight your way out. Just help
me out here and it's yours. Not sure when I'm going to get
around to telling you that it doesn't work anymore. Pretty
clever, huh?* Yeah, well, I'm done."

She sheathed the knife. "I'm staying here. But not with
you. I'm staying because I realized *I* want to find her. For all
I care we can go our separate ways. See who gets there first."
She started walking.

"Will you listen to me for a minute?" the ghost said. "I
know you don't owe me that. I'm asking."

"And I'm telling you I don't care," she said. "I don't have
time for this."

"I'm asking for *one minute.*"

Wasp stopped. "You get five seconds."

"The truth is nobody told me those things about you."

"Yeah, I gathered that. Two seconds."

"I wouldn't have believed them if they did."

"Outstanding. One second."

"Everything I said I saw for myself."

"I'm not interested in you trying to make nice with—"

"I wouldn't know how if I wanted to. It . . ." The ghost
paused, momentarily at a loss for words. "It isn't easy for me
to learn to work with someone . . . new. After working with .
. . with Foster . . . my whole life, you understand, my *whole
life*, I—" It made a noise, not quite a laugh, short and sharp.
"Clearly I didn't work with her as well as I should have, either,
or you wouldn't be here."

"Clearly."

"I should never have deceived you. I realize that. I didn't
want to do it. But I needed your help, and I had nothing else to
offer. If I had, I would have offered it. All of it. Anything. I've
tried for so long to do this on my own, and I . . ." The ghost's face
twisted, and there was a space of silence before it continued.

Wasp could hear the *can't* it hadn't said. She didn't push
it. It wasn't a word she much liked having to say herself.

"As for your methods," the ghost went on. "Maybe you think I don't mind in the slightest, standing by and letting you browse through my memories, knowing full well that I will never see them again for myself." It gave her a long cold look. "You would be mistaken."

"I'm not trying to *pry*," Wasp shouted at it. "I'm trying to *help*. You think this is only hard for *you*? At least *you've* done this before! How easy, exactly, do you think it is for *me* to learn to work with *anyone*?"

"Going by what I've seen of your predecessors," the ghost said drily, "I can see how that might be difficult." It sighed. Shook its head very slightly. "You're far from the first Archivist I tried to convince, you know. I don't even remember when that started. Or why. It feels as though it's been going on for some time."

"They didn't take the same shit from you, huh? Lucky me."

"That isn't what I meant. Of all of them, you're the first who was willing to listen. To look for her. To help *me*. You put your life on the line for two dead soldiers you never knew. And in return I betrayed your trust, as I betrayed her trust, and lost her. For what it's worth, even if you go no further, I'm grateful you were willing to come this far."

"Agh," said Wasp, uncomfortable. "This is getting way too dramatic for me. I'm going now, if you're finished. Like someone told me a while ago, I don't have all day. Up to you if you want to follow."

She took off walking. The ghost followed.

Chapter Seventeen

They tromped through the snowfield for ages. They passed things that, to Wasp's eye, might have been waypoints. A wind-shredded orange plastic tent. A cave hung with icicles that were mottled gray with ash. A distant huddle of dark birds circling and alighting on an unseen mass. A tiny pond, perfectly round, frozen into a mirror upon which no snow settled. The metal skeleton of something that had fallen from the sky and smashed there, its nose plowed deep into the earth. They walked on.

Wasp was getting tired, and the cold was ridiculous. The wind was whipping up in gusts that stung her eyes, then settling for just long enough that the next one surprised her into cursing. She could barely feel her legs, the sensation in her hands and ears was long gone, and the only thing that proved her nose was still there at all was that it was running freely, which didn't seem at all fair, considering.

The ghost kept moving at the same measured, even pace, oblivious to the cold. Wasp knew it would slow down if she asked, and did not ask.

Miles later, she tripped on something in the snow and went down. Digging revealed nothing there that should have caught her up. She stood, brushing herself off. She reached her hip and froze. The knife was gone.

"No," she breathed. It shouldn't have been possible. Above, it had never fallen out of its sheath, not once, and now this was twice in one day, it made no sense. She splashed around in the snow, flinging it up in powdery armfuls. She couldn't tell how far down it went, or if there was a bottom to it at all. The ghost stopped and helped her, kicking the drifts, fishing with the sword.

They found it eventually, yards away. Not back the way they'd come, either—alone, with no footprints in a solid four-foot radius of the knife. It had to be ten feet from where she'd fallen. They stood above it, staring down.

"No way," Wasp said. Her skin was prickling, and not just from the cold. She looked at the ghost. It shrugged. "Glad one of us is used to this place anyway," she said, stooping to swipe up the knife before something weirder happened to it, "because it is really, *really*—"

From beneath the snow came a muffled metallic sound, and Wasp stopped midsentence, mouth open, snot freezing on her lip. Poked around a little in the snow with the knife. Whatever was below it clinked when she tapped it. The ghost was beside her before she called. They shared a glance, then started digging.

It was a door, set into the ground beneath the snow, like the hatches that led down into the white tunnels beneath Sweetwater, ancient and lousy with ghosts. Even touching it she got a strange feeling in the back of her neck, like someone was watching her. Like she had back in the hedge-maze, staring up at a monster made of leaves.

There was a wheel on top. They cleared the snow away and turned it. The door opened onto light of the same greenish cast as the fires. Wasp, not relishing the notion of another jump, peered down.

There were the bare bones of stairs here, rusted and creaking, completely mismatched to the foot-thick metal door that had led down to them. They descended a few steps and pulled the door shut behind. Wasp descended the rest, while the ghost hung back, opening and shutting the door at intervals. A few knocks, listen, open, snowfield, shut, wait a bit, repeat.

Wasp took this opportunity to explore.

She couldn't tell if this room was almost unbearably cold or almost unbearably hot. The walls looked like ice, but also like the fires she'd seen lit amid the snow. She was shivering and sweating at once. Words were scratched down the length of one long wall, in a language she couldn't read. The tunnel went back and back, the walls shading to a dark glassy green farther down.

Shredded remnants of ghosts lay in the corners like wind-blown trash. Wasp took a few steps toward one pile, and a sound echoed up from the depths beyond.

It was like the howls of the lurchers on her scent—yet not. It was a shriller call, from something much larger or more numerous. It sounded like sheet metal tearing. She could feel the vibrations of it in her ribs.

She drew her knife and started backpedaling for the door. "Hey—" she said.

"Any minute," said the ghost, pushing the door up and out. Snowfield. Leaden sky. Flare of greenish light as one of the pits erupted. Pulled it shut again.

"We don't *have* any minute."

The shrieking resumed, closer now. The walls were changing color, purpling like a bruise.

"I'm not staying here. That door locks from the top, and I'm locking it. Staying or going?"

Other hand on the door, the ghost set one finger to its lips. *Hush.*

She could not hear so much as feel something approaching. There were no footsteps, no sound of wings or slithering. The shrieking had not returned again. It came to Wasp that whatever was causing it might be right in front of her, savoring her confusion, breathing down her neck, choosing the choicest bite, and she *simply could not see it.*

Her flight instinct almost picked her up bodily and hurled her up the stairs.

"Fine. You're on your own. Let me through."

At that, whatever the light source was, it guttered wildly and went out.

Suddenly Wasp's knife seemed very small.

The ghost rapped at the door with its knuckles. This time it sounded different.

An unseen hand locked around Wasp's wrist and she yelped. "It's me," said the ghost. "Hold your breath."

Then it opened the door.

A wall of water slammed into her. Water went cascading down the steps, down the throat of the cave in the dark. The shrieking came again, horribly close—then receded, accompanied by a sound she couldn't begin to place, not claws or fins or wings or feet, but all these things at once, or none, as whatever made the noise was borne away on the rising tide. The lights stayed out.

The amount of water was astonishing. The cave was filling fast, and in the dark she had no way of measuring how long she'd stand there gasping like a landed fish before the water level rose and caught her up behind. Wasp wound her arm around the stair-rail to keep herself upright as the force of it battered her, held her head free of the waterfall that used to be a doorway and started shouting at the ghost to close the door. Even as the words left her mouth, she realized that the door had opened *outward*, with all the colossal weight of the water against it. The fact that it had opened at all amazed her.

The ghost's voice, near her ear. "We're going up."

"Through *that*?"

"That's our door."

Wasp looked toward the water, looked toward the ghost, and wrapped herself tighter around the railing. "I can't swim."

"You don't need to. Just let go."

It was that or drown. If she could drown. She pictured one of those silvery ghost-rags, filling with water at its nose and mouth until it ballooned and burst.

She let go of the railing.

"On three I'm going to lift you through," said the ghost. "Hold your breath. Close your eyes. You're not going to like this."

Wasp considered the awful force of that water. Though it made her shiver to say it, she said, "We can wait here until the room fills, and—"

"I don't know how long the door will hold. Whatever's next might be worse, and trust me, it could be. I'll be right behind you. On three."

Wasp inhaled until her lungs burned. *Be through there, Foster,* she thought. *Please. I can't take much more of—*

"Three."

She felt herself being lifted into the water. It bore down on her. She thrashed her way up through it. Made no headway. Her lungs were on fire. Her entire body stung. It felt like the water was flaying her flesh from her bones.

Just when she thought she couldn't take any more, the pressure was gone. She was through. Still underwater, still in the dark, flailing and breathless, and the suction from the whirlpool started pulling her back in. She gritted her teeth, got her feet under her, and pushed off against the silt and sand beneath.

She was strong but the water was stronger. She was starting to black out. Frantically she paddled forward, gaining no ground. In the dark she couldn't see if there was anything along the bed of the—what? Lake? Sea?—to grab hold of. She reached down to sweep the ground blind in front of her and the current whipped her legs out from under, hauled her back down, convulsing now, willing herself not to breathe—

Suddenly, below her, the room had filled. The whirlpool stopped. All was still. She marshaled the dregs of her strength and kicked off again, as hard as she could. She couldn't see light above. For all she knew she wasn't even aiming *up*. Her arms scooped water, pushed it aside. Her legs kicked and floundered. Her chest felt like it was imploding.

Then the ghost's hand found her wrist in the dark, and she was being pulled upward with such force and speed that she couldn't keep the air in her lungs. It exploded out of her, and she clamped her free hand over her nose and mouth to keep from gasping water in. She shut her eyes and waited for her resolve to fail.

As her face broke the surface, it did.

For some minutes after she did nothing but breathe, glorying in the swelling and shrinking of her lungs, kicking feebly at the water as the ghost towed her to shore.

It seemed to be some kind of lake or inland sea, dotted with rotten boats. Like the river they had crossed and the pond with its tree of bone, the water was black. "It draws all the colors out from the ghosts that die in it," the ghost explained to her unasked question, and Wasp was suddenly very careful to keep any of that water from splashing into her mouth.

After a while, the ghost pulled her up onto shore. Ageless houses lined the bank of the water, gangrenous with flamboyant mold. They seemed unoccupied. Wasp sat up, feeling the beach shifting oddly beneath her. She looked down to find the ground composed of countless objects that looked like wide flat pebbles made of metal. She picked one up. A locket. If it once had an engraving, it had long since eroded to a smudge. She popped the catch with a thumbnail. The hinge had rusted and the whole front snapped off. Inside was a spider crouching on an apple seed. She bent to flick it at the black water. It skipped once and sank.

"What now?" she asked. But she already knew the answer. She sighed and tilted her head toward the houses. "I'll look around in there."

She stood. Her legs trembled but held. She picked a house and tried the door. The handle was gone, but the door gave way to her shoulder, splintering damply.

Inside was darkish, lit only by one high warped stained glass window. A wide staircase rose up before her, and a hall swept off to either side of it, lined with bloated doors. The air smelled of salt. It was as though the sea had reared up and drowned this place some time ago, maybe more than once. Wasp, having seen enough water for the day, hoped it wasn't due to do so again anytime soon. Quickly she opened what doors she could, found nothing approximating a waypoint, turned around and left the house to try the next one.

In the following three houses there was nothing. In the next, she'd taken a few steps down a dim hall when she stopped dead, knife-hand on the hilt. Movement out of the corner of her eye. *Not now,* she thought, her muscles still shaky from lack of oxygen. She pulled her knife and turned.

It was a mirror. Cracked across, its frame tending toward verdigris, it still showed her the clearest reflection of herself she had ever seen. She gave herself a once-over, head to toe, and scowled. The mirror-Wasp scowled back.

Without warning the ghost appeared beside her in the mirror and she jumped, cursing. "Don't *do* that!" As the shock wore off, she began to notice something. This mirror was giving her the same unnamable feeling she'd had looking at the overgrown bear-thing in the maze, the hatch hidden in the snow.

She nodded at their reflections, "I think . . . this looks like it might be something."

The ghost followed her gaze to the mirror. It didn't appear to share her confidence.

"The mirror?"

Wasp nodded.

"In what way?"

"It's *huge.*"

By its standards, the ghost looked amused.

"Not only that," she snapped. "It looks . . ." She thought of the dry well in the desert of rocks, the bear-thing in the maze, the door in the clearing she had stepped through, long ago. "Out of place."

The ghost raised one eyebrow faintly. "Out of place."

She wanted to dismiss the feeling, but it wasn't going away. Instead she fumbled for words. This time she'd get it right. "Like it's supposed to be a door. It just isn't yet. Like something's in the way?"

The ghost *hmm*ed at her. Raised one hand to set its glove to the reflection of its glove. Pushed forward lightly with its fingertips, and the glass cracked around them into webs. It took its hand back and stepped aside, deferring.

Wasp stared her reflection down, recalling how she had gotten below Execution Hill to begin with. The ghost's voice ran through her mind. *Don't think: the rock is insubstantial. It isn't. Think: I am stronger than the rock.*

"Open up," she demanded. "Let me in."

It did not.

"There are other houses to check," said the ghost. "No time to linger here."

"You go on," she said. "I'm going to figure this out."

"Splitting up could be dangerous. What happened in the maze could have gone a lot worse. You were lucky."

"So you keep telling me." Wasp turned to eye it straight. "Okay, so you've been looking for Foster for a long time. You know how the waypoints work. I don't. I get it. But if what you were doing was *working*, I wouldn't *be here*. You brought me down here to figure this out, and I'm going to figure it out. If you don't want to split up, then help me. Or find a chair and sit in it."

The ghost held her gaze. "I'm going to check the last few houses," it said at last. "First sign of trouble, run outside. I'll find you."

Wasp nodded absently, still inspecting the mirror. She wedged her fingers in behind the frame and pulled. It was boltcd to the wall. She slid a grimy fingernail into the long crack down the middle of the glass, as though she could pry the two halves of the mirror apart.

Still nothing. Nothing, and her time down here was still ticking away. Soon she'd have to go find the ghost and let it heap its silent scorn on her stupid stubborn head and show her the waypoint it had taken ten seconds to find.

Well, she wasn't backing down quite yet.

She paced back and forth before the mirror for a minute, thinking. As she turned, the harvesting-knife caught hard on a chair-back, making her stumble. "Weird," she muttered. She hadn't thought she was standing that close to anything.

Her hand dropped to rest on the hilt, and she stopped walking. She bit her lip and looked sidelong at the mirror. Then she drcw her blade.

The point of the harvesting-knife tapped against the mirror, like any blade-point against any glass, so she set it next to the palm of her off-hand and pressed until a few drops of blood welled up onto the blade. Again, no vision came to her when she did. Perhaps when she became a ghost for good, it would be different. Wouldn't be long now.

This is stupid, she thought. *Stupid and desperate.*

She set the blade back to the glass, and this time it sank in.

Wasp couldn't help shouting. Inside five seconds, the ghost was there. She turned to it, beside herself with triumph. "*Look.*"

She bloodied the knifepoint again and set it to the mirror, right inside the frame. It sank in to the exact depth of the bloodstain on the blade, and she drew it down the length of the glass, then across the bottom, then up and across the top to end the line where it began.

The mirror did not shatter or fall in as Wasp half-expected it to do. In fact it looked much the same, except for the line she had drawn, which shimmered wetly, though was not wet.

The ghost stared. "What did—" it began, and stopped. The look on its face suggested it didn't like being outdone any better than Wasp did. She was beginning to enjoy this.

"It looks like," she said, trying to keep the *I told you so* from her voice and doing a wretched job of it, "I made a door."

She stepped toward it, fixing that moment once again in her mind: crossroads, bodies, Foster—then drew back. She had no idea if she could make another door. She had no idea how she'd made this one. Maybe a ghost-culling knife and some not-quite-ghost blood were actually able to, if not tear the fabric of this place wide open, at least snag it a little and ladder it down. Or maybe there was a door there all along, waiting to be found. Or maybe it was just this place messing with her.

In any case, she couldn't afford to waste it. She had to be sure.

The city appeared so often in the ghost's memories and in Foster's, it *had* to be right, had to if anything was, but maybe her focus was slightly wrong. She replayed the memory in her mind as best she could.

Start talking, the ghost had told Foster. Just as it had said to Wasp, back on Execution Hill. If there was any proof that this was the moment the ghost couldn't move past, it was—

She froze.

If she was right about what was causing her thread to dissolve so quickly, she was about to embark on a terrifying prospect.

But as far as finding Foster went, it might just be enough.

"So I've been . . ." The time for secrecy was past. She had to level with the ghost. At least to a point. "I've been trying to control the waypoints. As we go through them."

The ghost narrowed its eyes. "Control them."

"Get them to take us to where we want to go. Concentrate on . . ." She ran an impatient hand through her hair, back and forth. What she really wanted to do was start squinting at the thread, gauging how much more decay it could take before it dropped her, but if she did that she might well lose her nerve, and then they were done. "Okay, so it hasn't worked. But this—" she gestured at the door—"*this* is new. If we can just . . ."

She trailed off, feeling childish. Wishing on stars. As though stars had ever brought her anything but misery.

"The memories I see keep showing me this city, right? Foster freeing the hostage. I keep trying to get there, and I can't. Here's the thing. When I first met you. On the ledge. You attacked me." She didn't wait for a response. "Do you remember why?"

The ghost looked faintly puzzled. "I blacked out. I *said* it was an accident. I don't see—"

"You attacked me because you took me for Foster," Wasp said.

It favored her with a withering stare. "Now why would I have—"

"I have no idea. But you did. What you said to me was *exactly* the same as what you said to Foster when you caught her freeing the hostage. You were *there*, in that memory, more than you were on the Hill with me. After I saw it for myself, I knew why. That's the moment you can't move past. So that's what I was trying to get back to. For most ghosts it's their death, but—"

"I don't see what this has to do with—"

"*There were two,*" Wasp said, her voice catching in her throat with excitement. "You said that stuff, same as in the memory, and then you sort of *flickered*, faded out but then back in. Then you told me . . . you said the plan changed. You told me to get up. You said we were leaving."

The ghost paused a moment, narrowing its eyes at the wall.

"Nothing?"

The ghost looked away.

She didn't like reminding it of its lost memories, but Wasp couldn't afford to back down now. "Your memory of the city isn't getting us anywhere. I saw it when I read her blood, too, so I thought it was working, but it's *wrong*. All this time I thought we were looking for the back door in. So maybe what we're looking for is the *back* back door."

She took a deep breath. "Whatever that other memory is, I haven't seen it yet. Maybe you don't remember it anymore. But it's *there*. You said she was tortured to death," she plowed on, her mouth outrunning her common sense, not able to look the ghost in the face as she said it. "Maybe you tried to bust her out. *Get up. We're leaving.* Okay, but maybe it was too late, she was too far gone. Most ghosts, they . . . they imprint on their deaths, on the very *moment* of—"

As she said it, she remembered standing on the ledge of Execution Hill, nothing but a knife and some salt and a wild guess keeping her alive. Drily she thought to herself: *how far I've come.*

She waved the knife at the door. "I saw the room where she was tortured. If she died there she might still *be* there. But I can't—"

I should probably have told you about the thread, she thought. *Well, I might fall down dead after this, but there are worse ways to die than trying. The only way out is through.*

She palmed the knife and flipped it over, holding it hilt-out toward the ghost. If the ghost noticed her hand shook, it said nothing. It looked unaccountably preoccupied.

"I need to try to see what you saw," she said. Talking through her teeth to ground herself. Repeating those few phrases in her mind—*the plan changed, get up, we're leaving right now*—as though she could pull herself along them, down into the dark or out of it. "I need to see where she died."

†

She was in a tiny white box of a room, smaller even than her house. There was a kind of shelf built into one wall that she assumed was a bed. A kind of pot built into a corner, whose use she also guessed. The door had no handle, and on it, from around the level of her ribs to a bit above her head, was the second-largest single piece of mirror she had ever seen.

Foster was sitting on the edge of the bed-shelf. Her weapons and uniform had been exchanged for a simple jumpsuit, and she bore about as much resemblance to her old self as a pile of ash did to a wildfire, but Wasp knew her at a glance.

She looked like she'd recently lost a fight. Badly. Or that she had, long ago, and then something had gone very wrong with the recovery. All the injuries Wasp had seen Foster take during her interrogation had been healed almost completely, leaving just enough for her to remember them by. Keeping the memory of the last round of questioning fresh for the next one, maybe for the one that would kill her. Her hair fell around her face, doing nothing to soften it.

Less subtle were the horrors Wasp could read in Foster's hands. It was as if every bone in each hand had been methodically snapped, and healed, and re-broken, and healed, more times than Wasp could guess at. There was a lattice of scars on the back of each hand as well, as though each were a fish that had been gutted, then meticulously— almost—repaired. Wasp's own voice in her head: *You die that way, you're a long time dying. It's a little late now.*

Wasp thought of Foster cuffed to a chair at a table, refusing to talk. *Let's take a look at those famous hands.* She thought of the little chirping device with which the ghost had healed Wasp's fractured ankle, back in her house on the hill, a lifetime ago, and felt sick. She thought of Foster's sword and the mastery with which she wielded it—then looked again at those mangled hands and felt worse.

The jumpsuit covered the rest of Foster's body, but her posture also spoke of recent damage. There had been an upstart, years ago, who had run off to find her parents. When the shrine-dogs chased her down and brought her back, she was dragged before the assembled upstarts, so that an example could be made of her. She'd come in, hands bound, head bowed, defenseless, and the Catchkeep-priest had stood the upstarts in a ring around her and forced each to take a turn with the whip, around and around, for a quarter hour. The next quarter hour was his turn. Before the girl had finally died of her wounds two days later, oozing and untouchable, begging the upstarts to smother her, she'd sat the way Foster was sitting now.

There came a commotion outside the door. A voice, panicked, terrified: "Sir—you can't—I'm sorry—express orders—"

Another, with an icy calm Wasp knew too well: "I'm countermanding them."

"Sir, with all respect, you don't understand. My orders were specifically that under no circumstances—"

"It's late. Why don't you go get some sleep."

"But sir, the—"

"I *said*," and now there was no mistaking the warning in the voice, "get some sleep."

"Yes sir. My apologies. Thank you, sir."

Footsteps receded quickly down the hall. From the door, a few beeps and then a hissing as the lock released. Foster watched it open, watched the ghost step through, looking like he hadn't slept in a while. Foster, for her part, was furious.

"What in the *hell* are you—"

What he was doing was drawing his weapons. Staring down the open door as though daring someone to come through it. Spoiling for a fight. Wasp had never seen anyone look so desperate to kill something in her life. "We're leaving," he said. "Right now."

Wasp's breath caught.

"That was *not* the plan," Foster said. Spending no small effort to keep her voice pitched so it wouldn't carry. "The plan—"

"The plan changed. Get up."

Foster didn't move. "Do you know what I had to go through to make this work? Do you have the faintest idea?"

A silence, and when he spoke again, his voice was dangerous. "Did they hurt you?"

Wasp found it difficult to believe he was oblivious to the evidence on Foster's face and hands, but there it was. At that moment it came to her that no matter how calm the ghost might seem right now, it was a lie. He was utterly beside himself.

Something in Foster's face wrung and smoothed. Whatever decision she was trying to reach, it took her a few seconds to get there. In the end, she stood.

"No," she said, giving him a look of insulted incredulity. She walked over, managing not to limp, and punched him in the arm. If Wasp expected her to wince when her ruined fist made impact, she was disappointed. "Not me."

The tension in the room being what it was, this attempt at playfulness only looked grotesque. The ghost was staring at Foster, stricken, in a kind of rage. "Not you," she added softly, but didn't move to touch him again.

He made a contemptuous sound in his throat, then turned on his heel and stalked out.

As the door shut behind him, he stopped. Wasp could see now that what had been a mirror on the inside was, on the outside, a window into the room. He stood for a moment, perfectly still: back to the door, head cast downward, eyes shut. Then turned. Through the window, Foster was standing in the middle of the room, her back to the door.

His hand went to the control panel by the door and hovered over it for a long moment without activating it. He appeared to be about to say something, then didn't. For a second that rage got the better of him and he struck out at the wall opposite, denting the concrete.

"Idiot," he said, and walked away.

Wasp came out of it grabbing at her thread. The integrity of the thing was shot beyond hope. It looked like a strand of syrup, all beads and gaps, and mostly gaps. Yet somehow, for the moment, it held.

The ghost was staring at her. It didn't seem to have even noticed her thread.

"It wasn't the same room," she said slowly, and the look on the ghost's face, on anyone else, she would have called alarm. She was getting the distinct impression there was something it wasn't saying. "Like a white box, with a white hall outside. It . . ." *Looked familiar,* she'd been about to say, but that made no sense, so she discarded it. "She didn't die there. At least, not then."

"What you saw," the ghost said, finding its voice. Its gaze flicked to the door shimmering in the wall. "Can you use it?"

Wasp made herself shrug. She felt like if she so much as sneezed, the thread would go. "I have to."

She set her hand to the mirror and gestured to the ghost to do the same. She closed her eyes, unsure now of which memory to focus on. Thought of Foster in the white box. Foster lying about her injuries to the ghost. Foster in the torture room, staring down her interrogators unflinching, her eyes lit by something Wasp did not know by name. Thought *take me to her.* Steadied her hand against the glass and pushed—and her hand sank in to the wrist.

Her guess was that if she lost focus, she would lose any chance she had at making this work, so she stifled the reflex to turn wide-eyed to the ghost: *See? See?*

Instead she pushed her arm in farther. Instinctively she expected to hit an obstruction of some kind. The far side of the wall, maybe. The outside of the house. But she was to the shoulder in it, twisting to hold her face away, and her fingertips brushed nothing. It was like heading into deep water and trying to touch her toes to the bottom without letting her face slip under.

Foster gazing out at her from the picture. *Find me, little girl-with-a-knife. Find me if you can.*

Trusting the ghost would follow, Wasp stepped through the glass—and it must not have worked, because Foster was nowhere to be seen.

The city, however, was.

Chapter Eighteen

She was struck by how huge the city was close up. Even from a ways back, they stood almost in its shadow. Whether it was because their wanderings had taken longer than she'd thought, or because the city brought its own sky and its own time with it, the sky was blood-colored with the setting sun, and the city's million lights were being turned on one by one.

The city looked very different than it had from the far side of the river, or from behind the black pond. Its buildings were higher and more regular. On each wall of each one was far more glass than Wasp had seen anywhere in her life. On each of these walls the sunset was reflected, so they all looked like they were in the process of burning to the ground. There were no outlying buildings, no gradual climb of rooftops from low to high, no gradual procession from grass and dirt to paths to small streets to big ones. No roads at all led in. There was the meadow, and then there was the city, disembodied, rearing up like a wall of spikes before her. It was as though the city and its concrete footprint had been cut cleanly from whatever map, whatever time, whatever world they belonged to, and dropped out of the sky to land here.

Except for the combat damage, the explosions and gunfire, and the time of day, it looked a lot like the city she had seen with her hand on the harvesting-knife, reading the ghost's blood, and Foster's.

An awful lot.

The whole place was foreboding. She thought of those wide streets from her vision, those blind alleys, the unearthly silence of the lurchers coming through the cabin windows. Indefensible. It took a lot of effort for her to step forward, nearer whatever might be lurking between those buildings.

If stepping forward even *brought* her nearer. If she didn't keep walking in place like last time, trapped in the unseen current of the meadow as the city kept its distance. If she didn't blunder through some unseen door and get zapped to Chooser-knew-where, and have to start all over again from the beginning.

But she walked, and the city grew nearer, and soon she began to notice something odd.

The city was full of ghosts.

It was nothing like the few ghosts they had come upon, from time to time, in their journey to this place: heads down, eyes averted, listless and quiet. Here there were thousands, climbing around and over each other in a mass, setting the city boiling like a kicked anthill.

Even stranger, while many kept their feet on the ground, there were those that seemed to be climbing or descending stairs—where there were no stairs. Crossing bridges—where there were no bridges. Entering doors—where there were no doors.

If she put her head back and shaded her eyes with a hand, Wasp could discern the tops of all the buildings. By some illusion they seemed to sway, and she had to suppress a twinge of sick worry that they'd come down on her head.

The ghost, catching her staring up into the sky, glanced at her in some surprise. "You see it, too?"

"The city?"

"*This* city. Look at them." It raised its chin at that seething mass of ghosts. "What they're seeing isn't what you're seeing. Where they are isn't where we are."

Wasp watched a ghost walk straight through a concrete pillar holding up a building whose footprint was the size of most of her town. It did not reappear out the other side. A child-ghost sat five feet in midair, swinging its legs over an unseen ledge. A group of three ghosts, carrying a fourth, bypassed a staircase leading underground in favor of descending straight through the street.

She thought of the waypoints, the doors leading nowhere or elsewhere, the ghosts navigating cities she couldn't see. She could remain down here for centuries and she was certain she still wouldn't understand a fraction of it.

The ghost spoke without looking at her. Still staring at those buildings. "It's the same, though, isn't it. What you see."

Wasp didn't need to ask what it meant. From here, she couldn't see the crossroads with its ring of bodies, Foster standing in the middle, the hostage hidden down the alley, but—"Yeah," she said. "But how—"

"We've met your monsters," said the ghost. In its voice was a kind of awe, which she had not heard there before. Also a kind of fear. "I think this is one of mine."

They continued forward, toward that endless wave of buildings and the ongoing chaos between them. Wasp saw soldiers and buskers, wanderers and suicides, gangs and loafers, workers and thieves, in armor and uniform, finery and rags, work boots and combat boots, aprons and robes, bell-skirted dresses, suits with ties and shiny shoes, as if every jar every Archivist had ever filled had been upended in this one place at once. Each ghost or group of ghosts was oblivious of the others. Each ghost or group of ghosts passed through the others when they touched.

The closer it got to the city, the more noticeably the ghost was losing some of the inhuman smoothness of its movements, as though whatever it was holding in abeyance inside it was rattling its cage. Wasp, for her part, was mostly ready to do whatever they could do here and get out. It was not lost on her that stepping over the threshold of this city might well be more stress than her thread could take, and given a choice between facing the Catchkeep-priest again or being stuck in this place for eternity, she hadn't quite decided yet which was the least of evils. Either way, she hated to leave business unfinished. And this business, like most business, wouldn't finish itself.

As they stepped out of the grass and onto the pavement, all the ghosts around them disappeared.

They were left facing down a long straight road, from which other long straight roads branched off. These roads all were exactly alike. Most of the buildings had no doors. Above, the crimson clouds stuttered across the sky. It was less like a city than a dream of a city, an idea of a city. Or a memory of a city so often replayed that its details had started to blur and fade, like an ink drawing of a city left out in the rain.

"She's here," the ghost was saying. "This is where she has to be."

It seemed wrong to Wasp. The moment she had stopped focusing on the city, it appeared before her. Then she thought of the bridge they had crossed so long ago and felt like an idiot for not guessing at it sooner. *You don't travel in straight lines in this place.*

Despite that, she didn't have the feeling about the city that she had about that thing in the hedge-maze, the hatch in the snow, the mirror in the rotting house. In its absence she could almost begin to describe it: like an itch she could only scratch just shy of. She paused and assessed. Nothing.

"You never made it here before?" she asked. "Not once?"

The ghost gave the slightest shake of its head. "I used to get close," it said. "That was a long time ago. I never found the way in."

It slid a sharp look from Wasp to the harvesting-knife. It looked about to say something, then didn't.

"I don't know," said Wasp. "I don't like the look of this place."

It wasn't just the buildings leaning on her. Or the way the sunset reflecting off the glass-walled buildings painted the street before her red. Her skin was crawling like she had her back to the Catchkeep-priest, and she didn't know why.

Still, Foster might be in there.

"Ghosts don't like to be kept waiting," she told herself.

She took a step forward, then another.

And something dropped down from a building behind her, landing neatly on the blood-colored street.

Wasp whirled, knife out.

What stood before her wore a knee-length, greasy dogleather coat. Four parallel scars raked down its cheek, temple to upper lip, investing its mouth with a permanent sneer. A tangle of many-colored hair, interwoven with bullets, bones, and charms, was pinned up with a skewer into a heap on its head.

It carried a knife. A long knife. A knife with sixteen dark stars inset on the flat of the blade.

Its coat was rent in places with puncture holes two inches across. Wasp's coat bore the same holes, in the same places, stitched over in her own shaking hand when the coat had passed to her and she had scrubbed it until her fingers were raw and bleeding and the coat was as clean of gore as it was going to get, which was not terribly.

More of the same punctures were in its exposed throat, and there was a gash down the unscarred temple where Wasp's knife had missed its mark and gone skidding down the outside of the eye-socket toward its ear.

Wasp could hear herself, in her head: *Because when it was my turn to fight the Archivist, I poisoned my blade and stabbed her full of holes. Then I became Archivist.*

"No," she said.

The ghost was beside her. "You know her?"

Wasp clenched her teeth to keep them from chattering.

"I killed her."

The Archivist smiled, its teeth dovetailing strangely where they'd been filed down to points. Dipped its burdened head at her in mock respect, caught its harvesting-knife in a reverse grip and regarded Wasp over it. "Hello again, upstart," it said, its voice only slightly distorted by the green stone in its mouth. "Allow me to return the favor."

Then it caught sight of the ghost.

The smile fell off its face, then came back deeper, more calculating. Wasp's memories of that smile were not fond.

"You again."

The ghost drew but did not advance or bother to reply. Wasp was not used to seeing it hanging back from a fight. It unnerved her into doing the same. Maybe the ghost was thinking it could wring some answers out of this Archivist, who might, after all, have caught or destroyed Foster's ghost. It wasn't, she thought, an unreasonable idea. They stood behind their weapons and waited.

The Archivist went on: "Weren't you the one who came begging for my help?"

Wasp's educated guess was that *begging* was something of a stretch. Still, for some reason it came as a bit of a shock, seeing the ghost recognized. *She's different from the other girls who'd come before her, even though they'd carried the same knife, worn the same scars.* Maybe for the first time it hit her fully, how long it must have searched. She thought of those dead Archivists, killed by ghosts nobody ever caught. She wondered whether this ghost might know anything about that.

The Archivist tapped its scarred cheek, making a show of remembering. "Oh, what was it now? Looking for some dead bitch, wasn't it? Well. Guess you found someone to do your hunting for you," it said, its glacial eyes raking at Wasp. "Too bad for you. This one never did understand how to keep her head down to a task."

Wasp spat at its feet. "Didn't have much trouble killing *you*," she lied.

The Archivist ignored her. It was smiling tenderly at the ghost. Its teeth were bloodied. *From its death?* thought Wasp. *Or because it's basically talking around a mouthful of knives?*

"You were a slippery one," the Archivist was saying to the ghost, its tone friendly. "Crazy and confused. Don't think I forgot you almost killed me." Pensively, the Archivist stroked the place where the halves of its coat-collar joined, at a knot of scar tissue which Wasp's fight had not put there. "I never could catch you. Not until today." Its grin put Wasp in mind of lurchers. "So. Was your bitch even down here? Did you find her? What were you after anyway, hmm? Give her a big kiss hello? Stick it in her one last time for old time's sake?"

Bad idea, thought Wasp. *Very, very—*

The ghost paled, inasmuch as this was possible. It looked slowly down at the Archivist in a cold fury.

Too late, Wasp saw the trap.

She lunged to intercept the ghost—but it had already shot past her, already gotten the Archivist's head wrenched back by one fistful of hair and its blade laid against the Archivist's throat. In an eyeblink the Archivist's head would roll. If its neck didn't snap like a daisy-stem first.

"You will *not*—" the ghost began, and stopped.

The Archivist was smiling.

"No," Wasp breathed. Her mouth took over where her brain left off and she kept saying it. "No no no—" She leapt with the knife, swinging down toward the Archivist's hands before it could—

The Archivist's fist came up fast between them, closed around something. It set its lips to the opening at the end and blew. Something came out, a kind of crystalline powder. Finer than what Wasp had used for her own work, but essentially the same.

Salt.

This Archivist's ghost-binding ability had been legendary in life, and immediately, finally, Wasp saw why. This salt was reddish with the blood this Archivist had dried into it, and glittered here and there where she'd added specks of holy metal filed from the harvesting-knife itself.

It gusted into the ghost's face, its particles ground fine enough to find their way into mouth and nose and eyes, sink in through the pores.

The amount was minuscule. It was enough.

"I bind you," the Archivist crooned.

And Wasp's knife came down. It was no sword, but it cut deep, lodged in the bones of the wrist, and she almost lost it when the Archivist wrenched its hand away.

The ghost was frozen in place, flickering like a candle in a drafty room. The Archivist didn't have to disentangle the fist from its hair, the blade from its throat—the ghost flickered out for a split second and the Archivist simply stepped back through where it had been, leaving it, when it flickered back in, in the absurd position of menacing someone unseen.

"Well, now that *that's* out of the way," said the Archivist, advancing.

Wasp remembered this Archivist all too well. She was ducking before she'd even seen the knife move in its hand. She was rewarded by the sound of it slicing air six inches above her head, and the Archivist stumbled a half-step forward, unbalanced by the contact it hadn't made. Wasp readied her foot and shot it at the inside of the Archivist's knee. There was no crack and no cry. The Archivist, now unbalanced completely, fell to that knee but stood swiftly, unharmed. *Okay,* thought Wasp. *I have to make it bleed.*

She lashed out high and fast with the knife. The Archivist, apparently judging the damaged arm useless, threw it up to block the swing. But Wasp knew this Archivist better than that. At the last second she turned her wrist to send the blow glancing up that arm and toward the Archivist's face, slicing at its eyes to blind them. At the same time she gathered all her strength in her legs and sprang.

They came down in a heap. The Archivist found the lurcher bite-wound in Wasp's arm and dug its fingers in. Wasp screamed and backhanded the Archivist across the face with her fist, then felt a hot spike of pain as the Archivist's harvesting-knife began to sink into her side. Reflexively she twisted away, which she soon regretted as the harvesting-knife opened up a long gash, ribs to hipbone. Deep but not deep enough to stop her. Not quite yet. She swung her leg up and brought her heel down hard on the Archivist's mouth. It spit a couple teeth but appeared otherwise unbothered. The sudden warmth running down Wasp's ankle would be from the hole it was stabbing in her calf.

She thought of those broken ghosts, reduced to silver cutouts, thrashing down the river. She wondered how much more of this she would be able to take before she joined them.

A ways away, the ghost was still flickering, out and in. It was up to Wasp to protect herself. To protect them both. To do what they came here to do and get back to her body in time to run. This time the Catchkeep-priest wouldn't bring her back. She'd escape or die fighting her way free. And she'd let the Ragpicker eat her and shit her out before she let this dead Archivist get the better of her.

Twisting and cursing, Wasp fought her way to the top. She got the Archivist under her, its shoulders pinned under her knees, the harvesting-knife pointed at its throat, both of her hands on the hilt.

She didn't hesitate. She plunged it in, then pulled it out and plunged it in again. A few more times and she was panting and the Archivist lay still.

"That's twice," said Wasp, and gave it one more stick for good measure.

Oddly, the Archivist didn't dissolve into black slime the way the lurchers did, or turn silver like the other dead ghosts. It lay there on the street, inert as any corpse. Wasp got one arm planted and leaned on it hard until the darkness around the edges of her vision passed, then wiped the knife and sheathed it. She was bleeding freely from at least three deep wounds. Her whole body hurt.

A few yards away, the ghost shook free of the salt. Wasp glanced up at it, amused by the alarm on its face. She realized amusement was rather out of place, all things considered, but between blood loss and nerves she was unable to tie down any other particular emotion to what she was seeing. She watched, then, a strange empty half-smile frozen on her face, as the ghost reached for its sword, the Archivist opened its eyes beneath her, the ghost blurred and was suddenly behind the Archivist, blade streaking down to cut off its head as the Archivist slid its harvesting-knife in between Wasp and the thread connecting her to her body, and sliced it cleanly through.

Wasp's hand went to the broken thread, a slow sick shock welling up in her. She felt as though she'd stepped on an old mine and was beginning to realize why she couldn't feel her legs anymore. Her eyes went to the ghost. The ghost was looking at her, in part, the way a warrior looks at a weapon that has failed him in the thick of battle. And in part, the way a warrior looks at a fallen comrade, whom he, in turn, has failed.

The other end of the thread fluttered softly down from the Archivist's blade, across its crumpling coat-sleeve. It had the weight of breeze-borne spider-silk, the color of lightning. Where it touched down it withered dark and brittle, then fell to powder, vanished completely to Wasp's sight. The colors of the Archivist's body all drained and silvered as the body collapsed in on itself until it resembled a sun-bleached blanket left discarded in the street.

The thread, she thought wildly. *The thread was fading anyway. Now I'm stuck here for good. At least now I can find her. I can do something. It's better this way. There was nothing for me up there.*

What would happen when she became a ghost? Had she become one already? Or was she on the verge of disappearing entirely? She seemed no different. She held her hands out to inspect them, turning them back and forth in the light.

And then, all around her, there came a great rushing of wind. She braced her legs and leaned into it. It seemed to be coming from the ground beneath her feet, flung up in a cylinder with her in the middle. The Archivist-coat whipped up into flapping wings, the harvesting-knife rattled in its sheath at her hip, her legs and arms were lashed with uprooted chunks of concrete, and if she hadn't cut all of her braids off already she might have lost an eye.

The ghost, evidently untouched by this wind, was shouting something at her through it. She couldn't make it out. At the look on its face, the shock wore off and panic took over. Maybe this was what disappearing felt like. Or being undone. Getting caught in-between, like Aneko's ghost, drifting back and forth, her feet never touching the ground. Or maybe her wounds had been too great for her ghost-form to withstand and she'd melt to black slime like the lurchers, or be rendered down to a silver rag, hands flapping, eyeholes agape on nothing.

She tried to calm herself. It didn't take.

"I can't hear you," she screamed over the wind. If her voice made it out, the ghost's voice didn't make it back in. She was on her own.

Could she push her way out? She doubted it. Something about the wall of wind kept her from setting her hand to it directly. She rifled her pockets. Firestarter, saltlick, jar. Of these things she judged the jar the least likely to be missed if it broke, so she held it out before her, pressing it gently into the wind. When the barest edge of the jar made contact, it was torn out of her grip and spun out sideways, hard and fast. Too fast to duck. It hit her above the eye and she reeled, one side blinded, and fell back into the arms of the wind.

And everything went dark.

Chapter Nineteen

A different wind woke her back up.

It was colder, crisper, and smelled of winter: frozen earth, warn-fires, snow. It brought her straight back to the time she had left her little house on the hill to find that a ghost had turned the tables and hunted her instead. Except that, as far as she knew, that had been two days ago. And from the smell of the air, here, now, many weeks had passed since then. She might have been back in the snowfield where she'd found the hatch. She might be someplace new.

She couldn't see. Why couldn't she see? She could feel the warmth of the sun on her face, so it wasn't because it was dark. She reached up to her eyes—or tried to. There was something in the way. Something like a blanket tucked too tightly, something like a cocoon, which gave way and tore as she moved . . .

Oh no.

She froze. As slowly as she could, she tucked her arm back in. Forced her breathing to remain shallow and slow. Squeezed her eyes shut fiercely, like a child awakened by a dream with hours left till morning.

Too late. The spiderweb-thing was falling to brittle pieces around her, each piece still in the shape of the part of her it had molded to, right down to the ears and eyelids and fingernails, the way a shed snakeskin holds the shape of the snake that has abandoned it. Eyes shut, she could feel flakes of the thing falling from her cheekbones, forehead, chin. Out in the elements for so long it had lost all resilience and now felt like the rough thin paper they made in town out of used or scavenged paper-scraps soaked and pounded and spread out to dry into patchy sheets in the sun.

She sat up and they rained from her, head to toe, apart from a few large areas where blood congealed them to her wounds: her forearm, her calf, her side, the fresh gash above her eye. Noticing this was what finally drove the terror she'd been suppressing to the surface.

She had been seriously wounded down there, in that world below. Along with the harvesting-knife and the coat, those wounds had come back up with her when that place had spit her out at last. Not only that, but she had gone weeks with no food or water, in a kind of sleep, and now that she was awake her body's weakness was all too apparent. And she was stuck at the top of a mountain she had no hope of descending in one piece, and certain death awaiting her in the off chance she happened to succeed.

Weakly, she began to laugh. It was winter now, deep winter. She had been gone at least a month, maybe more. In this cold, the Catchkeep-priest must have called off his search for her weeks ago. If she had cut her thread yesterday and been done with it, she wouldn't have been so badly wounded, her body not so weak. She probably could have climbed down and walked off whistling.

And now, she couldn't get back down, and she couldn't get back in either. She had no more little green pills, no more camouflaging spiderwebs, no way of cramming the bulk of her body through a solid rock wall. She had a knife in its sheath and the things in the pockets of a greasy coat and a precarious ledge not much bigger than the cot she slept on back in her house on the hill. And that was all.

She was well and truly stuck.

For a second she thought maybe the ghost would come and find her. It didn't take her long to shoot that notion down. After all, they had reached the city, which by its own admission the ghost had never found on its own. It was hardly going to leave that place behind, put however many waypoints between itself and the place where Foster might be, to come after Wasp. *Their* partnership was temporary, a means to an end. Now that the end was in sight, she was alone.

As far as she could tell, she had two choices. Stay up on the ledge and die. Or attempt the descent and, if she made it, run with all she had left in her. Maybe this time the One Who Got Away would finally smile on her and she'd reach a town where nobody would recognize the scars on her cheek and the knife in her belt, where she might scrabble out a foothold for herself. Roof, bed, garden. She might live. Blade under her pillow, watching the roads, waking from nightmares of huge bright dark creatures like dogs, but not dogs—but she'd live.

Until she died. And then it would be straight back below with her, with no friends and no companions, just that empty bleak vastness that went on forever. She could see herself now, walking on and on toward a horizon that grew no nearer, hoping to encounter someone on that endless road whose life her life had touched.

Already she knew there would be none.

What came back to her now was the scribbled fragment of writing beneath the bloodstain on the ghost's paper: *don't want to have died for nothing.*

It was a sentiment she could understand.

She gave her wounds a second, closer inspection. The one in her arm, comparatively, was trivial. The single stab in the muscle of her calf was a bleeder but nothing next to the long deep slash in her side, which she didn't dare probe deeply for fear of what it might reveal. It was almost identical to, though on the other side from, and larger than, the wound she had taken in single combat against the last upstart she had fought, which had scabbed and flaked and scarred over as she'd slept that death-sleep on the ledge. The other difference was that now she was desperately weakened and had nothing with which to bind off the blood flow. For all she knew, standing up would be all it would take to send her insides slopping out. She shuddered. At this rate she would be dead within a couple of hours, and likely less.

Suddenly Wasp found herself on the verge of what was quite probably the worst idea she'd ever had. But on that ledge, in that wind, all but bled out, and so thirsty she felt like any minute she'd crumble to dust and blow away, it looked to her like genius.

She picked the rest of the papery stuff away from her wounds. It caught and tore against what blood had clotted, and she hissed between her teeth as the flow redoubled. For a moment blind panic overtook her and she pressed both hands against the long wound, nearly weeping with pain and fear, blood coursing through her fingers. Eventually she calmed enough to let go.

Now all she had to do was wait and watch for her moment. And then be very, very fast.

Half an hour later she was still waiting, and staying awake was proving harder than she'd anticipated. Even the day after an escape attempt, or a near-thrashing in a knife fight, her muscles had never felt so useless, her arms and legs so heavy. Each breath felt more and more like trying to thread rope through a needle. The gash above her eye throbbed. Half-delirious, she could have sworn she could actually *feel* her life dripping out of her with every beat of her heart, which kept on pumping away, oblivious of the fact that it was busily, dutifully bleeding her out on the stones. She dozed off, then jerked awake, more times than she could count. She kept her hand on the wounded forearm and poked it now and again, focusing on the pain to chase the sleep away.

The sun went down, and the air grew colder. Wind whistled through the holes in the Archivist-coat, snuck in the back of the collar where her braids used to hang. For a while, it hurt to shiver, but she couldn't make herself stop. Eventually it stopped hurting, but by then she had stopped shivering anyway.

She couldn't feel much of anything, really. No pain, no cold, no thirst or hunger. No desire to get up. No desire to do anything. What a relief it was, after spending so long wanting so much, or rather wanting so little so badly, to reach a place where she wanted nothing at all.

Her eyelids were getting heavy again, and she poked at the wound in her arm, gently at first, then harder, digging her thumb in until it hit bone. But that trick wasn't working anymore.

Anyway, she'd only sleep a minute. A minute couldn't hurt.

She woke, unsure how much time had passed. Her body felt strange, like it wasn't hers. Like it was a chair she sat on, or a bed she'd woken in, ready to kick off the covers and stand.

So she stood. It was surprisingly easy. She felt so strong, so light. She looked down at her wounds—and noticed the thread, thin as spider-silk, white as lightning, emerging from her chest and wrapping around her side to keep going on behind her.

If she turned to see her body in the state in which she knew she'd left it, she was sure she'd lose her nerve. It was only the thread, thinner and more tenuous than the first one but still *there*, still connecting her to the three-quarters-dead body on the ledge, that gave her the strength to walk away, able to hang all her hope on the one quarter that still pumped blood, drew breath.

She descended to the lower ledge and stood facing the wall she had passed through before. What she hadn't understood at that time, and thought she did now, was that this wall on this ledge on Execution Hill, along with the other places where Archivists relied on ghosts to pop up out of the ground like weeds, was something like the waypoint-doors she'd traveled through below. And she hadn't yet been able to shake the idea that maybe those doors might be directed or controlled in some way, if only she knew how.

Either she had tried once already and failed—or Foster *was* in that city, and the waypoint in the mirror had simply dropped them off on her doorstep.

And there was only one way to find out which was true.

Wasp drew the harvesting-knife and bloodied the point of the blade, then set the point to the rock face of the wall. The stone parted for her knife-blade, then sank back behind it like wet sand a stick has been dragged through, leaving a thin line, behind which a greenish light glimmered. She dragged it in a rectangle, tracing the rough shape of a door.

Before she could change her mind, she set her hands to the wall. She fixed the ghost in her mind's eye as clearly as she could. Its face and its stance and the odd mannerisms of its movement, as though it fought a constant inner battle between the explosive, destructive grace that Wasp had come to think of as its weapon-ness, and the iron discipline that kept it in check. Its cold humor and its colder rage. Its studied impassivity as it sat with its boots on her tabletop, narrowing its eyes over her field notes . . . which was different from its studied impassivity as it held the spiderweb-thing away from her face as she gasped in those final breaths . . . which was different from its studied impassivity as it unfolded the bloodied paper it had carried around with it since well before the world had died . . . which was different from its studied impassivity as it obliterated lurchers with that monstrous ease, all to keep her safe—no: as it obliterated lurchers *beside* her, *with* her, each of them keeping the other safe. *Two against the world,* Wasp thought, and did not allow herself to think it again.

It was haughty, selfish, temperamental, deadly, insufferable. It was the only Ragpicker-taken excuse for a friend she'd ever had.

"Take me to him," Wasp said, not even noticing until later what was different about her choice of words. And pushed her way into the wall.

This time, the wall pushed back.

The wall pushed back, and the ghost stepped through.

Wasp gaped at him. She'd sooner have expected to be hit by lightning from a stormless sky than see him standing here before her. He returned her gaze coolly, taking in the rents in the coat, the bloodstains, the thread. One slightly raised eyebrow was his only comment on her state.

"I thought you might be here," he said. "Although I didn't expect you'd be alive."

"Give it a minute," she said. "I've got one try left in me, and I don't know where to try *for*. If she's not in that city—if I can even get *back* to the city—"

Wasp cast one last glance toward the higher ledge, where her body waited. Unprotected this time from the elements, its own thirst and hunger and blood loss, it would not wait long. The road she walked could well be endless, and the thread was so frail, so fine. In places it had darkened like a rotten fruit. In places she could see through it.

For the thousandth time since she began her descent from that ledge, she thought about returning. Throwing herself on the mercy of the Catchkeep-priest. Going home, Trying to escape again after her wounds had healed and she regained sufficient strength to run or fight her way out.

If the Catchkeep-priest didn't cripple her outright. Or throw her to the upstarts. Or to the shrine-dogs. Fight? Run? She was close to dead and getting closer by the second. She was no match for anyone. She thought of inching down Execution Hill, spending the last of her strength to come up with a speech that might move the Catchkeep-priest to mercy. She thought of bowing her head and begging forgiveness as the whip came down.

When I am a ghost, she thought, *this will be the moment I can't move past. When I stood between living a life on someone else's terms, and facing an almost certain death on my own terms, and chose.*

Then it struck her.

She wasn't the only one who had made that choice.

"She didn't die from being tortured," Wasp said quietly. "Did she."

The ghost said nothing.

The knife was already in her hand. She held it out to the ghost. The ghost did not look at it. The ghost looked everywhere and anywhere but at it. "No more secrets. I have to know."

Nothing. She didn't like the faraway look on the ghost's face. He'd had centuries enough for brooding. Right now, Wasp's patience was wearing thin.

She reached up and backhanded him hard across the face. Anger brought him back. *Good,* she thought. It was better than no focus at all, or worse, focus on something he— and she—could no longer undo or repair. She shouted in his face. "Listen, do you want to find her or not? We don't have time for—"

The ghost said something softly. So softly she must not have heard him quite right, because it *sounded* like he had said—

Suddenly she felt a sharp tug in her chest. She looked down. The thread. It had eaten up all its slack and was spooling up to where it had come from, tightening against her until it must either snap or pull her back to where it started. Back into her body, which had only enough strength left in it to die.

At last it had happened.

She had run out of time.

As soon as she realized what was happening, the tugging intensified, turned her completely around, and started reeling her in. She dug in her heels, leaning back against the pressure until it nearly swept her feet out from under her and dragged her up the Hill on her ass. She planted her feet and leaned harder. Either it would drag her back, or break. Either way she was dead. At least this way she'd die fighting.

The thread yanked her forward a step, then two. Then she stopped. The ghost had caught her and held on, stronger than the thread.

The thread pulled back, and she cried out. Any minute she expected it to tear free of her chest, and that would be that, and she would be done. The idea of dying so—she couldn't honestly say *so close to what I came for*, as she had no certainty of that, but *so far from where I've come, and so near to it*—infuriated her.

"Don't let go," she heard herself say.

"Do you see me letting go?" the ghost replied.

"I screwed up," said Wasp, with a deathbed honesty. "I couldn't find her. I should never have said I could. When you asked me to find a ghost, what I expected was . . . well, it sure as hell wasn't *this*."

"And I never meant to get you hurt," said the ghost. "I gave you plenty of reason to want to walk, but you stayed. Despite everything, you stayed. For what it's worth, I was glad to have you fight beside me. I had . . . almost forgotten." A pause. "She would have liked you, I think."

"Then you can tell her all about me," said Wasp, "when you find her."

The ghost either laughed or sighed. She couldn't tell which. She let her head fall back and found herself gazing up at the sky, where Catchkeep's sixteen stars twinkled serenely, riding low over the hills. *Maybe you're real,* she thought at them, *and maybe you're a lie made up by men who got too used to living off of other people and giving nothing back. And maybe you're something in between. But if you're up there listening, you mangy bitch, know this. You owe me.*

She would never know if what happened next was coincidence or not.

Everything went still. Wasp hadn't really noticed the small distant sounds of the place—breeze, nightbirds skirmishing in the orchard, late work-noise carrying up from the town, someone laughing on the road—until they stopped.

Then out of nowhere came that same ferocious blast of wind that had brought her back to the peak of Execution Hill when the Archivist had cut her thread. And out of the crack in the rock past the ledge there came ghosts.

They were small, flickering in the onslaught of that wind, but she recognized them. Every one of them was a ghost that the Catchkeep-priest had ordered her to destroy and she instead had set free. The one that had torn up the baker's kitchen just before her last fight was not among them, but she recognized others. One that had struck her and fled when she'd tried to capture it, and she'd respected the fight in it enough to let it go. Several that must have died during infancy or childhood and so were useless as specimens for study. One that had kept clawing back toward the rock it had come from, mewing a name over and over, until Wasp had released it to find whoever it was calling out to. There were dozens.

And then there was one she knew at once for an upstart, from its clothes and its scars and from the way it kept going after her knife instead of the salt.

It walked a little funny, as though a leg had been broken in life, and its left ear was shredded, and it had blood in its ponytail, like someone had cleaned a knife on it. Strangely, it was swollen up around its many wounds, as though it had taken longer than most upstarts did to die.

Wasp stared at it, wide-eyed, but didn't dare call to it by name for fear it would not answer.

The ghosts gathered around her in a faintly glowing silver mass. Each of them was doing something complicated with its hands. It was like and unlike the string-games the town children played, stretching cups and watchtowers and wolves between their fingers. It wasn't until their color started fading that Wasp realized what the ghosts were doing—but by that time each had gathered a handful of silvery strands from the fabric of its form, and one by one, bit by bit, they began feeding the strands into Wasp's thread.

Above or below, it was the first and only time she had seen lone ghosts unite in anything like a common goal. She stared, and the ghosts slowly faded, and the thread slowly lengthened, and was reeled in, and the ghosts worked faster, and for an instant the thread fell slack.

The ghost didn't hesitate. He seized her arm and pulled her back around, and the wind ate her shriek as she felt her shoulder give, then pop. Still the ghost didn't let go. He pressed her hand to the wall and held it there. She couldn't see what the other ghosts were doing, down on the ledge. Whether they would keep on feeding themselves into her thread until they vanished down to disembodied pairs of hands plucking at each other, until those vanished too.

The tearing in her chest felt like it was about to rip her heart out. She felt her feet leave the ground. Still holding her hand to the wall, the ghost set his other hand over hers. Wasp understood instantly. She got the harvesting-knife in a death-grip and poised the point over her hand, the ghost's hand, and the wall beyond, then glanced one last time at the ghost.

The ghost nodded once. Wasp nodded back and plunged the blade in.

The last thing she thought on her way through the door was this.

Whatever the ghost had said to her so softly, just now, right before her time had run out for good and her thread began pulling her back toward her body, she had to have heard it wrong.

Because what it had sounded like was *I should have killed her.*

Chapter Twenty

Wasp stepped through into a long dark room lit by small running lights of such pure high vibrant colors that they hurt her eyes.

She had seen this place before. The beds full of doomed children were gone but otherwise it appeared much the same.

Her wounds burned cold. Her arm hung useless at her side. The thread pulled but not so sharply as it had. She pictured the ghosts unraveling themselves into it and knew she couldn't have much time. She began walking forward, into the room.

As she did, lights came on overhead, so white that she saw spots.

In the middle of the floor where the beds had been, there was a chair. Foster sat in it. She was wearing the jumpsuit. Her weapons were gone. She was cuffed to the chair twice at each arm, twice at each leg, with a wide belt around her middle. She was sitting uncharacteristically still. There was something strange about her hair.

The ghost was standing in front of the chair, at the head of a group made up partly of men and women in white coats and partly of uniformed men and women with guns.

At first Wasp thought the guns were trained on Foster. They weren't. They were trained on the ghost.

Wasp got closer. The strangeness to Foster's hair was that in places it had been shaved off. Where it had been, there were scars on her head, where incisions made by something not a knife had been cauterized.

"—thought you might want to see her," one of the men in white coats was saying to the ghost. "Now that she's stable. She was all over the place there for a while." He tapped a screen on a stand beside the chair. Wires snaked from it to Foster. "It took some doing, but we got her back in the green. Truth is, this *all* took some doing. More than it should. You wouldn't believe how much sedative we had to shoot her up with just to get her on the table. She's . . . well, she's really something." The others were nodding a little at this, grimly, as at an unpleasant memory put behind them. "As I'm sure you are aware."

Nobody was looking at the ghost. Nobody but the guns.

Finally he spoke. "What did you do to her."

The man looked offended. "Do to her? We saved her life. She just couldn't take the stress anymore. She was getting paranoid. She was getting people *hurt*. Our people. You know we can't have that. If we hadn't intervened, it would have . . . ended badly. For everyone. But mostly for her." The man cleared his throat. "Don't worry. She's still herself. She could still kill me with her pinky finger without breaking a sweat. So cheer up. You'll get your partner back. As soon as she earns her way clear of the meds, she'll be right as rain."

The ghost looked at Foster. Foster looked through the ghost.

"She doesn't know who I am."

The man in the white coat took another of those lit panels out of a woman's hand and tapped at its screen with his fingertips. "Now that we're not sure about. It might come back in time. Some things already have. Some things haven't yet, but should. Some of it—" he gestured, tipping his hand back and forth like a balance that wouldn't calibrate—"comes and goes. We'll have a better sense of what's on which list the more time goes by. Already we're seeing improvements. We ran some psych tests, tested some basic self-help skills. Even managed to get her in the combat simulator for a few minutes last night. Things are progressing. Eventually her weapons and uniform will come back out of the vault and she'll go back into the field. But that'll be some time coming." The man checked a device on his wrist. "Now. She's due for Program reintegration therapy in five minutes, but, well, she'll be sitting through that three times a day for the foreseeable future. Missing a few minutes from one lousy session won't kill her. Not for an old friend."

He turned to Foster, and suddenly his tone changed, as though he were speaking to a child. "Would you like that, Kit? You probably don't remember me, but I remember you, and when you were just *this* high, five gallons of trouble in a pint glass, we used to call you that. What do you say? Want a few minutes alone with your partner? Have a nice chat? Get all caught up?" He patted her head. She looked up at him, then back to the ghost. Wasp couldn't read her eyes. Nor could she read the ghost's. "Consider it a welcome-home present," the man said. "For services rendered."

He raised his voice. "Okay, let's clear it out." Then, quietly, to the ghost, as the others filed out the door: "The room is covered. I know they're calling you a hero now, but— let's not try to be one today." *A hero?* Wasp thought, then remembered. *What did you leave at the bridge?* she'd asked. *A medal,* the ghost had replied. *The medal they gave me for turning her in.*

"I don't want to go through all that again," the man was saying. "Any funny business, they might well just shoot you down like a dog. Both of you. Loose cannons. Tragic accident. I can see the headlines now." He clapped the ghost on the shoulder and walked out, leaving him and Foster alone in the room.

The ghost knelt, the better to see into her face. "Foster," he said. "Foster." A pause, and then: "Kit." Her eyes drew him into focus, but in the way a person's eyes focus on something in the distance through a window.

"You don't know me," said the ghost. "Do you."

Foster furrowed her brow, tugging cauterization scars out of true. "I," she said. She sounded thirsty. "I'm not sure."

Suddenly she was holding something. Even now, wrecked, she was so fast that Wasp couldn't tell where it came from. First her hands were empty, and then she held a piece of paper, folded into a square. Foster shook it by a corner until it unfolded. On one side was a lot of printed text, above and below an image of an armed man and woman standing together in front of a ruined building. On the other side there were a lot of words, scribbled in a cramped and desperate penmanship.

Wasp would have known it anywhere.

Foster was looking from the picture on the paper to the ghost and back. At this point she seemed to notice the restraints on the chair, and tore herself free of them. From the look of it, they might have been made of lint.

There was some commotion from the observation deck running the length of the room. "Oh, *shit,*" Wasp heard someone say. Then many heavy footsteps, sprinting.

Foster was oblivious. "I think," she said, holding the paper out, "this is for you."

Until this moment, Wasp had never seen the ghost look unsure of himself. He reached, and did not take, then took the paper.

"Hey," someone shouted from the observation deck. "Drop that and step away from her. That's an order." He ignored it. A rifle fired a warning shot. It embedded itself in the wall, and everything he was clamping down on began to leak out. He drew his own gun, held it out to the side, and fired back without bothering to sight or even look. One shot toward the shot that came, then three more shots toward targets Wasp couldn't see. It was blindingly fast and over quickly. In the ensuing silence, he began to read.

Here I am writing a letter to someone I don't remember. Well, they keep saying my ideas were irrational. What's one more? I took this paper off their table. This pen too. I don't have much time. I've forgotten so much. I know I have, even if I can't remember what it was. They tell me I'm imagining it, bad dream, there there, here's something to help you sleep. But they're wrong. I know they're wrong. I have to get this out before I forget it too. There's a photo on this paper. I see me in it. Looks like a copy of a newspaper. You're there with me, whoever you are. You look like Latchkey. Like an operative. Like me. Maybe we worked together. Trusted each other with our lives. I'm trusting you with mine now. If we were friends, if you ever cared about me, hell, if you ever owed me a favor, I need you to pay up now. I need you to kill me. They say I was sick and they fixed me, but I don't feel right. They put me in the simulator and I can still fight, and I can feed myself and lace my boots and spell these words, but I don't feel like me. I don't even know who I'm writing this to. I should remember you. I look at this photo and I know I should remember you. Anyway, this is what I want. This is all I want. I'm begging you to help me. I don't want to have died for nothing but I don't want to live for nothing either. And that's what it feels like they've left me with. Nothing. I'm asking you to help me because I look at you in this photo and something makes me think you understand. Either way, I guess this is goodbye. I can't say for sure but I bet it was fun while it lasted. See you around.

His hands went to fists. The paper crumpled. He stood there, head down, eyes shut, for a moment. "I can't," he said. "You know I can't."

Foster smiled. "'Course you can. Look at you. I bet you've killed a million people."

"That isn't," he said, and then the door burst in, and, too fast for Wasp to track, he was there to greet what came through. Shots rang out, but none of them were his. He didn't even bother with the gun.

A moment later, the door was still banging shut, and the floor was littered with bodies. The ghost slung the blood off his sword and turned back to Foster—and stopped dead. The look on his face was like nothing Wasp had ever seen before or ever wanted to see again.

Wasp turned and stared, her breath caught in her throat like a fist.

Foster had taken a few steps out into the room. Wasp hadn't seen her so much as get up out of the chair. The expression on Foster's face suggested she'd gone out there with a purpose, and Wasp had no way of knowing whether the bodies at her feet were ones Foster had put there with her bare hands, or whether they'd landed there when the ghost was done with them.

There were two neat holes punched in Foster's jumpsuit, below the collarbone, under the ribs. Reddened around the edges.

As Wasp watched, Foster's expression turned to bewilderment. She set a hand to her belly and brought it away slick with blood. She looked at the ghost. The ghost looked back at her. His eyes were terrible.

He didn't move. He seemed to have forgotten how.

Foster stumbled back a few steps and went down, hitting her head on the leg of the chair. Not noticing. "There," she said, or tried to. She sounded winded, as if she'd run too fast too long. "Makes it easy for you."

Still the ghost did not move. "I can heal you."

Foster grinned, then winced. "You're a terrible liar. It'll be over soon and you know it." Her wounds drooled dark blood, black in the light. Her teeth were red. "Come on, don't make me break my own neck. If someone has to do this, I want it to be you." Her laugh was despairing. It sounded like syrup boiling down to jam. "Whoever you are."

She got up, tottered sideways a few steps, and fell. She lay there, her breath racketing in and out of her. "Don't leave me like this," she said. "You could at least let me die with—with some kind of dignity."

Unbidden, the image came to Wasp of the fallen upstart Aneko kneeling in the sand, expecting a moment of pain and getting days of it instead. To see Foster like this, now, was unbearable. Unlike the upstart, though, Wasp blinked but could not banish her.

The ghost was still standing rooted to the spot. He was hanging back as though there were an invisible line between him and Foster, and if he crossed it, that horrible noise of her breathing would stop altogether. He stood there like a spring too tightly wound, like an undetonated bomb.

From his distance, he spoke, his voice desolate. "Why didn't you run?"

"I was going to." Foster's whole chest was working much too hard to gather air, and her voice was down to a whisper. "They snuck me. Had a needle. Whatever was in it . . . was new. Couldn't fight. I couldn't . . . couldn't. Three days. That was important. I don't know why. Three days. Three days. But they—"

Her eyes wandered to the ghost. In them, Wasp could almost see the spark of her awareness receding, like a torch dropped down a well. "It's weird," Foster said. "There was someone in the picture with me. Someone I had to write a letter for. For a minute I thought it was you. But I guess I was—"

She went silent.

A long moment passed.

The ghost dropped the sword and knelt beside her. He had that device in his hand, the one he'd healed Wasp's ankle with, ages after Catherine Foster fell, was translated into memory, the memory in turn half buried or half lost. He set it to the hole beneath her collarbone. Lights came on and the device chirped and hummed, gauged the wound beyond the scope of its treatment, then beeped its condolences as it gave up and shut down. He powered it back up immediately and set it to the exit wound in her back. Lights, chirping, beeping, shutdown. He tried the wound in her belly. Again the same.

"No," he said. "Get up. You idiot, you can take worse than this, don't you dare let them break you, get up." He shook her. He slapped her. Blood ran out of her mouth. He lowered her back to the floor, his grip so tight Wasp heard bones crack in Foster's shoulders. "Not like this, Kit," the ghost was saying, softer now. "Not like this."

He let go and knelt beside her, eyes shut, face a blank. He did not close Foster's eyes. He stayed there for a long time before Wasp joined him.

"I always thought I was the one with . . . with more discipline," he told her. Not looking at Wasp, not at Foster, not at anything. "I followed orders. Whether I wanted to or not. I was—" his mouth twisted—"*reliable*. To all the wrong people."

He paused, and Wasp settled in to wait him out, not daring to break that silence.

"Most of us, we . . . we took the easy path. We did what they told us because we had nowhere else to go. We had no idea how to live out in the world. We never would have passed for people, real people, living normal lives, with—with—families and houses and—and pet dogs and—"

He trailed off, a muscle working in his jaw. Clearly at a loss. "Leaving this place is the hardest thing any of us could possibly have done. And she was the only one willing to do it. She was the only one of us who'd rather die her way than live theirs. That was Foster's discipline." A long pause. "She trusted me. After . . . after everything, there was still some part of her that trusted me. And I failed her. The last thing she ever asked of anyone, and I failed her. I let her bleed out on the floor of a place she spent her life trying to escape, let her lie there drowning in her own blood while I stood there and *watched*—"

"But you didn't want her to die," Wasp said lamely. Realizing how stupid it sounded. Realizing she had to say it anyway, say something, say anything, to try and block out the pain and rage and shame in the ghost's voice, if only for a moment. It was a ragged voice, frayed to breaking, like a thing too often mended to be saved. It was a voice like the sword you fall on when you see no better option, and Wasp found herself wondering, suddenly and for the first time, how this ghost had died. "You wanted her to live."

But then the upstart Aneko was back in Wasp's mind, festering at a dozen wounds, dragging herself through town on that broken leg, scratching at doors that would not open, and Wasp's wanting-her-to-live had been worth its weight in shit.

She shut her eyes.

"She didn't even know me anymore," the ghost said softly. "Our whole lives together and she had no idea who I was. What I can't stop wondering is, if I'd given her a reason to trust me— if I'd done as she asked and cut her down—in the split second before her mind shut down, *would she have remembered?*"

Wasp swallowed, or tried to. Her mouth tasted like dust. "I don't know," she said.

Gently Wasp took Foster's hand in her own. It was a darker brown than hers, and, except for the blood smeared on it, much cleaner. Its nails looked chewed. Wasp was down to one useable arm, so she passed Foster's hand to the ghost and drew the knife. Set the blade, already slick with her blood and the ghost's, red and silver, to that dead palm. Blood welled up. Wasp shut her eyes.

†

Foster got up out of her body, off the floor. Her ghost did not match her corpse. Her corpse was wearing a bloodied jumpsuit and had strange sutures on its head. Her ghost was back in the uniform of a Latchkey operative, with the sword and gun at its belt.

Foster's ghost walked to the door and tried it. Locked. She drew the gun and shot the lock off, but the door still wouldn't open. Pushing at it with all her impossible strength couldn't break it. Battering at it with her fists couldn't dent it. The sword couldn't cut it.

The Catchkeep-priest's voice in Wasp's head from a lifetime ago. *What are you proving? She's still dead, and people are saying her ghost will walk for all time because it's caught in-between and Catchkeep can't take it across.*

And something else, something the ghost had said. *Down here, you die alone, you walk alone. Unless you find the ones you walked with, up there in the world, and keep moving, and keep reminding each other, and when this place pulls on your mind you pull back harder.*

She didn't want to think about the other thing the ghost had said a minute ago. If he was right, and if the wounds on Foster's corpse had been from his sword instead of Latchkey bullets—

She's stuck, Wasp realized. *She's been stuck here all this time. Because she can't remember having anywhere else to go. Or anyone else to go there with.*

Foster's sword came into the light, and Wasp, getting her first good look at it, was struck by how similar it was to her harvesting-knife. The sword was much longer, of course, but the shape of the blade, as well as the hilt and the guard, bore an uncanny resemblance. If someone took the sword and broke it, then set sixteen dots of contrasting metal into the flat of the blade and wrapped dogleather around the grip of that hilt that was always too big for any knife, howsoever holy, it would be hard to tell the two weapons apart.

Wasp narrowed her eyes. "What in the—"

Up until this moment she hadn't even been sure if she and the ghost had truly passed through a waypoint or only strayed into a memory, or a bit of both, but when she spoke, here, now, Foster turned and saw her.

Then she saw the ghost.

The silence lasted a full minute before the ghost broke it.

"I've decided," he said.

Foster tilted her head to study him, face and uniform and the odd ashy sort of no-voice he had spoken in. She looked confused, as though the ghost had addressed her in a language she used to know, and had mostly forgotten, and she was trying to piece a translation from what few words remained to her.

In the end she said nothing. It came to Wasp that perhaps she didn't remember how.

Whatever invisible line the ghost had been hanging back from, he stepped over it now. He stopped before Foster, took the folded paper out of his pocket and pressed it into her hand. Then stood, hands in fists at his sides, watching her unfold it.

Foster looked from the ghost to the photo on the paper and back.

"Come with me," said the ghost, so soft and low Wasp might have been imagining it.

The last thing Wasp saw was Foster's eyes widening.

And the pressure on the thread, which Wasp had been ignoring or enduring, finally gave way. This time there was no wind, no ghosts, no door. There was nothing. She was there and then she wasn't. She was nowhere at all.

Time passed. Maybe a moment, maybe a day. A year. A lifetime. Dimly she was aware of footsteps approaching her. Booted footsteps, two separate sets of them, walking together. They vibrated in her head. She must have been lying with her ear to the ground. She couldn't get up. She couldn't feel her legs. Maybe that was because she was dead and her body had gone to the shrine-dogs already. Her mouth tasted funny. Maybe it was the taste of a green stone, which would taste like defeat. The footsteps stopped, and there came a sound of rustling fabric very near her head, as of someone squatting down beside her, rummaging through coat-pockets. Momentarily, something emitted two little chirps and started humming in a way Wasp could not hear so much as feel: belly, scalp, and teeth. One by one, her wounds began to burn, worse than ever, as though they were being seared down to the bones. She preferred feeling nothing to feeling this. It went on for a very long time. She rode the pain the whole way down—or tried to. She fell off somewhere along the way.

Chapter Twenty-One

Winter had come to lay its claim on Wasp's town. Snow lay in the branches of the apple trees, buried all the hill paths, stood knee-deep in her abandoned little house ever since the door had blown off in a storm. Around the Catchkeep-shrine the upstarts piled it away from the doors, and the shrine-dogs yellowed it with piss.

Ghosts walked in it, leaving no footprints. Silver on white, back and forth, disobeying the shapes of the roads. Some walked singly, some in pairs or groups. Some bunched and swarmed like bees. There used to be a network of tunnels below the town, before it collapsed, leaving white walls crumpled like paper, doors the thickness of a waist popped off their hinges. It had always been a prime hunting-ground for Archivists. It was rumored that these ghosts were coming from down there.

But there was no Archivist anymore to cull them and keep them in line, no knife and coat to pass hands. The Archivist who had kept them was gone, her body never recovered, and the tokens of her office were lost with her, somewhere beneath the snow. In the spring it would melt, and a green stone could be placed in her rotten mouth, and these things could be recovered. For now, the people of the town walked single-file down the snow-walled paths, and ghosts walked through them.

If any were left alive who knew the story it might have seemed fitting, for it was down in those tunnels that the man who would become the first Catchkeep-priest had found the broken blade that would become the harvesting-knife, back in the days when the town of Sweetwater was little more than a few lean-tos on a lakeshore. He brought it home and gave it as a gift to his daughter. She was a bright girl with a keen eye and an inquisitive heart, who, in the way of children leaving dishes of milk out for stray cats, left pinches of salt out for the dead.

Upon discovering the blade's strange power over ghosts, she gathered the townspeople together and told them that the only way to learn about the world Before was to pay attention to the dead and archive what they knew. Some believed her, some did not. But after that, whether in mocking or respect, they all called her Archivist.

Soon after, she died young in an accident that left the right side of her face torn open, temple to mouth, as though she had been raked by giant claws. Already the people of Sweetwater regarded this ghostcatching girl as sacred in some way to Catchkeep, whose dominion was ghosts. The manner of her death only sealed it. She left nothing behind but a long knife, some salt, a notebook of ghost-sketches, and a father who'd gotten used to living off the respect and fear his daughter's work had brought to his house.

Before all that, though, down in those white tunnels, he'd found the harvesting-knife in a room whose widest wall was lined with huge drawers made of some lasting kind of metal, etched with names and numbers. There'd been twelve of them in all. There had been paper in them, lots of it, all ruined. Photographs and guns and child-sized uniforms. Devices whose purpose nobody could guess. Half an inch of reddish slime sloshing in sealed, lined boxes, four feet or so by a little under two, set with dials and gauges, all broken now. And one drawer was empty altogether. But another held the blade.

In the Catchkeep-shrine, built above the deepest reaches of those tunnels, that story was barely recognizable anymore. All that was left to it was a blade underground, and a girl to whom it was given. Another story had slowly crept up to eclipse it, as stories will, about a star that had been knocked loose from the sky to fall to earth as a knife, but nobody knew anymore where that part had come from. Catchkeep Herself, and all the others, up in the stars: the Ragpicker, Ember Girl, Carrion Boy, the Chooser, and the One Who Got Away—as far as anyone knew They were as old as the tunnels or older, when They had gone on other business, under other names, along dead roads in an unknowable world.

Now it was morning, and a low sun glittered on ice that had fallen overnight. In a space swept clear of old snow, ten upstarts stood in a ring around two in the middle. Behind them, the people of the town had gathered, talking amongst themselves, pointing, elbowing at each other, while the ten upstarts stood in silence and watched their sisters fight. The Catchkeep-priest sat on a high chair, cloaked and blanketed against the cold, squinting in the winter sunshine.

There may have been no harvesting-knife and no Archivist-coat, but the system that was built up around them had four hundred years of resilience behind it and it did not die so easily.

So the girls in the ring slashed at each other, their flimsy shoes skidding in the slush. Their hands were blue with cold. First blood spattered the snow, and there were those in the crowd who cursed under their breath and emptied their pockets clandestinely to their neighbors.

And a hooded figure in a long coat pushed through the crowd, through the ring of upstarts, to where two girls, one cut, one limping, glared at each other across the few feet of space the ring allowed. The figure stood between them, put back its hood, drew a long knife from its belt, and leveled this at the Catchkeep-priest in his cozy chair.

"Get down here," it said. "Get down here and fight me."

The figure's face was unrecognizable, gaunt and haggard, and its hair was cropped short enough in places to stand up in spikes, and it looked just about weak enough to fall over in the snow and not get up again, but the Catchkeep-priest's eyes went from the coat to the knife and widened. "*Wasp?* But you're *dead.*"

Wasp dropped a mocking little bow, wincing only slightly as what was left of the deep wound in her side complained. "We'll see."

The upstarts were watching her the way they might watch the Chooser if She came dancing down to earth, all bone cape and empty belly. Now they looked to the Catchkeep-priest, to see what he would do. The Catchkeep-priest saw them looking.

"Wasp, our Wasp," he crooned, playing to the crowd. "Our best and brightest, returned."

"None of that," she said. "You have two choices. One is climb down and defend yourself. Two is pack your things and walk, and don't look back."

The Catchkeep-priest whistled up the shrine-dogs. They did not come. Wasp shook her head. "They can't hear you."

His face hardened. One hand came out of the cloak, something glinting between the fingers. A throwing knife. He flung it at her head. She brought up the harvesting-knife and cut it from the air. People scattered away from her, upstarts and townspeople alike. Scrambling up snowdrifts if they had to, sinking in to the knees. Wasp wasn't sure if they were more afraid of the Catchkeep-priest's knives or of her. They looked at her like she was a ghost herself. A few of the upstarts hurried back off toward the shrine and returned momentarily, armed.

"You've gotten faster," he said. "But still not quite fast enough."

Wasp spread her arms. "Show me."

He did nothing. She did nothing. Nobody intervened.

"While we're waiting," she said to the crowd, "let me ask you a question. Sort of a puzzle really. Maybe we can solve it together. Don't you think it's strange that none of these upstarts came from families here in town? None of you recognize them, do you? None of you saw them born with Catchkeep's mark. They don't even know who their families are. Who they are. Who they should have been, if Catchkeep hadn't chosen them for holy work. They just . . . sort of . . . appeared. With the clothes on their backs and the scars on their faces. With *him*. Can't Catchkeep find babies *here* to trust to do Her work? Here, where Her ways are kept?"

The next knife went flying past her head and embedded itself in the snow. A warning shot. She didn't flinch. To strike her now would be to prove her right, and she knew he was nowhere near that stupid. She guessed she had a minute or two for him to try and discredit her first. Whether she walked away from this depended fully, she knew, on whether or not he succeeded.

"On what grounds are you wasting our time here, Wasp? Playing back-from-the-dead is amusing, I'm sure, but if it's a battle you're itching for, there are two perfectly good upstarts here who are all warmed up already."

He gestured to them. They looked at each other, then at Wasp. They didn't move. They were listening.

"Have any of you looked at those scars?" Wasp went on, not taking her eyes off the Catchkeep-priest, who paled very slightly though his composure did not slip. "Really looked? Do they look like the scars made by Catchkeep's giant claws? Or are they more like what you'd get if you, oh, I don't know, cut into a screaming baby with a knife?"

Most of the upstarts scoffed, or rolled their eyes, or spat and cursed at her, and soon were laughing. But a couple began inspecting each others' scars, one girl taking the other by the chin and turning her face into the light. It was almost as good as looking into a mirror. One by one, most of the others stopped laughing and joined in. After all, the upstarts knew knife wounds better than anyone present. They began muttering amongst themselves.

"You want to leave?" the Catchkeep-priest said. Louder now, as if to drown her out, though she wasn't even speaking. "You want to turn your back on your honor and your calling and go shiver in some cave and hoard your freedom? It will not feed you. It will not warm you. But I grant it to you. It's yours. Take it and go."

One of the upstarts, the one who'd drawn the fight's first blood, had begun circling around behind Wasp, knife in her sleeve. At the Catchkeep-priest's words she stopped dead. "Why does *she* get to leave?" she demanded, and got no reply. The upstart looked from the Catchkeep-priest to Wasp to the other upstarts, still touching each others' cheeks and talking amongst themselves. Their voices were getting louder now. None of them were laughing at Wasp anymore.

The upstart's eyes went wide. "You're trying to get rid of her because this horseshit she's spouting is *true*?"

Most everyone stopped talking at once. All eyes were either on the upstart, on the Catchkeep-priest, or on Wasp. Wasp spoke into that near-perfect silence.

"I'm not fighting you for my freedom," she said. She lifted her chin at the upstarts, glanced over her shoulder pointedly at the one who'd been sneaking up behind. "I'm fighting you for theirs."

Now the silence was complete. Everyone was staring at Wasp. Her throat felt like she'd eaten sand. She cleared it and kept talking.

"They're standing here in rags and you're up out of the snow in a pile of blankets. They sleep on stone, you sleep on a feather bed. Their hands are cracked and callused and raw.

Yours are smooth. The townspeople feed you and the upstarts get the scraps. No wonder they hate each other. No wonder they fight each other. No wonder they climb up each other to get out of the pit of this place."

Wasp turned to the upstarts and pitched her voice as clear and loud as she could, which was not very. "Catchkeep didn't choose you. Any of you." She pointed at the Catchkeep-priest. "He did."

The Catchkeep-priest coughed a laugh. "You can't seriously be listening to this," he told the crowd. Some of the crowd laughed back, half-certain. He played to them. "Listen to *me*. She's lost her mind. Too much Waste, too much winter. Wasp, sweetness, climb down off it. Nobody's interested in—"

"I'm interested," one of the upstarts called out. Wasp recognized that voice. *Maybe some of us look at that and see weakness. Maybe some of us see something else.* Wasp never did return that blanket. "What's the harm? It's just a story. We're all comfortable." The upstart smiled up at the Catchkeep-priest. "Unless you have something to hide."

It bought Wasp another moment of quiet, another moment of no knives flung at her throat. She spoke.

"Maybe Catchkeep's real and maybe She isn't. I don't know. Maybe this knife fell out of the sky and maybe it didn't. Maybe there *was* a man, a long time ago, who thought he could talk to the stars, and a girl with a scar on her face who thought those stars chose her. Maybe she picked up the knife and realized it let her hear ghosts, and so she learned to listen. I don't know when the system fell apart. When it turned into something that calls girls upstarts and sets them at each other's throats. Something for people like *him* to hide behind."

Wasp beckoned with the long knife. "Well, you're done hiding. I'm calling you out. Stand and face me. Or walk."

First she thought: *Don't walk. I would love for you not to walk.*

Then she realized she didn't care anymore. Looking at him now only made her tired.

Some of the townspeople still seemed torn between seizing her and hearing her out. She addressed them. "Is he the one removing the ghosts from your houses? Or bringing you ghosts, if you need them?" She looked to the midwife, standing with her hands on her niece's shoulders. The midwife gave her the shadow of a nod. *Probably for the best it didn't work out,* Wasp thought at them. *It wasn't going to end well.*

"Is he the one who captures ghosts and learns from them and speaks for them? No. You keep him fed and comfortable when he does nothing. You let him take babies and raise and beat them into *more* people who keep him fed and comfortable. But as far as you're concerned, I'm the one who's a monster. Me and the ghosts I protect you from."

Foster's voice went streaking like a comet through her head. "Well, if I'm going to be a monster, I'm going to be my own monster." She pointed to the upstarts. "And so are they."

Out of nowhere, the Catchkeep-priest flung another knife. Wasp was half-turned, facing the people. *Never should have turned my back on him,* she thought wildly. *Stupid, stupid—*

She hurled her arm up to fend off what she could of the blow—but the blow never came.

The upstart who had been sneaking up to stab her in the back was now standing before her, the Catchkeep-priest's knife stuck quivering in the makeshift shield on her arm.

The look on the Catchkeep-priest's face. Wasp would have liked to preserve it in stone and keep it forever. She realized the look on her own face was probably similar.

The upstart eyed him levelly, her voice bitter and thick. "I *asked* you if it's *true.*"

He forced another laugh. "Don't be stupid, girl, of course it isn't. Our Wasp here always was a little bit on the—"

"Then where did we come from?" said the upstart who'd lent Wasp the blanket, long ago. "If she's lying. Tell us that."

"And our scars," said another.

"The rest of it's true enough," said another, hesitant. "We do all the work."

"And sleep on stone," said another one.

"Don't forget the whippings," said another.

"Tess died," another added, softly, staring at her feet. "Because she tried to find her parents." Her gaze hardened as she raised it. "He killed her. He made us help." A pause. "She brought me soup one time, when I was sick."

"And he steals the shrine-offerings people leave for Catchkeep," said another. "I've seen it. I saw a starved old man leave food there and fall down dead the next day in the street, while this one fed the food to the dogs."

"I saw him take a necklace a girl left," said another. "She left it and asked Catchkeep to help her sister's ghost find its way. She said it was all she had left of her."

Now the townspeople were muttering like the upstarts had been. The upstarts, for their part, were shouting now. It brought the Catchkeep-priest to his feet, a knife in each hand. But he still didn't come down.

"I've wanted to kill you as long as I can remember," Wasp said softly. "Today, I was ready to say what I just said, tell the upstarts you're mine, and cut you down." She shrugged. "But I'm looking at them, and they're looking at you, and I'm not sure I've ever seen them want something so badly. And, well, nobody's really ever *given* them anything before."

She turned to the upstarts, their knife-hands and their hungry eyes. "I changed my mind. He's yours."

Winter passed, and spring came. Ice cracked. Snow melted. Cold mud shot up greenery, then flowers. As the roads became passable, one or two of the upstarts left the Catchkeep-shrine, set off to look for the families they'd been taken from, the lives they should have had. A couple chose instead to start a family of their own. Some dispersed into the town to take up trades: one brought her keen eyes and strong stomach to learn healing from the midwife; another took her muscled back and shoulders to the blacksmith, and learned to turn scavenged scraps into tools. Others learned to bake bread or draw maps or keep bees or brew beer, or took posts at the warn-fires, weapons at the ready, eyes scanning the hills beyond. They found the clay of their lives taking slow shape under their hands.

Others stayed, and some of the ones who had left came back, bringing their new skills and knowledge with them. They divided what of the Catchkeep-priest's things would help see them through long winters and burned the rest. They scrubbed the living-quarters top to bottom, and aired the whole building out for three days straight, in case any girl-ghosts were still trapped there in the stone of it, but none were seen to leave. They still maintained the shrine, and saw to it that Catchkeep's pedestal gathered no dust, and that no offerings were subtracted.

For the time being, when the company didn't chafe her, Wasp stayed with them. In the absence of the Catchkeep-priest, the absence of Archivists and upstarts, they began to call each other by the names they remembered, and those who no longer remembered theirs made up new ones.

Isabel had never before gotten to know the upstarts at all. There'd seemed to be no point. As an upstart herself, she'd looked at them and seen nothing but rivals. As an Archivist, she'd looked at them and seen nothing but her death. Now she learned which one sang under her breath as she swept the floors, which one had an eye for healing plants, which one sleepwalked, which one never learned to read, and which one was willing to take the time to teach her. Which ones couldn't shake the taste for combat, and sparred in the fields in the moonlight when the nights were warm.

If Catchkeep looked down and noticed the dereliction of their duties, or the absence of Her priest, She never once complained.

When the earth thawed they tended the orchard, tapped sugar maples for syrup, went foraging for wild greens, and planted vegetables, fencing them off from browsing deer. In summer they picked wild blackberries in the woods, and harvested more beans than they could eat, so they dried them for winter. In the autumn there were tiny wild grapes, powdery with yeast, and they made wine, and hunted, and set apples in the sun to dry, and traded for what they could not make or grow themselves. In the winter they never locked their door, and they kept a fire roaring in the great stone hearth, their table big enough and full enough for anyone who wandered in out of the cold.

Sometimes ghosts came, too. Isabel never encountered another that could speak to her, but there were still those with a dying word or a name to repeat, and she wrote them down with diligence and respect. She began bartering for paper-scraps, and learned to soak and pound them into sheets. She learned to make ink, and carve a pen. She sketched every ghost she saw, and recognized none.

Her harvesting-knife was useless now. Like a key handed down across centuries until nobody remembered anymore what lock it belonged to or what door it opened, it had waited, as Foster had waited, until it had fallen into the hands of someone who, not knowing the door, was willing, against all odds, to try and find it. It had gone there and returned, and now it was just a big knife with an outsized hilt and a guard like a sword. Isabel pried out the constellation and unwound the dogleather from the grip, and kept it always sharp and always by her side.

From time to time she wondered whether it would go with her when she died, down to that other world below. Whether it would cut through the fiber of that place, leaving doors she only had to step through to get where she wanted to go. She didn't allow herself to dwell too long on where that might be.

One day, in late autumn, she was out back of the shrine, building a wooden box for the coming year's field notes, when she heard footsteps approaching from behind. One pair stopped, then the other. She didn't need to turn to know who was standing there.

"I suppose you want this back," she said, touching the knife in her belt.

"Keep it," said Foster, and in her voice was the wry smile Isabel remembered. "I have my own." A pause, which Isabel could not read. "You have my thanks. For everything."

Isabel nodded, stalling. She didn't know what would happen if she turned. She didn't trust herself to chance it.

Behind her, she heard Foster stand aside, heard the ghost step forward and draw his sword.

"If you want to come with us," he said, "it'll be quick and painless. You have my word."

Something pulled within her chest, in the place where a silver thread used to be, and Isabel found herself grinning. It fit her face and her feelings badly, but it was either that or cry.

Blinking hard, she stared off into the distance, where even from here she could make out a silvery mass on the lower ledge of Execution Hill. Countless ghosts wandering, toward or from whatever drove them, unhindered by scarred girls with knives who'd thought they understood the world.

From there, her gaze was drawn downward. Toward the shrine outbuildings, the town, the fields they had cleared and planted, the buildings they had built—the thousand ways in which those girls had set their hands together to that world and changed it, or changed themselves, until the one could finally fit comfortably inside the other.

"I'll hold you to that," she told him. "But not today."

Acknowledgments

First and foremost, my thanks go to Ysabeau S. Wilce, patron saint of this book, without whom it would have languished.

I am endlessly grateful to Small Beer Press for taking a chance on Wasp and her specimen when everybody else told me they were unmarketable. My editor, Kelly Link, is the most careful, insightful, and incisive reader I've ever had the pleasure of working with. Any good parts in this book were helped made so by her wizardry; any soggy bits left over are all mine.

Likewise, Kate McKean at Howard Morhaim Literary Agency has proved invaluable in the short time I've worked with her, and I'm looking forward to having her in my corner for some time to come.

Thanks also to my amazing first reader crew: Mike and Anita Allen, Patty Templeton, Caitlyn Paxson, Julia Rios, Ysabeau S. Wilce, Autumn Canter, Dominik Parisien, and C.S.E. Cooney. My family chimed in on this one too with interesting and useful perspectives, so thanks also to Matt, Steve, and Char Kornher. Also to everyone else who provided advice and support along the way, or listened to me whining about query letters, finding agents, etc., including but not limited to Francesca Forrest, Erik Amundsen, Jeff VanderMeer, Ellen Kushner, Amal El-Mohtar, Leah Bobet,

Sally Harding, and Alex Dally MacFarlane. Apologies and thanks to anyone I may have accidentally left out. You know who you are.

Mike and Anita Allen published my short story "On the Leitmotif of the Trickster Constellation in Northern Hemispheric Star Charts, Post-Apocalypse," which eventually, in a very different form, became this book. Thanks again to them, and also to Alex Dally MacFarlane, who reprinted it in *The Mammoth Book of SF Stories by Women*.

And to Dan Stace, who, despite having never written a word of fiction in his life, remains the best book-brainstormer I've ever met. I don't understand it but I've learned by now not to question it. Thanks, dude.

About the Author

Nicole Kornher-Stace lives in New Paltz, NY, with two humans, three ferrets, and more books than strictly necessary. Her short fiction has appeared in numerous magazines and anthologies. *Archivist Wasp* is her second novel.

More Big Mouth House titles from Small Beer Press

"Mining folklore for ideas is routine in modern fantasy, but not many can add the surprising twists and novel logic that Peter Dickinson does. These are beautiful stories, deft, satisfying, unexpected. They deserve to become classics of the genre."
—Tom Shippey, *Wall Street Journal,* Best Fiction of the Year

Earth and Air: Tales of Elemental Creatures
paper · $14.95 · 9781618730381
ebook · 9781618730398
Junior Library Guild Pick

Cara's mother has disappeared and Cara is realizing her mother is not be who she thought she was—and that the world has much stranger, much older inhabitants than they had imagined. Includes a sneak preview of the second book in the Dissenters series, *The Shimmers in the Night.*

★ "Lyrically evocative. . . . A lush and intelligent opener for a topical eco-fantasy series."—*Kirkus Reviews* (starred review) Best of the Year

The Fires Beneath the Sea
paper · $12 · 9781931520478
ebook · 9781931520416
Junior Library Guild Pick

weightlessbooks.com
smallbeerpress.com